THE IMPOSTOR

THE IMPOSTOR

A Novel

by

JUNE DRUMMOND

St. Martin's Press
New York

Library of Congress Cataloging-in-Publication Data

Drummond, June.
The impostor / June Drummond.
p.   cm.
ISBN 0-312-09385-3
I. Title.
PR9369.3.D7I47   1993
823—dc20   93-18411   CIP

First published in Great Britain by Victor Gollancz Ltd.

First U.S. Edition: May 1993
10 9 8 7 6 5 4 3 2 1

For Lily

THE IMPOSTOR

I

'The fact is, Finch,' said Mr Lychgate, 'Hubert's right. You're wastin' your talents. Ain't makin' the best of yourself.'

His companion, who reclined in the far corner of the travelling coach with his feet on the opposite seat, gave no indication of having heard this stricture. He appeared to be blissfully asleep.

Mr Lychgate raised his voice.

'Wycombe? You listenin'? D'you recall what Hubert said? Called you a frivol. Called you a flibbertigibbet. Called you a . . .'

'Slubberdegullion,' supplied the other. He opened very blue eyes and smiled at Mr Lychgate. 'In full flight was our Hubert, though sadly inclined to mix his metaphors.' He adopted a rhetorical tone. 'I take leave to warn you, Hector, that your head is in the clouds and your feet are on the primrose path to hell! It is time to set your shoulder to the wheel and your nose to the grindstone!'

'He never spoke of a grindstone,' protested Mr Lychgate.

'Only because it slipped his mind.' Lord Hector Amory Finch Wycombe removed his boots from the leather upholstery and turned to gaze out of the carriage window. 'Lord, what a downpour. I doubt we'll reach Leicester tonight.'

'Never mind Leicester,' said Mr Lychgate. 'I'm talkin' about you. Seems to me you go out of your way to provoke Hubert.'

'He brings out the worst in me, Freddy. He's so pompous, so worthy.'

'Well, as a man of the cloth he's bound to take a sober view of things. Besides, he's fond of you and wishes to see you succeed in life.'

'But I do,' said his lordship reasonably. 'I'm all the crack, just now. *Succès fou.* Ask anyone.'

Mr Lychgate considered his friend dispassionately. Not the harshest of critics could fault Lord Hector's appearance. The perfect set of his coat, the elegance of his pale grey pantaloons, the glossiness of his Hessians were the envy of every aspiring blade in Town. Nor could he be accused of foppishness; he indulged in no extremes of fashion, wore no jewellery save the signet ring on his left hand. He looked what he was, an athlete in the prime of his powers.

Mr Lychgate sighed. 'It's true you're very well liked,' he conceded, 'and a pink of the ton . . .'

'Why, thank you, Frederic.'

'. . . but that don't make you a man of sense. Take your gamblin', for instance. I hear you lost twelve thousand at the tables last week.'

'You're misinformed. I won seven.'

'The point is,' said Mr Lychgate, stabbing the air with a minatory finger, 'you play for dangerously high stakes.'

'It relieves the tedium.'

'You'll find yourself rolled up one day; consigned to a debtors' gaol!'

'You begin to sound like Hubert.'

'I'm speakin' as a friend. You ain't usin' your head. Mean to say, Finch, you have brains. Not like me; I'm not bookish. I'm content as long as I can ride my acres and pay the occasional visit to Town. I know my limitations, but you can be anything you please, if you'll only set your mind to it.'

'"How dost thou wear and weary out thy days, Restless Ambition, never at an end."'

'Eh?'

'The melancholy truth, Frederic, is that I lack ambition – unlike my brothers, who take their father as their pattern. Papa desires John to succeed to his title and manage the estates. Hubert is to become a bishop and Robert a general. Given the formidable power of Papa's will, these things will certainly come to pass.'

'He's ambitious for you, too. He's made every effort to see you creditably established . . .'

'. . . in a position of his choosing . . .'

'. . . because he cares about you.'

'You think so? He has a strange way of showing it! I have never in my life won his unstinting praise. I have never made him happy. In my younger days I strove with all my might to please him. It was wasted effort. I don't intend to prolong the exercise.'

8

There was a hardness in his lordship's voice that warned Mr Lychgate not to pursue the argument. He was uncomfortably aware of the strained relations between Hector and his father. Julian, Duke of Wycombe, was of the old school, impossibly high in the instep, unbending in his decisions, and contemptuous of any display of emotion, which he held to be a mark of low breeding.

Frederic's own papa categorised the Duke as a martinet. Certainly he was not a man who inspired affection. His manner was austere and cold. His several houses were furnished, staffed and run with a grandeur and formality that did not accord with the relaxed style of the present day.

'Wycombe is the prisoner of his own conceit,' said Lord Lychgate bluntly. 'He's his own worst enemy.'

Lady Lychgate was kinder in her judgement. 'Julian wasn't always so stiff-necked,' she said. 'I remember him as a young man, as dashing a gallant as one could wish. It was only after Genevra died that his nature changed. He held Hector responsible for her death, you know – though how anyone could blame a four-year-old child, is beyond me. The trouble was that though Hector had the Wycombe cast of feature, in character he was remarkably like Genevra, a constant reminder to his father. For more than a year, Julian couldn't bring himself to look at the boy. He sent him to stay with Genevra's mama, who idolised him, spoiled him, and encouraged him to be as little like a Wycombe as possible.

'By the time Julian brought Hector home to Fontwell, the damage was done. The scene was set for a feud between the Wycombes and Otilie Frasier, with poor little Hector tossed like a shuttlecock between the two camps. Otilie was French, a great beauty and a brilliantly clever woman; but her character had been shaped by her upbringing at the court of Versailles. She was imbued with all the silly protocol of that place, but she had no true sense of decorum, no real consideration for others. She was vain, wilful and wildly extravagant. Her husband was always at his wits' end to know how to curb her spending, and after he died she was free to indulge her smallest whim. She was an inveterate gambler and by rights should have ended disgraced and a pauper; but she had a shrewd French head on her shoulders, and amassed a fortune through wise investments and foolish lovers. She died when Hector was eighteen and left everything to him. It was her parting blow at Julian Wycombe.

'Hector inherited not only his grandmama's money, but some of her faults, and I believe he flaunts those to annoy his father. That's very wrong in him, but one can't help thinking that if Genevra had lived, things would have been very different. Hector may favour his mama in character, but he also has a lot of his father in him: his sense of loyalty, and his courage, and his sharpness of intellect. It's a great pity he doesn't put it all to better use.'

Which was the burden of Hubert's song last night, and of Frederic's today.

Hector and Mr Lychgate had been staying at Lincoln for two weeks as the guests of Lord and Lady Hubert Wycombe. It was an experience Mr Lychgate wished to forget.

Heavy rain had ruled out all hope of hunting, and though Hubert possessed a fine library it held no charms for Frederic. He had been forced to endure a great deal of Hubert's conversation, which centred on the mundane affairs of his parish. Hubert was not a tolerant man. He disapproved of London, of Society, of the Royal Family, foreigners, reform, and other people's children. His own brood numbered six and Mr Lychgate thought them uniformly poisonous. Lady Hubert indulged them shamelessly, lauding their pert remarks as witticisms, encouraging their tale-bearing, and pressing them to eat far more than was good for them.

Mr Lychgate found his temper sorely tried, and marvelled at Hector's forbearance, particularly in regard to his sister-in-law. Emily Wycombe was an acidulous female who delivered sly digs in the guise of Christian counsel; and on the last night of the visit she took as her target Hector's reputation as a leader of fashion.

'In my humble view,' she said, 'clothes do not make the man. I cannot admire those who strive to outdo one another in vain show. We country bumpkins do not prick ourselves out in fine feathers, but are content to wear the breastplate of righteousness and the helmet of salvation.'

The image of Emily in armour cap-à-pie brought an unholy glint to Hector's eye, but he said nothing, and disaster might have been avoided had not Hubert chosen to enter the discussion.

'Speaking of clothes,' he said, 'I wish you will be so kind, Hector, as to convey to Fontwell a trunkful of cast-off clothing for distribution among the servants there. The articles are too good to be sent to the poorhouse. I am disposing of them only because I have gained a little embonpoint. I fancy that Herrick and Bogget and the rest will find good use for them, and the gesture will please Papa. If Frederic can find space for the box in his luggage-chaise, you may take it on from Leicester.'

Hector shook his head. 'Unfortunately I shan't be visiting Fontwell until the autumn. Send the trunk by cart, Hubert, it will get there far quicker.'

'And the expense?' demanded Hubert. 'We aren't all as rich as Golden Ball, you know. We must count our pennies with care.'

Since he knew Hubert to be the possessor of a very comfortable competence, Hector did not take this remark too seriously.

'I'll be happy to meet the cost of carriage,' he said. 'I'll call in at Plinlimmon's in Leicester and arrange for them to collect the trunk and send it south.'

Emily became waspish. 'I am persuaded,' she said tartly, 'that you will go to any lengths to save yourself effort!'

'Why yes,' Hector agreed. 'I'm incorrigibly lazy.'

'And selfish!' Emily had quite lost control. 'Could you not for once alter your plans, to serve others?'

'I'd be delighted to oblige you, Emily, but I have engagements in London which I can't break.'

'And what are those, pray?'

'An appointment with my tailor,' said Hector blandly, 'and an invitation to dine at Curzon House. I suppose I might risk offending the Curzons, but Weston is another matter.'

As Emily opened her mouth in fury, Hubert intervened.

'Let us say no more on the subject,' he said. 'If Hector is unwilling to undertake this small mission, then that is that.'

'I'm willing to have the trunk conveyed to Fontwell,' pointed out Hector, 'but not to accompany it.'

'The truth is,' said Hubert, very red in the face, 'you will not do anything that might please Papa!'

He had stepped on to Tom Tiddler's ground. Leaning back in

his chair, Hector spoke with dangerous quiet. 'I fail to see, Hubert, how Papa will be pleased by the sight of either a trunkful of old clothes, or me.'

'He will be gratified to know that you have performed a charitable act.'

'Won't it be charitable if I pay for the carriage?'

This logic infuriated Hubert past bearing. He struck his fist on the table so that the cutlery danced, and said in a thundering voice, 'Do not quibble with me, sir! Slick replies don't disguise the fact that you're breaking our father's heart by your dissipations. You gamble, you carouse, you consort with ruffians . . .'

'Oh, come! I've never run with the Carlton House set!'

'Do not interrupt! I speak for your own good! I take shame to see my brother a frivol, a flibbertigibbet, a slubberdegullion! You are idle, sir, idle! I'll wager a hundred guineas to a shilling that you're incapable of doing an honest week's work!'

Hector regarded his brother steadily for a moment, then drew a shilling from his pocket and tossed it on to the table. Hubert brushed it aside.

'Don't be ridiculous,' he said. 'The jest's in poor taste.'

'It's no jest.' Hector's smile was seraphic. 'A bet is a serious matter. We'd best set a time limit, however. Shall we say that if, during the course of the next month, I succeed in doing an honest week's work – duly attested to by a reliable witness – you will pay me one hundred guineas?'

Hubert began to look uneasy. 'I'm sorry,' he said stiffly. 'I went too far. I should not have spoken so to you. I exceeded my duty as a brother and a host, and I beg you will forgive me.'

'Certainly I forgive you, but the wager stands. I hope you don't mean to renege.'

'It is not a question of reneging,' said Emily, bridling. 'A man of God does not lay bets.'

But Hubert held up a hand. 'On the contrary, if it takes a hundred guineas to persuade Hector to undertake some worthwhile task, then it's money well spent.' He met his brother's eye. 'It must be worthwhile, you understand? No sinecures, no fudging.'

'Agreed.' Hector returned tranquilly to the enjoyment of his claret, and it was left to Mr Lychgate to restore some cordiality to the gathering.

'That is settled, then,' he said cheerfully. 'I shall take the trunk of clothing to Leicester in the chaise, and Hector will arrange for it to be sent on from there.'

Hubert thanked him for this gracious offer and the conversation moved on to safer, if duller, ground.

II

Lord Hector and Mr Lychgate left Lincoln next morning, bound
for the Lychgates' home near Leicester.

The rain had not abated, and they found the rivers overflow-
ing, and the roads in a shocking state. The travelling-coach,
which belonged to Frederic's father, was of old-fashioned design
and inclined to flounder on the muddy stretches. The luggage-
chaise in which rode Hector's valet Peck, and Frederic's man
Dooby, fared even worse.

By midday the entourage had come no further than Bingham.
Here they learned that the main road south had been blocked by
a mud-slide and that they must make a detour through the side
lanes. These proved to be little better than quagmires, and after
an hour the carriage slowed and came to a dead halt. Veitch the
groom came to tap on Frederic's window.

'What is it?' demanded Mr Lychgate, lowering the window
enough to let his voice be heard.

'It's Valiant, sir,' the groom replied, wiping water from his
eyes. 'Gone lame in the left fore. Not surprisin' in all this muck.
Morrison says I'd best lead 'im to the village.'

'What village? Where the devil are we?'

'Couple o' mile from Nether Kettleby, sir. Good inn there, wi'
stablin' fer the 'osses.'

'And plentiful ale, I make no doubt?'

Veitch grinned. 'Aye, sir, an' a nice side o' beef, too.'

Mr Lychgate shook his head. 'We can't break our journey.
Lord Hector is pressed for time.'

'Not so pressed as to risk your cattle in this weather,' Hector
said. 'Besides, I'm devilish hungry. My vote goes for Nether
Kettleby.'

Frederic accordingly instructed Veitch to unharness the lame
leader. This having been done, he rapped on the carriage roof as
a signal to Morrison to drive on. The carriage remained station-
ary. There was the sound of altercation in the roadway ahead,
and presently Veitch returned to the window.

'Beggin' yer pardon, sir,' he said, 'but there's a gennelman a-settin' in the road. Won't move, noways. Says 'e's waitin' fer a sign.'

'Then give it to him, Veitch,' said Mr Lychgate irritably. 'Remove him bodily, if need be.'

'Don't see as I can, sir. Wouldn't be right, seein' as 'e's a parson, sir.'

Mr Lychgate sighed, turned up the collar of his drab-coat, clapped his hat on his head and climbed down from the carriage. Lord Hector followed suit.

Seated on a battered valise in the middle of the roadway was an exceedingly wet parson. Water streamed from his drooping clerical hat and sodden black raiment. He seemed to be oblivious to the rain, to the carriage-horses champing impatiently not two yards from his nose, and to the furious glare of Mr Lychgate. His body rocked to and fro, his eyes stared blindly skyward.

Mr Lychgate bent towards him. 'Sir,' he said loudly, 'you are blocking the road. Be so good as to move to one side.'

The only response was a strangled sob.

Mr Lychgate tried again. 'Pray where are you from, sir, and where are you bound?'

The man lowered his gaze. His pale lips whispered. 'I come from Hell. I hope to go to Heaven.'

'Well, yes, some day no doubt you will, but in the meantime, perhaps you could wait somewhere else?'

'All the trumpets,' declared the man, 'will sound for me on the other side.'

Mr Lychgate looked at his lordship. 'The fellow's three sheets in the wind.'

'I don't think so. Can't smell it on him.'

'Mad, then. A case of religious mania. Dangerous, I shouldn't wonder.'

Hector shook his head. 'I don't think he's drunk or mad. I think he's suffering from shock.' He put a hand on the man's shoulder and shook him gently. 'Will you ride with us to the village, sir? I'm told the inn there is tolerable. At least it will be dry.'

For answer, the man seized the skirts of his lordship's great-coat and burst into fresh sobs. Hector took him by one shaking arm and pulled him to his feet.

'Come,' he said briskly. 'Veitch will bring your bag.'

'You ain't goin' to put him in my carriage,' protested Mr Lychgate. 'He'll ruin the upholstery.' But he nodded to Veitch to hoist the valise up to the coachman's box.

'I hope you know what you're doin',' he grumbled, as he helped Hector ease the clergyman into the coach.

'I'm saving a fellow pilgrim from the Slough of Despond,' said Hector cheerfully.

'And after that, what then?'

'I've no idea. One step at a time, Frederic. On to Nether Kettleby! A plan will come to us when we've drunk a quart or two of ale, and sampled the side of beef.'

Mr Lychgate was gripped by deep foreboding, but could think of nothing to say. The coach and chaise moved slowly along the road, with Veitch and the limping Valiant bringing up the rear.

Twenty minutes later they arrived at the Cap and Bells, a solid hostelry of Jacobean brick, with a good yard, ample sheds, and a fair-sized barn.

The landlord hurried out to greet his guests and assure Their Honours he was able to house and feed the whole party; a servant came to help Dooby bring in the luggage from the chaise; Mr Lychgate went off with Veitch and the two coachmen to see to the stabling of the horses; and it was left to Lord Hector and his valet to convey the sodden pilgrim within doors.

He had recovered a little from his early trance-like state, and though his teeth chattered with cold, he succeeded in identifying himself.

'M-my name, sir, is B-Bumper. Eb-Eb-Ebenezer B-Bumper. I am d-deeply obliged to you for b-bringing me here. When we met I was n-not myself. I fear I c-caused you a great deal of inconvenience.'

'My name's Wycombe,' Hector said. 'This is my man Peck. He'll help you to your room.'

'There's n-no n-need,' began Mr Bumper, but his lordship cut him short.

'You've suffered a shock, Mr Bumper. Get out of those wet clothes, and give them to Peck to be dried. Mr Lychgate and I will be dining an hour from now. I hope you will join us.'

He did not wait to receive Mr Bumper's stammered thanks, but sauntered off to the private parlour indicated by the landlord and set about ordering a substantial meal, adding to the roast sirloin a saddle of mutton, some glazed capons, vegetables, bread and cheese. The landlord promised ale, burgundy, claret and a nice bottle of brandy to round all off.

These matters settled, Hector repaired to his bedroom. He shed his greatcoat and jacket, slipped off cravat and shirt, and was rummaging through his valise for fresh linen when there was a tap on the door and Peck appeared bearing hot water and towels.

Peck had been a footman at Fontwell in his youth, and was aware of all the circumstances of the Wycombe family. When Hector left home at the age of eighteen, Peck accompanied him as his valet. Over the ensuing ten years they had learned together the ways of the beau monde and had reached an excellent understanding of each other's gifts and failings.

Peck emptied the can of hot water into the basin on the washstand, arranged the folded towels next to it, and came to remove a bundle of cravats from his lordship's grasp.

'The Reverend Gentleman, my lord,' he suggested, 'is a very rum touch.'

'Very,' agreed his lordship, crossing to the washstand and beginning to sluice his face and torso.

'Told me he walked from Great Kettleby,' continued Peck. 'That's twelve miles, they tell me, across the fields. Carrying a bag, it's a goodish step.'

'It is.' Hector dried himself briskly and allowed Peck to help him into a clean shirt.

'Demons,' Peck said. 'He spoke of being tormented by demons.'

His lordship smiled bleakly. 'Perhaps he has brothers, Peck.'

Peck shook his head unhappily.

It had in no way surprised him when his master chose to offer Mr Bumper a ride in the carriage and a seat at the dinner table. There were some that might consider such actions to be beneath their dignity, but Lord Hector wasn't one of them. Nothing top-lofty about him. Did as he felt he should without troubling himself over what others might think.

Yet Peck sensed that this rescue of Mr Bumper was a sign of a crisis in his master's life. The discussion in the servants' hall last night had been all of the squabble between the two brothers. Peck knew that though Lord Hector might put on a smiling face, he was angered and hurt by the insults dealt him.

It was one thing for the old Duke to come the heavy – a father was entitled to speak sharpish to his sons – but when his lordship's brothers tried the same trick, it was time to run up the storm signals. Milords John, Hubert and Robert were quick enough to come to Lord Hector when they needed a spot of the ready, or a favour done; but between times they treated him as if he was still wet behind the ears. Jealous of him, if the truth be known, and working it off in uncalled-for advice. Lord H had been patient with 'em till now, but he was about ready to boil over, any fool could see.

Peck cleared his throat, wondering if he dared speak his mind. 'The question is, my lord,' he said, 'what's to be done with the Reverend?'

Lord Hector smiled. 'Why, he must be fed, Peck, and allowed to enjoy a good night's rest. Then we shall see.'

He took the cravat held out and moved to the looking-glass. Wrapping the muslin round his throat with slow, precise movements, he tied an intricate knot. He surveyed the result with a critical eye, then gently lowered his chin causing the fabric to form three parallel creases. Again he considered the effect.

'It will have to do,' he decided. He put on waistcoat and coat, slipped his watch into an inner pocket, nodded dismissal to Peck, and left the room.

Downstairs in the parlour, he found Mr Lychgate standing before the fire, a tankard in his hand. Hector helped himself from the stoup on the table and came to join him.

'How's Valiant?' he enquired.

'Settled nicely. It's no more than a strain. Veitch knows what to do.'

'Good.' His lordship took a pull at his ale. 'I must warn you that I've invited Ebenezer Bumper to dine with us.'

Mr Lychgate, like Peck, was conscious of unusual tension in his friend but, unlike Peck, he was not afraid to challenge it.

'Why?' he asked bluntly.

'Vulgar curiosity. I want to hear his story.'

'Well I don't. At best, the fellow's touched in the attic. At worst he's a desperado, after easy money.'

'Desperado,' mused his lordship. 'One who is devoid of hope. You may be right.' As Frederic seemed ready to protest further, Hector smiled. 'Indulge me,' he said. 'After all, no other entertainment is available in this backwater.'

At that point, Mr Bumper himself arrived in the doorway. Now that he had shed his hat, his features could be clearly seen. The pointed nose, the tremulous mouth, the pale protuberant eyes suggested that here was a man who lived always on the brink of hysteria. He came towards them, nervously wringing his hands.

'Lord Hector, I beg you will forgive me! Had I guessed your identity, I would never have presumed to intrude upon your privacy. I am here only to express my deep gratitude to you, after which I shall depart to dine in another place.'

Hector smiled, extending his hand. 'I doubt if there is one, Mr Bumper. You're very welcome. May I present the Honourable Mr Frederic Lychgate? It was his carriage that brought you here. Any thanks are owed to him, not to me.'

'Yes, yes, so I collect, and indeed I do thank you, Mr Lychgate, and offer you my abject apologies. I was not myself when you discovered me, not at all myself. I blush to recall my sad want of conduct.'

Frederic demurred politely, and Hector poured burgundy into a glass.

'A little wine, Mr Bumper, to steady the nerves?'

Mr Bumper's eyes glistened. 'Such kindness,' he cried. 'Such condescension! To have caused inconvenience to men of consequence like yourselves must put me quite beyond the pale.' He sat down, accepted the glass and drained it with remarkable speed. Hector refilled it.

'Thank you,' said Mr Bumper. He blinked rapidly. 'You are right, my lord. My nerves have been sadly overwrought of late. I have suffered unimaginable torments. Unimaginable.' He shuddered.

'In hell, I think you said,' prompted his lordship, sitting down and waving Frederic to a chair.

Mr Bumper coughed deprecatingly. 'That, my lord, was of

course a figure of speech. I did not refer to the Hell of Holy Writ, but to Hell on Earth.'

Mr Lychgate shifted uncomfortably, and Mr Bumper turned to face him. 'I beg you to believe, sir, that I am not deranged, though my behaviour this afternoon may have led you to think so. I am as sane as you are, but I confess that the treatment I have received over the past month has reduced me to the pitiable wreck you now behold. I am broken in spirit, Mr Lychgate . . . or was, until you and his lordship appointed yourselves my guardian angels.' He drank some more wine and heaved a deep sigh. 'Ah, that is excellent. Ambrosial.'

Hector stretched a hand to the decanter, but Mr Bumper shook his head. 'No, no, I thank you. I must not add inebriation to my other sins.' Leaning back in his chair he closed his eyes. 'How deliciously warm it is,' he murmured. 'In that accursed house I was perpetually chilled to the bone. I must ascribe it to apprehension, for I admit there were good fires in the rooms, even the bedrooms.'

He seemed about to drift into sleep, and Hector said loudly, 'What house do you speak of, Mr Bumper?'

'Eh?' Mr Bumper opened his eyes and sat up straight. 'Ah, my lord, on that point my lips must remain sealed. I am not the man to tattle about my employers. Mind you, that boy shouldn't be allowed to get away with it. He is a fiend. He put a toad in my pocket. He exchanged my breviary for a copy of the *Decameron*. He flouted my authority. He questioned my teaching. And last night he hid an object in my bed! When I climbed between the sheets expecting to sink into the arms of Morpheus, I encountered this . . . this horror. It was ice-cold and slimy to the touch. I envisaged snakes and sprang from the bed. Tossing back the bedclothes I beheld a human arm, a dead arm, speckled with blood! I shrieked and cast it from the window. Then I must have swooned for I woke to find myself surrounded by people who were dashing water in my face.'

'Whose arm was it?' asked Mr Lychgate, fascinated.

Mr Bumper drew out a kerchief and dabbed his brow. 'I learned this morning that it was not a real arm,' he said, 'and the blood was that of a chicken, but the effect was ghastly beyond imagining!'

'Nelson's Arm,' said his lordship.

Mr Bumper stared at him. 'Precisely. Don't tell me that you have suffered the same hideous experience?'

'Oh, yes, at Eton. It's an old ploy. Take a lady's kid glove, pack it with mud and grass, and leave it in the icehouse. When it is frozen, add a few decorative touches . . . as for example chicken's blood . . . and the result is enough to turn the strongest stomach.'

'I don't know about Eton,' said Mr Bumper with feeling, 'but I must tell you that to my mind only a demon could conceive and carry out such a trick.'

'A demon, or a schoolboy,' agreed Hector. 'How old is this one?'

'Eleven; but I assure you that in the ways of wickedness he is a great deal older.'

'How came it that you . . . er . . . fell victim to him?'

'I was engaged to be his tutor. My bishop recommended me for the post. It was to be a month's trial on either side. I endeavoured to impart knowledge to the boy. It was useless. He was not only stupid, but depraved.'

'And the boy's parents? Did they do nothing to check him?'

'His mama is dead. His papa entertains the notion that his son is delicate and must be indulged in every way.' Mr Bumper looked wistful. 'I was not permitted to beat him. I had no recourse. I had to endure it all, but after last night's episode, I knew I could stand no more. I collected what was owed to me and left the house. I did not even ask for transport to the Seven Stars, where I hoped to find space on the stage coach to Derby. When I learned that the main pike was closed, I walked to where you found me.' A glazed look came into Mr Bumper's eyes. 'Tomorrow I shall beg a ride north from some farmer. I shall go home. I shall never again attempt a tutor's task; I am not cut out for it. Perhaps I shall enter a contemplative Order. The tranquil life of a monk . . .'

'Had there been other tutors?' enquired Hector, cutting short his guest's flight of fancy.

The clergyman nodded vociferously. 'Indeed, yes! It was because none of them stayed for more than a week that the bishop approached me. He said I must regard it as a chance to pluck a brand from the fire. All I can say is, I would not care if that particular brand burned to cinders before my eyes!'

Luckily the arrival of dinner prevented Mr Bumper from making any more unchristian remarks.

The landlord had spared no effort in providing a really excellent meal. Fortified by good food, a fine burgundy, a mellow claret, and a superlative brandy, the three gentlemen contrived to pass a pleasant evening.

At ten o'clock Mr Bumper rose to his feet, delivered a graceful if slightly slurred speech of thanks, wished his hosts goodnight, and departed to bed.

'Well,' said Frederic, as the door closed, 'now we may be at our ease. Shall I send for another bottle?'

'Not on my account,' said his lordship abstractedly.

Mr Lychgate poured the last of the golden liquid into their glasses and sipped his appreciatively.

'Might purchase a few bottles for myself,' he said. 'Smooth as velvet, and probably cheaper than what's to be found in Leicester. What d'you think?'

'That man,' said Hector, 'should never have applied for the post.'

'Probably didn't know what was in store for him.'

'He's totally unfit for such work.'

'Oh, I agree. Dicked in the nob, poor fellow. Mind you, the boy sounds an extreme case. He should be sent to school; they'd soon shake the nonsense out of him.'

'If he's frail, they'd more likely kill him.'

'Rubbish,' said Mr Lychgate, remembering Emily's undisciplined tribe. 'The brat's obviously spoiled past bearing. I doubt if any man could put up with such a situation.'

'I think I could.'

'You?' Mr Lychgate burst out laughing. 'Oh, that's a good one! You a tutor! I can just see you with your Euclid and your Greek grammar! And do you have algebra? That's required, these days, I believe.'

'I imagine I could handle most subjects, at the level of an eleven-year-old.'

'Yes, and then there's the remuneration to be thought of. I daresay you might earn as much as ten guineas the month. Very useful, in your straitened circumstances.'

'Not ten guineas,' said Hector. 'One hundred. You've forgotten the wager, Frederic.'

'Eh? You mean Hubert? Good God, man, he wasn't serious!'

'Hubert laid odds of a hundred guineas to a shilling that I wouldn't in the course of a month do an honest week's work. I accepted the odds and tonight I find there is a post vacant, a post I believe I can fill.'

'Not a gentleman's post, Finch. Not a post for a Wycombe of Fontwell!'

'Why not?'

Mr Lychgate peered more closely at his friend. 'You must be foxed,' he decided.

'I'm dead sober, Freddy, and I mean to apply for the position of tutor to this boy.'

'It's madness,' cried Mr Lychgate, desperately casting about for a sound argument. 'Lord, man, you'd be found out in a trice.'

'How?'

'Your clothes, f'instance. Coat by Weston, boots by Hoby, fob-chain from Asprey's. You look like a chalk-pusher, don't you!'

His lordship was taken aback for a moment, but quickly rallied.

'I shall wear Hubert's cast-offs,' he said. 'They're well-worn and they won't fit me. I shall look suitably shabby-genteel.'

'It won't fadge,' Frederic said. Hope dawned in his eyes. 'Besides, you don't know the name of this gentleman, nor his direction. You can't hope to find the house.'

'Peck told me Bumper walked from Great Kettleby. Once I'm there, I'll easily discover where he was employed. You may drive me to the village tomorrow morning.'

'I'll do no such thing!'

'And if you will be so kind as to take Peck with you to Leicester, he may travel to London on the stage coach.'

'Your engagements . . .' said Frederic feebly.

'Peck shall carry letters of apology. It's no use arguing, Freddy, my mind's made up.'

Mr Lychgate saw that this was true, and decided that all he could do was see to it that Hector's latest freak didn't reach the ears of the outside world.

'Very well,' he said. 'I'll do as you ask. I'll drive you to Great Kettleby.'

'Thank you.'

'Don't thank me! I don't like this prank.' A thought occurred to Frederic. 'What if I need to write to you? How shall I call you? Lord Hector Wycombe won't do.'

'Quite right. I shall be Mr Hector Finch,' said his lordship. 'A man of respectable family, who is forced by unhappy circumstances to earn his bread and butter. And now, if you please, sit down and write me a testimonial. Make it as glowing as you can, with particular emphasis on my erudition, my high moral character, and my ability to handle refractory schoolboys.'

III

Peck's reaction to his lordship's plan was as unfavourable as Mr Lychgate's, though for different reasons.

'It'll come to no good, my lord,' he said. 'You'll find yourself telling a pack of lies, gettin' in deeper and deeper. And how will it look if you're taken up by the Law as an impostor? What will your father say to that, I'd like to know?'

'Something vitriolic, I've no doubt.' Hector handed Peck the key to Hubert's trunk. 'Open it up,' he ordered. 'I must choose a wardrobe proper to the role.'

Peck opened the box and Hector bent over to lift out a folded coat of black broadcloth. He tried it on, grinning at Peck's pained expression.

'Fits where it touches, eh? But the material is good.'

'It has no buttons,' pointed out Peck.

'So it hasn't. I expect my sister-in-law purloined them. You'll have to find substitutes. Cut them off something of mine.' He examined a pair of pantaloons and tossed them aside. 'No use. Hubert has indeed put on weight. It must be my own breeches, and his coats. That should give a sufficiently dowdy impression.' He hesitated over a bundle of clerical collars. 'I'm tempted,' he said, 'but perhaps that would be going too far. Besides, I've a feeling my prospective employer may have had his fill of the products of Mother Church.'

He completed his selection, and ordered Peck to pack the garments into his own valise.

'That'll give the game away, for sure,' said Peck. 'Pigskin, your case is.'

'I shall pass it off as the last vestige of my vanished fortune,' said Hector cheerfully. He strolled towards the dressing-table.

'Not your brushes, my lord,' Peck warned. 'They're monogrammed.'

'True.' Hector replaced them. 'I'll buy something less ostentatious; but my razors I must have.'

'And who's to shave you?' mourned Peck. 'Who's to polish

your boots, and press your suits, and turn you out as a gentleman should be?'

'I must take my chances.' His lordship weighed his watch in his hand for a moment, considering the Wycombe finch engraved on its back. 'I can't be without it,' he decided. 'My circumstances shall be represented as straitened, but not desperate.'

He took a roll of banknotes from his pocket, peeled off a few, and handed the balance to Peck.

'Use what you need for the journey to Town,' he said, 'and give the rest to Purdon to put in my safe.'

'You'll come short,' said Peck with conviction.

'In seven days? I think not. I shall have free bed and board, after all. Start packing, please. I have letters to write before I go to bed.'

Though Mr Lychgate and Peck renewed their pleas next morning, Lord Hector turned a deaf ear to both. At eleven o'clock, amid a welter of unsolicited advice, he was set down on the outskirts of Great Kettleby.

The rain had ceased, but the weather was still cool, a fact for which he was grateful as he had perforce to carry his baggage a quarter of a mile to reach the Seven Stars.

The village was large and looked to be prosperous. The stalls on the central square were doing a flourishing trade, and the inn yard was crowded with farmers' drays, gigs, even a brace of carriages.

Lord Hector entered the public taproom and looked about for the landlord. He quickly discovered that between Hector Wycombe, driving up in his curricle behind his blood bays, and plain Mr Finch arriving on foot, bag in hand, a vast gulf stretched. No one in the room paid him more than a cursory glance, and the potboy was far more concerned to serve the noisy group of farmers seated at the table by the window.

Setting down his valise, he made his way through the press to the bar counter. Two people were serving there; a thin, weasly man in a soiled apron, and a buxom woman with a knowing eye. Hector ordered ale, paid for it, and addressed the woman.

'Beg pardon, ma'am, perhaps you can assist me?'

Her sharp stare took in his ill-fitting coat and muddied boots. She sniffed.

'Stranger to these parts, be ye?'

'I am, yes.'

'From the stage, is it?'

As Hector looked puzzled, she spoke more loudly. 'I say, did 'ee come off t' stage coach?'

'Oh! No, ma'am. A friend was good enough to bring me here.' He gave her his most charming smile, and she relaxed a little.

'Wantin' a room, was yer?'

'No. In fact, I'm seeking an acquaintance of mine, a Mr Ebenezer Bumper, and I wonder if you can . . .'

''Ow come you know Bumper?'

'I met him by chance. He was stranded on the road near Nether Kettleby, and my friend assisted him.'

'Huh!' She tossed her head scornfully. 'That Bumper's on'y got fifteen ounces in 'is pound, if you ask me.'

'He mentioned that he had been employed as a tutor to the son of a local gentleman. I fear he didn't supply me with the name . . .'

The woman stared at him closely, then turned to the thin man beside her. 'Wragge,' she said sharply. 'We're nigh out of porter. See to it, will 'ee?' The man moved off and the woman leaned massive forearms on the counter.

'You after the job? That it?'

'I thought I might make enquiries . . .'

She leaned closer. 'Not a job I'd choose me'self,' she said hoarsely. 'Not in that 'ouse.'

'Indeed? Why do you say so?'

'Reasons.'

'The boy is . . . difficult, I gather.'

'Malarky!' The woman looked contemptuous. 'Boys'll be boys, the world over. Jason Carey's no worse'n most. If you ask me, it's the missus that's the trouble. I never could abide them 'oley-moley ones.'

Hector put on what he hoped was a downtrodden expression. 'I'm afraid, ma'am, I'm in no position to pick and choose. I'm ready to accept the difficulties – provided it's honest work.'

'Oh, it's honest, a'right, an' the pay's good, simly.'

'Then I'll be obliged to you if you'll tell me how to reach Mr Carey's residence.'

'Admiral,' she corrected. 'Admiral Sir William Carey, Bart. It's a ways up t' Kegworth Road.'

'Thank you. I'm most grateful for your help.'

'Ah.' She gave him another of her hard stares, then said, 'D'ye have much to carry, sir?'

'One valise.'

She nodded, scanning the faces in the taproom. Presently she raised an arm and bellowed 'Sam! Sam Hemming! Over yere, a moment.'

A young man with ginger hair made his way across to them, leaned to plant a kiss on the woman's cheek, and grinned broadly at Hector.

'What's Moll Wragge bin tellin' yer?' he demanded. 'Pack o' lies, I'll be bound. Proper ol' liar, is our Moll.'

Unruffled, Mrs Wragge tapped Mr Hemming's chest.

'You've 'ad more'n enough, young Sam. Time yer went 'ome to Dorcas, an' yer can take this gennelman wi' yer, so far as t' Manor.' She glanced at Hector. 'What's yer name, dearie?'

'Finch. Hector Finch.'

'Go an' fetch round the trap, Sam. Mr Finch is wishful to leave as soon as may be.'

So saying, she moved to the far end of the counter and began to berate the potboy for not clearing the dirty tankards. Hector collected his valise, and followed Sam Hemming out to the yard.

The journey in Hemming's trap was quickly over and Hector found himself once more on foot, this time tramping up a long, well-tended driveway. The Manor, when at last he reached it, proved to be surprisingly large; two houses run into one, the west wing Elizabethan, and the rest more modern. Capacious stables lay at the rear, backed by a home wood. To the left was a shrubbery, to the right a rose garden, with wide lawns between.

The only people in evidence were two gardeners, and they paid him no attention. Hector was not sure of the protocol involved in applying for work, but he decided that a would-be tutor should approach the front rather than the back door, and he climbed a shallow flight of steps to ring the doorbell.

This was presently opened by a black-clad butler. Hector gave his name and asked if he might speak to Admiral Carey. The butler shook his head, none too graciously.

28

'Sir William is from home this morning, sir.'

'Then perhaps I may await his return?'

'May I first enquire, sir, what is the nature of your business?'

It was an impertinence, and Lord Hector was on the point of dealing the man a sharp set-down, when he recalled his new role. He said quietly, 'I wish to enquire about the post of tutor to Master Jason Carey.'

The butler hesitated. He was at a loss to gauge the visitor's social status. His voice identified him as Gentry, but that coat! Moreover, Sudbury knew that no gentleman arrived at the door, baggage in hand. This man might be a sharp, in which case he should be sent packing; but if he was what he claimed to be, then he must be persuaded to remain at least until Sir William had had a chance to size him up.

As Sudbury stood irresolute, there was the sound of footsteps, and a girl came running down the stairway.

She was small and slender, dressed in a riding-habit the skirt of which she had looped over one arm, affording a generous glimpse of polished boots. She carried gloves and a riding-crop, and a tall hat was set on her brown curls, though the veil that would secure it was not yet tied. Reaching the hallway she paused, stared, then came across to the two at the door. Giving Hector a brief nod, she said crisply, 'What is it, Sudbury?'

Sudbury sighed. 'Mr Finch, Miss, desires to see Sir William on a matter of business.'

The girl's eyes, of an unusual grey-green colour, surveyed Hector dispassionately.

'What business, sir?' she asked.

'I wish to apply for the post of tutor, ma'am, if it is still vacant.'

She smiled faintly. 'It's vacant.' She continued to study Hector. He found it disconcerting. Young females were wont to look at him in a very different way. They might bat their eyelashes or lower them demurely, they might gaze at him languishingly or in open invitation, but they did not stare at him with such cool detachment. He began to feel a certain sympathy for Mr Bumper.

At last the girl reached a decision. 'My uncle should return within the hour, Mr Finch. If you care to wait, Sudbury will show you to the library.'

Bestowing another of her brisk nods on them, she hurried away.

Sudbury was far too well-trained to question her decision, but the rigidity of his back as he led Hector to the library, and the regal manner in which he withdrew from the scene, left no doubt of his disapproval.

Abandoned, Hector studied his surroundings. The room expressed very clearly the character and taste of its owner. Several of the bookcases had been altered to hold racks of maps and nautical charts. The pictures on the walls, with one exception, displayed battles at sea. A large cabinet housed a compass, a sextant, and a ship's bell. A pair of cutlasses was slung one each side of the chimney-piece, and on the vast chart-table that occupied the centre of the floor were ranks of miniature ships, arranged, Hector thought, in the fighting formations of the Battle of Trafalgar.

He was still admiring the model when the door behind him opened and Admiral Sir William Carey strode into the room. He was a small man, thickset, with a red face, and grey hair tied back in an old-fashioned *queue*. By his expression it was obvious he had come to repel boarders.

IV

'I'd have you know, Mr Finch, that the opinion of that donkey Bumper cuts no ice with me, none whatsoever.'

Admiral Carey stood straddle-legged on the hearthrug. His black eyes sparkled with rage.

Hector inclined his head. 'I understand your feelings, sir. I assure you I don't rely on Mr Bumper's recommendation, but on that of Mr Lychgate which you hold in your hand.'

'Never met the fellow!' The Admiral scowled at Frederic's letter. 'Acquainted with his papa, however. Lord Lychgate's word is good anywhere in this county.'

'If you require further testimonials, I'm sure Mr James Cavendish of the Admiralty would speak for me . . . as would Mr Arthur Spender of St Martin-in-the-Fields, London.'

'You've been employed by these gentlemen?'

'No, sir. To be honest, I've never before worked as a tutor.'

The Admiral's eyes narrowed. 'Then why start now? Eh?'

'Necessity drives me, Sir William.'

'Rolled up, are you? Pockets to let, that it?'

'Let us say,' replied Hector carefully, 'that gambling has brought me where I am today. I seek to redeem myself in the eyes of my brother who doesn't think me capable of earning my bread, even for a limited period.'

Sir William grunted. His suspicious glare and out-thrust jaw put Hector in mind of a singularly ill-tempered bulldog his brother John had once owned. When Towser was out of humour, the only safe course was to stand still and say nothing. Hector waited quietly for the Admiral's next words. He found them surprising.

'Tell me, Mr Finch, do you speak French?'

'I do, yes.'

'How well?'

'With fluency.'

'Aha! And do you have any French blood, Mr Finch?'

Hector was beginning to think he had stumbled into a nest of lunatics, but he answered the question.

'My maternal grandmother was French,' he said.

'She was, was she? What was her name, may I ask?'

'She was born de Montfort, and became Frasier on her marriage.'

'Frasier sounds English enough.'

'My family is English to the core, sir. My grandmother was . . . er . . . a mere flash in the pan.'

'Hmm.' The Admiral seemed to feel he should explain his last remarks. 'I can't abide the French,' he said. 'Fought 'em all my life. My first wife, Jason's mama, died in France.' His gaze lifted to the portrait above the fireplace; a young woman in a blue cloak, fair-haired, with a face both charming and wilful.

'It was enteric fever,' Sir William said. 'Georgina died of it. Jason took it too, but he recovered. It left him delicate. He's subject to bilious attacks and requires special care. I can't send him to school. He must have a tutor, but not an idiot like Bumper. Jason's as sharp as a needle; his mind needs to be challenged. It's hard to find a man who has both academic skill and the ability to set the boy an example of gentlemanly behaviour.'

Hector reflected that to hide a dismembered limb in a man's bed was hardly the mark of a gentleman, but he forbore to say so.

'My wife – my present wife – was confident Mr Bumper would fill the bill, but she was wrong.' Sir William wandered over to the chart-table and with a flick of one stubby finger demolished a large section of the French fleet.

'Scuppered the brutes,' he said with satisfaction. He turned back to Hector, his black eyes challenging.

'You a fightin' man, Mr Finch?'

'I was taught to fence and box, sir.'

'And you ain't craven, I hope? Bumper was craven. Swooned like a girl at the mere sight of blood.' He sighed. 'Well, I suppose beggars can't be choosers. You've the manners of a gentleman and, if that reference is to be believed, you're literate. I agree to employ you, Mr Finch. One month's trial, either way, at a salary of ten guineas the month.'

Hector drew a deep breath. 'I believe, sir, that one week should suffice for either one of us to know his mind.'

The Admiral scowled as if he would contest the point, but after a moment he nodded.

'So be it. One week's trial at two and a half guineas.'

Hector bowed. 'And when shall I meet your son, sir?'

'Later. He's from home this morning, visiting neighbours. I don't permit him to loiter in the village on Market Day. Too much raff and scaff about. He's out of harm's way at the Broughtons'.'

'I see.'

'No, you don't,' said Sir William snappishly. 'And I don't propose to discuss it. Just accept what I tell you, Finch, and we'll get along famously.' He pulled a turnip watch from his pocket and consulted it.

'We're accustomed to assemble for a glass of sherry at one o'clock,' he said. 'I suggest you join us. Give you a chance to meet the whole boiling – my wife Lady Carey, my daughter Laurel, my niece Miss Osmond, and of course Jason himself. Now I take it you'd like to be shown your room.'

He tugged sharply on the bellrope; a footman quickly appeared, and led Lord Hector away to begin his life as a working man.

The room allocated to him was nicely judged to suit his new status, being situated neither in the servants' quarters in the attic nor among the large front bedrooms on the first floor, but in the Elizabethan wing at the west end of the house.

Its decoration reminded Hector very much of that at Fontwell. The walls were panelled in dark oak, and the corniche of the ceiling was carved with Tudor roses and what he took to be the Carey crest. Above the fireplace, the massive overmantel depicted Adam and Eve and a smugly smiling serpent.

The appointments of the room were not lavish, but they were comfortable. The curtains at the windows and round the four-poster bed were of chintz, faded but crisply laundered. The bookcase proved disappointing for it contained little modern writing and few novels. However, there was a good selection of classical works, and a full shelf of school texts, which Hector resolved to study that night. Somehow he must contrive to stay one jump ahead of his pupil.

The view from the window was expansive. Beyond the shrubbery stretched open country, ploughed fields showing the first shoots of wheat, and pasture where sleek cattle grazed. This was Leicestershire, prime hunting country that he'd ridden over many times, yet he could not recall having seen Sir William at any of the meets. Not a hunting man, apparently, but an eccentric, something of a tartar, who kept his son very close at heel.

Molly Wragge blamed the lady of the house for that, but Sam Hemming declared that Molly Wragge was a liar. Only time would show where the truth lay.

Hector transferred his possessions from the valise to the wardrobe and dressing-chest, exchanged his muddy boots for black shoes and put on a clean cravat. His hair, cut in the fashionable windswept style, presented a problem, but by parting it in the middle and flattening it with pomade he achieved an effect that was downright staid. Even Emily must have approved of his appearance, he thought.

Grinning a little, he went in search of his new employers.

The drawing room of Kettleby Manor was a handsome apartment, its chairs and sofas upholstered in plum-coloured brocade, and its floor covered by fine Turkey carpets. A harp stood in one corner, a pianoforte in another. The cabinets flanking the fireplace contained several good pieces of Dresden china. There were no pictures on the walls, not so much as a family portrait, but the family itself was very much in evidence, clustered at the far end of the room and engaged in furious argument. Mr Finch, waiting self-effacingly in the doorway, was able to study the Careys at leisure.

In the centre of the fray stood the Admiral, pounding a fist into his palm and shouting that Henry Nettlebed was a great fool, and he'd tell him so to his face. To the Admiral's right, and making ineffectual attempts to stem his tirade, was a small plump woman in a grey silk dress, whom Hector judged to be Lady Carey . . . the ''oley-moley' of Molly Wragge's description.

Next to her ladyship, but taking little interest in the altercation, was the young woman Hector had met on his arrival at the house. She had exchanged her riding-habit for an afternoon gown of sea-green cashmere that admirably set off the whiteness of her skin. Hector guessed that this was the niece of whom the Admiral had spoken.

Facing Lady Carey were two exceedingly handsome young people: a girl of some sixteen summers, and a boy rather younger. Both had corn-gold hair, large blue eyes, and a fine-boned cast of countenance, and both stared mutinously at the Admiral who was now reaching the height of his peroration.

'I will not be defied,' he roared. 'You were directed to spend the morning with Martha and Pelham Broughton. You chose to disobey me. Why, I'd like to know? Answer me!'

The boy lifted his eyes to stare at his father. 'Martha is ill, Papa,' he said. 'Mrs Broughton thinks it's the mumps. She said we mustn't risk taking the infection.'

'You could have come home, couldn't you? But no, you must needs go gallivanting off to the Nettlebeds. How many times have I told you that I won't countenance such a friendship?'

'Come, my love,' said Lady Carey in a coaxing tone. 'You've no reason to dislike the Nettlebeds. They're everywhere accepted, you know, and most regular in their attendance at church. Really, one can't take exception to them.'

'I take strong exception to 'em,' retorted the Admiral. 'Henry Nettlebed is a radical, ma'am, a red revolutionary! Why, I've seen the writings of Rousseau and the like on his shelves! Only last week he had the effrontery to tell me that His Majesty King George III lost us the American colonies! He said that the men who threw the tea into Boston Harbour were Englishmen one could be proud of! If Nettlebed has his way we shall see our Army and Navy pensioned off, and the country handed over to a pack of sansculottes!'

'Dearest, I concede that Mr Nettlebed talks like a free-thinker, but one cannot question his patriotism. After all, he lost his oldest boy at Genappes, and his youngest is in the Hussars.'

'Crosby Nettlebed is in the Hussars because he hasn't the wit to be anywhere else,' said Sir William. 'He's a clodpole, a clunchhead, and I won't have him casting sheeps' eyes at my daughter, d'ye hear?'

This was too much for young Miss Carey. 'Crosby isn't a clunchhead,' she cried. 'If he had been, the King would never have granted him a commission!'

35

The Admiral burst out laughing. 'That's all you know, Miss! The reason your beau ideal can call himself "Ensign" is that his father was able to fork out the dibs for a set of colours. The army is the place for dolts and incompetents, and I'm sure Crosby will be very happy there, but he needn't think he can come dangling after you, for I won't allow it.' He swung round to glare at his son. 'As for you, Jason, I've a bone to pick with you. I watched you ride home, young fellow-me-lad! How many times have I warned you not to gallop about in that harum-scarum fashion, especially when there's been heavy rain? I didn't raise you to have you break your neck at some stitcher that's way beyond your capabilities.'

'I am capable, Papa! Ask Wiske, he'll tell you. The trouble is, Peppercorn's too small for me now. If you would only allow me to have a proper horse . . .'

The Admiral drew breath for another blast, but before he could speak, his wife caught sight of Hector standing in the doorway, and raised a cautionary hand. Sir William turned about, stared, then beckoned Hector forward.

'Come in, Mr Finch, come in! My apologies, I didn't see you there. Amelia my dear, allow me to present to you Mr Hector Finch, who comes to us on the recommendation of Lord Lychgate's son and heir.'

Lady Carey extended a small, plump hand. She was some years younger than her husband, and had a fresh, open countenance with a high complexion. Her brown hair was arranged in neat coils over her ears, and her grey eyes peered at him through spectacles which were attached to a silver chain about her neck. Her gown was severely cut, and she wore no jewellery save her wedding band. Hector would have thought her plain had it not been for the sweetness and warmth of her smile.

The Admiral indicated the next member of the group.

'My niece, Miss Serena Osmond.'

Miss Osmond did not offer her hand. 'Mr Finch and I met this morning,' she said coolly. Hector bowed, and moved on.

'My daughter Laurel,' supplied Sir William.

This time Hector received a curtsey, and a quick dimpling smile. Observing the perfection of lustrous eyes, a small straight nose, a tenderly curving mouth, and a figure that not even a dimity gown could impair, Hector decided that she would have no difficulty in attracting suitors more eligible than an Ensign of the Hussars.

'And my son Jason.' There was a note of tension in Sir William's voice as he drew the boy towards him, and Hector could understand why.

Young Jason Carey brought his heels together and made his bow in the manner of a duellist about to engage in a fight to the death. Never had Hector seen such animosity in a child's eyes. The hand he held out was pointedly ignored.

The Admiral attempted to cover the awkwardness by saying jovially, 'Well, my lad, go and make yourself presentable before nuncheon. We can't have you coming to table in all your dirt. Be off with you now.'

The boy left the room, and a footman brought in a decanter of sherry. Sir William poured for the three ladies, then handed a glass to Hector. Tasting it, he found it to be of superlative quality, though a shade sweeter than he liked. He glanced up to find Lady Carey regarding him gravely.

'You enjoy wine, Mr Finch?'

'I do, ma'am.' Hector remembered Mr Bumper, and added quickly, 'Though not to excess, of course.'

She sighed. 'I fear there's a great deal of insobriety in modern society. My own dear father relishes a fine vintage, but he will utterly forgo the pleasure if he thinks that any of his guests might take more than is wise. One should set a good example, don't you think, particularly to the young?'

The Admiral chuckled. 'There speaks the daughter of a bishop! I agree that a man shouldn't be a slave to the bottle, but it's my opinion a youngster should learn to take his measure like a gentleman, in his own home. A half tankard of ale does no harm to a growing boy.'

At this point Jason returned, scrubbed and combed, and the company repaired to the dining room where a cold collation awaited them. Hector found himself placed between Jason and Miss Osmond. The boy remained silent throughout the meal, rewarding any remark addressed to him with a stony stare; but Miss Osmond proved a livelier companion.

She chatted easily, with none of the lisps and drawls affected by fashionable beauties. Her smile was ready and she had an engaging way of tilting her head as she listened, which made her look like a small bird on the lookout for crumbs.

She told Hector she had been staying with her uncle and step-aunt since early December. 'It was a great kindness of them to invite me, for nothing can be gloomier than to spend Christmas and the New Year alone.'

'Have you no closer family, Miss Osmond?'

'My father died two years ago,' she replied, 'and my mother prefers to spend her winters abroad. At the moment she's at a spa in Tuscany.'

'Taking the waters is said to do wonders for the constitution.'

Miss Osmond helped herself liberally from a dish of salma-gundi. 'Mama, as I understand it, is taking the mud. She writes that she spends her mornings sitting in a mudbath, and her afternoons sipping sulphur-water, prune juice, and parsley tea. She's pressed me to join her, but somehow I can't bring myself to do so. Luckily she has a boon companion in second cousin Sybilla Fortescue. The two of them plan to make the Grand Tour of Europe's health resorts. From Tuscany they go to Aix-les-Bains, and from Aix, if the weather is warm enough, to Baden-Baden. I hope Mama may be in London for my come-out, but I place no reliance on it.'

As Hector looked at her in mild surprise, Miss Osmond sighed heavily. 'Yes, I know I am shockingly long in the tooth to be making my début, but the melancholy truth is that I have never been presented at Court. My aunt feels the disgrace keenly, and has persuaded me to make my curtsey to the King this year.'

'It will be a case of gilding the lily, Miss Osmond.'

She shot him a quizzical glance, as if she found the flattery transparent. 'I shall enjoy visiting London,' she said.

'Have you never been there?'

'Oh yes, often, but not since I grew up. You see, when I was seventeen I became betrothed, and Papa held that as I was already spoken for, it would be the merest extravagance to parade me in the marriage mart. Later, when the engagement ended, Papa succumbed to a seizure, and our being in black gloves precluded our going to parties. Since Papa's death, Mama's health has been too poor to allow her to racket about Town. This year, however, no problem exists. Uncle William has rented a house in Bruton Street for the Season. We are to remove there at the end of this month, and I'm to be presented at the May Court with my cousin Laurel.' She smiled brilliantly at Hector. 'Are you familiar with London, Mr Finch?'

'I have lived there for some years.'

'As a tutor?' Her tone was innocent, but there was a glint in her eyes that warned Hector to be wary. He knew all too well how the public eye fastened on a man of wealth and title. Even as a child, Miss Osmond might have had Lord Hector Wycombe pointed out to her in the Park or some other public place.

He said carelessly, 'No, ma'am. This is my first post.'

Again she gave him that quizzical look; but she did not press the point, turning instead to converse with her uncle. Hector decided that in future he would give Miss Osmond as wide a berth as possible. Her questions came far too close for comfort.

V

In the seclusion of her own room, Miss Osmond sat down to think about Mr Finch.

There was something disturbing about him, though she could not precisely define it.

His appearance, for instance – those clothes must surely have been bought from a second-hand jobber, yet Mr Finch wore them with complete assurance. His manners, though well-bred, were too easy by far. Without question, he was a handsome man, but the gleam in his eyes when they lit upon Laurel – or for that matter, herself – was quite inappropriate to his station in life. He was too . . . too comfortable, that was it!

Remembering other tutors and governesses who had crossed her path, Serena realised that they had all one thing in common. They were anxious; anxious to please their all-too-demanding employers, anxious to exist on their meagre salaries, pathetically anxious to be afforded some recognition and respect by the gentry they served.

Mr Finch was not anxious. He seemed very well pleased with his situation.

She could not rid herself of the feeling that he was not what he claimed to be.

Yet what possible reason could he have for posing as a tutor? It couldn't be that he meant to rob the house. The Manor held no art treasures. Her aunt owned little jewellery, her uncle kept no stores of money about him, preferring to lodge them with his bankers in Leicester.

It would be of no use to carry her suspicions to Sir William. He had employed Mr Finch, and would dislike having his judgement challenged. As for Aunt Amelia, she had the kindest of hearts, but her nature was so trusting that she could never recognise duplicity in another human being.

There was nothing for it, decided Serena, but to hold her peace . . . and to keep a very sharp eye on the activities of Mr Hector Finch.

*

Downstairs, Sir William and his wife were instructing Hector in the duties that would fall to him as Jason's tutor.

The interview took place in Lady Carey's private salon, a room whose initial elegance had long since been obscured by a rash of handworked rugs and cushions with knotted fringes. On each side of the fireplace hung a double row of miniature portraits in gilt frames. The bureau in the corner bulged with papers and letters, and on the spinet near the window lay piles of music, a basket of lavender, an embroidery tambour, and a glass bottle filled with sea-shells. To the left of the spinet stood a prie-dieu with a large Bible open upon it.

Seated in her chair, her hands folded in her lap, Lady Carey looked the picture of goodwill and practicality, but no one could call her pretty. Remembering the portrait of the exquisite Georgina in the library, Hector wondered how the Admiral had come to choose such a homely female as his second wife. Perhaps he had wished for a kind mama for his motherless children?

Sir William produced a sheet of paper from his pocket.

'We wish Jason to follow a strict regimen of work and play,' he said. 'I've written it out for you, Finch, and I expect you to see that it's adhered to in every detail.

'Jason is to rise at seven sharp. After the necessary ablutions, he may read quietly until breakfast, which is at eight in the schoolroom. The footman Findlay will attend on you, and you will please apply to him for anything you require.

'At nine you will bring Jason downstairs to greet us and acquaint us with the arrangements for the day. At quarter past nine he returns to the schoolroom for his lessons. He is to study Latin or Greek for the first part of every morning; and history, mathematics, and the use of the globes for the second. Are you competent to teach all these subjects?'

'Yes, Sir William.'

'Excellent. In the afternoons Jason must take regular exercise. Nothing excessive, mind! His strength must not be overtaxed. Riding and walking in moderation, that's what's required. He may try to hoax you into taking him out with a gun, but that I utterly forbid. I've seen enough bloodletting in my time to give me a distaste for firearms. Is that clear?'

'As crystal, sir.'

'Finally,' continued Sir William, 'there's the question of

Jason's leisure hours. They must be put to good use. Boys learn by example, not precept, and for that reason I encourage him to spend time with his elders. He takes his nuncheon and dinner with us . . . as you will do, except on formal occasions . . . and he's permitted to share in whatever entertainment offers in the evenings. We frequently invite our friends to take their pot luck with us, and there are parties with dancing for the young contingent, and whist or piquet for the older folk. I think you'll find we contrive to amuse ourselves very well in Kettleby.'

Hector took the paper Sir William held out to him.

'One point does occur to me, sir,' he said.

'Well, what is it?'

'I imagine you will want Jason to meet with other children? I suppose there are boys of his own age in the village?'

Sir William stood up abruptly. 'There are, Mr Finch; rowdy boys, the sons of farmhands, whose habits and language make them unfit companions for my son. Time enough for fraternising when our neighbours' lads are home from school. And now I have business to attend to. Your duties start tomorrow. I shall see you at dinner, six o'clock sharp.'

With a curt nod, he swung on his heel and left the room. They heard his voice in the corridor bellowing for Sudbury.

Hector had never believed that high rank entitled a man to be rude to his inferiors, indeed he regarded such conduct as contemptible. On the other hand, he had never reflected on how it must feel to be constantly snubbed and made to feel one's opinions were of no value. His reaction now was to consign Sir William and his brood to the devil and quit the house at once. He was prevented by Lady Carey's saying in a timid tone, 'Mr Finch, if you care to see over the Manor, I shall be happy to accompany you.'

He saw that her plain little face was tense with anxiety, and guessed that she spent much of her life trying to gloss over her husband's boorish behaviour.

He smiled down at her. 'That will be delightful, ma'am,' he said.

Their tour began in the schoolroom opposite Jason's bedchamber, and continued through both the old and the new parts of the mansion.

Lady Carey was an accomplished guide. She knew the name of the Elizabethan craftsman who had carved the great oak staircase, and of the Italian master who had executed the plasterwork in the ballroom. She could identify the subjects of all the portraits in the Long Gallery, and supplied colourful details of each one's life and times.

When at last they emerged on the lawn before the house, she said with a deprecating glance, 'You'll forgive my transports about the Manor, Mr Finch. To me it's the most beautiful building in the county. I know the purists hold that the marriage of Tudor and modern architecture is a *mésalliance*, but I can't agree. When Tabitha Carey – Sir William's grandmama – prevailed on her husband to build the new wing, she urged him to demolish the old, but he refused. He said that the history of the Careys was enshrined in those stones and he wouldn't lay a finger on them. Perhaps that seems nonsensical to you . . .'

'Not in the least!' said Hector, thinking of how much he would resent any change at Fontwell. His words seemed to reassure Lady Carey, for she became more confident and accepted the support of his arm as they strolled along a gravelled path that led past the end of the shrubbery.

Presently they reached a small grassy clearing and she checked.

'This is the oldest thing we have,' she said. 'Legend tells us that it was here in late Roman times . . . that it was a temple sacred to Mithras. Mr Henry Nettlebed, who is something of an authority on such matters, says it has no links with antiquity, and is merely a mausoleum dating from the year 1500.'

Hector eyed the edifice in the centre of the clearing. It was solidly built of weathered stone and sealed by a copper door encrusted with verdigris. Guarding the door were two massive marble figures whose arms were folded crosswise over their breasts and whose heads supported the pediment of the roof.

'It's said to be haunted,' supplied Lady Carey, 'by the ghost of the unfortunate monarch, Charles I. The story goes that he took refuge at the Manor before the Battle of Naseby, and that Cromwell's soldiers searched the house but failed to find him because he was concealed in one of the tombs in the mausoleum. Mr Nettlebed says it's all nonsense, that the Careys were staunch

Roundheads not Royalists, and that Charles would in any case have suffocated inside a sarcophagus.'

Hector perceived that Mr Nettlebed was a killjoy. 'I've always preferred amusing fiction to dull fact,' he said, and Lady Carey smiled warmly at him.

'Oh, so have I! William calls me romantical, but I believe the old folktales should be preserved. This part of the country is my stamping-ground. I was born in Kettleby village, and my father leased the Manor for a time. Then Sir William returned from his tour of duty in the West Indies, and my family removed to Melton Mowbray.'

'So you've known the Careys for some time, ma'am?'

'All my life. William's brother John and sister Letitia were my childhood companions. It was I who introduced William to his first wife, my friend Georgina Marriott. She was a reigning toast, you know, with a great many suitors at her feet, but she chose William. I was her bridesmaid, and when Laurel was born, I stood godmother to her. She was left in my care when William and Georgina made their fateful journey to Marseilles.'

She spoke with evident distress, and turning away began to retrace her steps to the terrace; but after a few paces she stopped and faced Hector.

'Mr Finch,' she said, 'it's not my custom to bare my soul to strangers, but I must talk to someone or I shall run mad. Our situation here is desperate. I feel you were sent by Heaven to deliver us.'

As Hector gazed at her in astonishment, she went on quickly, 'It may be that as Jason's tutor you'll be able to influence him. Please believe that I'm deeply attached to my stepchildren, and strive to do what is best for them. Laurel is tractable and heeds my advice, but with Jason it is different. I can't reach him, Mr Finch. I have never been able to reach him. Try as I may, he sets a barrier between us. Yet he needs help, of that I'm sure, and if we cannot supply it, we'll lose him.'

'Lose?'

'I see you think I'm an hysterical female!'

'No, no. Perhaps if you'll explain a little . . .'

She spread her hands in despair. 'How does one explain a fear, a premonition? However, I will try.' She paused for a moment, then continued.

'William and Georgina took Jason with them to Marseilles. It was 1815, and William had been charged with the disposition of the French fleet after our victory at Waterloo. There was a widespread fear that Napoleon might once again break loose from captivity and return to ravage Europe.

'William was obliged to remain in the Mediterranean sector for many months. France was still in turmoil, and Marseilles a hotbed of political plotting, crime and vice; not at all the place to bring up a child. Yet William kept them with him. It's a decision he's regretted ever since.

'In January of 1816, there was an outbreak of enteric fever in the port. Hundreds of people were struck down, among them Georgina's abigail. Georgina and Jason took the infection from her. All three were placed in the care of the Sisters of Mercy at a hospice outside the city limits.

'In February, William wrote me that Georgina had died, but that Jason was making a slow recovery. I set out at once for France, and early in April I was able to bring Jason home to England.'

Hector looked at Lady Carey with new respect. For a lady of quality to travel across France so soon after the end of hostilities, while the government was in disarray and the countryside infested with bands of discharged soldiers, must have required a good deal of resolution. He began to think that his companion, for all her dowdy appearance, was not quite of the common order.

'It was many months,' she said, 'before Jason was well enough to resume normal life. He's still not robust. He suffers from digestive weakness, which the doctors say can be traced back to the damage inflicted by the fever. But that is not all. I fear that the harm lies much deeper . . .'

She shook her head, as if she dared not put her thoughts into words, and Hector said bluntly, 'Do you tell me, ma'am, that Jason's brain was affected by his illness?'

'No, of course not! What gave you such an idea?'

'Mr Bumper hinted that the boy was . . . well . . . slow to learn.'

'Rubbish! Jason is an exceptionally clever child.'

'Then why did Bumper think him stupid?'

'Because that's what Jason wished him to think! Jason dislikes tutors and does all he can to drive them away, but I assure you he's not stupid. Indeed I believe he knows a great deal more than he'll admit to. I've seen him poring over his Greek texts when he might be enjoying himself elsewhere. Yet for reasons I can't fathom he puts on this truculent, uncouth manner, and pretends to be as ignorant as any village boy. There's a contrariness in him that distresses me very much.'

Hector said carefully, 'I've heard that a severe fever can change the whole character of a victim . . .'

'I don't believe that's the case with Jason,' said Lady Carey. Her eyes searched Hector's face. 'Mr Finch, I'll be frank with you. I'm convinced it's Jason's mama who is the root of his trouble.'

'His mama? But you said she was dead.'

'Jason doesn't accept that. He cannot . . . will not . . . accept the fact that Georgina is dead. He believes that she's alive, that somehow we are keeping her from him, and that one day, if he can but keep faith with her memory, she will return to find him.'

VI

To Hector's relief, the Careys entertained no guests at the Manor that night; and Sir William expressing himself to be as drowsy as a dormouse, the company retired early to their beds.

Hector himself felt no desire for sleep. A great many questions were spinning through his head, the foremost being how he had allowed himself to fall into such a ridiculous situation.

He knew he had only himself to blame. For an instant he'd let his annoyance with Hubert cloud his judgement; with the result that instead of being comfortably ensconced in the Lychgates' home, surrounded by his friends and enjoying all the amenities of civilised society, he was marooned in this rural backwater among people of doubtful sanity.

The Admiral was a case in point. While pugnacity was to be expected in an old sea-dog, Sir William appeared to see enemies behind every tree. His hatred of the French was surely excessive, for while he might blame them for the War and the death of his wife, he must by the same token admit that French nuns had saved his son's life. The man's moods spun like a weathercock. Witness his outburst against the hapless Ensign Nettlebed. After all, Laurel Carey could be little more than sixteen years old. Chits of that age were forever tumbling in love with some hopelessly unsuitable *parti*, and no sensible father would fall into a tantrum over it.

Then there was Lady Carey – kindness itself, but possessed of some very weird notions. Her statement that young Jason believed his mama to be still alive was too bizarre to be given any credence.

Hector had been only five years old when his mother died. He remembered how he had fought against the idea of her death, how he had hoped against hope that one day she would come smiling into the room to embrace him, but the fantasy had lasted weeks, not years.

Lady Carey, he thought, must be one of those plain, prosaic-looking females who nurse a secret passion for gothic romance, and are forever looking for a spark of drama to enliven their humdrum lives.

Finally there was Miss Osmond; a quirkish girl, if ever there was one. Attractive to look at – a flawless complexion, magnificent eyes, a neat figure – yet unwilling or unable to put these charms to work. Her manner was disconcertingly blunt. She spoke of her late father's parsimony and her mother's hypochondria as if they were topics for amusement. She showed neither regret nor embarrassment for her broken engagement. If Miss Osmond had a heart, she kept it well hidden.

All in all, it was a thoroughly uncomfortable household and a wise man would leave it at once.

But that would be to confess defeat. Frederic Lychgate would never cease to roast him. Worse, Hubert would win his wager, and feel compelled for the rest of his life to pontificate about his younger brother's wastrelly ways.

There arose in Hector a determination not only to remain at the Manor, but to make a success of his task.

He sat for some time before his bedroom fire, considering how he might breach the barrier of Jason Carey's dislike.

After a while he crossed to the bookcase and selected certain volumes. Carrying these back to his chair, he settled to read in frowning concentration.

At breakfast next morning, Jason greeted Hector with politeness, if without enthusiasm, which led Hector to think Sir William had read the riot act about the proper treatment of tutors.

At nine, he took Jason downstairs to greet his parents, who were just completing their repast. Sir William at once called the boy to his side and began to converse with him. There seemed to be an excellent rapport between the two, Jason answering his papa's questions with alacrity, and both of them laughing heartily at some shared joke. Yet when Lady Carey addressed him, Jason answered in a perfunctory way, scarcely looking at her, nor did the Admiral offer any reproof for this show of bad manners.

At quarter past nine the interlude ended, and Hector and Jason returned to the schoolroom. According to the Admiral's neatly penned timetable, the first lesson of the day was to be Latin grammar, but Hector laid the primer aside and instead reached for his copy of Virgil.

'I gather you've been studying the *Aeneid*,' he said. 'How far have you come with it?'

Jason scowled. 'Book Three.' As Hector looked at him with raised brows, he added an unwilling 'sir'.

'Construe the opening passage,' Hector said.

Jason found the place in his own book and began to translate. His face, voice and posture expressed his contempt for the exercise, and after a while Hector stopped him.

'Tell me what you make of the passage,' he invited.

Jason shrugged. 'Nothin'.'

'Nothing? The state of Asia overthrown, Priam's people defeated, proud Ilium toppled, Neptune's Troy smoking on the ground, and you have no comment to offer?'

'Well, it was their own silly fault,' said Jason sullenly. 'They shouldn't have nabbed Helen.'

'Very true.'

Emboldened, Jason shot Hector a look under his eyelashes. 'Aeneas was a milksop,' he said flatly. 'Always goin' on about his duty, an' makin' sacrifices.'

'One must remember that his gods had very nasty ways of dealing with impiety. Aeneas might have found himself pushing a rock up a cliff for all eternity, or condemned to everlasting hunger and thirst.'

Jason's scowl deepened. 'I don't like Virgil.'

'You prefer Homer?'

Jason made no reply. If, as Lady Carey said, he made a habit of reading Greek on his own, he was not about to admit it.

Hector reached for the *Iliad*.

'Turn to Book Twenty-three.'

'I haven't studied that far,' protested Jason.

'You're about to do so. Find the place, please.'

Jason did as he was bid, and when he was ready, Hector said, 'At this point in the story, Patrocles, the great friend of the hero Achilles, has been cremated on his funeral pyre, and Achilles is arranging funeral games in his honour. Prizes have been brought from the ships, and the best drivers invited to compete in a chariot race.

'The contestants are Eumelos, who surpassed all others in horsemanship; Diomedes with the Trojan horses he'd taken from Aineias; Menelaos driving Podargos and the famous mare Aithe;

Antilochos with his horses from Pylose, which were exceptionally fast; and Meriones, whose animals had flowing manes but not much turn of speed.'

Hector glanced at Jason, who stared back with narrowed eyes.

'Now,' continued Hector, 'consider line 352. "They climbed into the chariots and placed their token-lots in the box. Achilles shook them and the first to fall out was that of Antilochos." In other words, Antilochos was drawn to start in lane number one. Menelaos drew lane two, Eumelos lane three, Meriones lane four, and Diomedes lane five. As a betting man, Jason, where would you put your money?'

Jason considered. 'Not on Meriones, I suppose, if his cattle were slugs. Menelaos and Antilochos had good teams. Eumelos was the best horseman. Diomedes . . . I don't know . . . on the outside, he couldn't be boxed in.'

'Right! So it was anyone's race. Now let's consider lines 362 to 372, which describes the "off". Look at the text, and tell me which words you recognise there.'

Jason pored over the page. '"Whips",' he said, 'and "horses".' He hesitated, then looked at Hector. '"Drive their horses"?'

'"Urge their horses" is better, I think.'

Jason nodded. '"Urge their horses . . . forward."' Again he studied the lines. '"Ships",' he said. '"Ships," and "wind" and chariots".'

'Good,' Hector said. 'Now I want you to listen while I read the passage aloud in English. Don't trouble with the text, just listen to the words and try to see the pictures they paint.'

He began to read.

'"They all held their whips lifted high above the horses, then struck with the thongs of the whips and shouted to urge their steeds to headlong speed. Swiftly they travelled over the plain and soon were far away from the ships. The rising dust clung under the horses' chests like clouds or a dust storm. Their manes streamed on the wind's blast, the chariots rocking dipped now to the earth who fosters so many, and now bounced up clear of the ground, and the drivers stood in the chariots with the spirit pulsing in each of them with the effort to win; and each was shouting to his horses, and the horses flew through the dust of the plain."'

Hector checked, and Jason looked up.

'What do you think of that, Jason?'

Jason seemed to be struggling with himself. 'It's good,' he said grudgingly.

'What makes it good?'

'That's what happens, in a race.' He rubbed his nose. 'Who won?'

'Diomedes. Turn to line 499. "And now the son of Tydeus" – that's Diomedes – "in his headlong course was close upon them, and he lashed his steeds continually with the whipstroke from the shoulder. They lifted their feet light and high as they galloped. Flying dust splashed the charioteer all the time, the chariot overlaid with gold and tin kept rolling hard after the flying hoofs of the horses, and the running rims of the wheels left small trace in the thin dust. The horses came in at a fast pace. Diomedes pulled them up in the midst of the assembled men, the thick sweat starting and dripping to the ground from his horses' necks and chests. He vaulted to the ground from his shining chariot and leaned his whip against the yoke."'

Again Hector paused, waiting for Jason's comment, but the boy did not speak. He sat quiet, running a finger back and forth across the page. At last he looked up.

'Do you know the whole of the *Iliad*, sir?'

Hector smiled. 'Not as well as I know this book. My father set me to study it when I was about your age.'

'Did you have a tutor?'

'Yes, until I was of an age to go to school.'

Interest died in Jason's face, to be replaced by the old sullenness.

'Papa won't let me go to school. He says I'm better off at home. I don't think I am. I'd like above all things to go to school.'

'Perhaps when you're a little older . . .'

'No.' The boy's eyes burned. 'Papa has made up his mind. When he does that, he never changes.'

Hector did not argue. He had satisfied himself that Jason Carey was no fool. He was not sure that the same could be said of Jason's father.

VII

Jason's programme for the afternoon was horse-riding, and at
two o'clock Hector went with him to the stable yard. This was
ruled with a rod of iron by the head groom, Samuel Wiske, a
man short and thickset as a beer-barrel, who in his youth had
served as a marine soldier aboard one of Sir William's ships.

Wiske was not a talkative man, and Hector could get little but
grunts from him as they crossed the cobbled yard. Jason's pony,
the despised Peppercorn, was already saddled and waiting; a
plump animal with a kind eye, but obviously no Pegasus. Hector
found himself hoping that the rest of the Admiral's string was of
a more mettlesome stamp.

He need not have worried. The looseboxes contained several
likely looking hunters and a match pair of carriage greys. Hector
stopped to admire them, and Wiske's manner warmed slightly.

'They're young 'uns,' he said, 'but prime goers. Short o'
schoolin' though.'

'Does Sir William drive them himself?'

'Sometimes, if 'e's naught better to do.' It was plain that his
employer's lack of interest was a sore point with the groom.

The last box on the row housed a magnificent black, who
watched their approach with pricked ears and enquiring nostrils.

'Now you're a splendid fellow,' said Hector, reaching up to
stroke the glossy neck.

''At's Sultan,' Wiske said. 'Nice paces, heart of a lion, but
well-mannered with it. Just as well, or Missy'd never 'old 'im.'

'He belongs to Miss Osmond?'

'Aye.' Wiske seemed to feel he'd said too much, for he moved
to another stall. 'I'll give you Roland,' he said brusquely. 'He's
about up to your weight.'

Roland, a useful bay with strong quarters, was presently led
out, and Hector swung himself to the saddle. A morose Jason
was already mounted on Peppercorn, and to Hector's surprise
Wiske joined the party, riding a rangy roan.

'Us'll go up Windy Hill,' said the groom, and started off,

signing to Jason to follow. Hector stifled an impulse to snub the man. A tutor, while he might not be on the wrong side of the baize door, was certainly not counted as gentry and need not expect the deference accorded to a Wycombe of Fontwell.

They headed away from the village, along lanes greening with buds, and climbed through woodland to a stretch of open country where they could gallop the horses. At the end of the run they reined in, and Jason pointed out the main features of Kettleby, the distant huddle of Nether Kettleby, and over to the northwest the shining course of the Wreake.

They took a different route home, riding in a wide circle to approach the village from the east. The last mile lay across pastureland and brought them eventually to a long field that sloped down to a massive stone dyke. They had reached the Careys' Home Acre, and the roofs of the Manor could be seen beyond the fence to their left.

Hector followed Jason and Wiske into the field, and was leaning to secure the latch of the gate when he heard the sound of thudding hoofs, and a wild shout from Wiske. Wheeling his horse, he saw Jason galloping towards the dyke, using his whip on Peppercorn's rounded flanks. After him thundered Wiske, lashing the roan and yelling like a banshee.

Hector saw that the boy meant to set his pony at the dyke. He urged Roland in pursuit, but knew he could not be in time to prevent disaster.

Luckily for them all, Peppercorn had a strong sense of self-preservation. Some ten strides from the stone wall he slowed, bucketed, and planted his little hoofs. Jason lurched forward over his neck and slid to the ground. As he scrambled to his feet, Wiske caught him by the collar, glared at him briefly, then turned to examine Peppercorn who stood trembling and sweating a pace or two away.

Hector dismounted and strode over to Jason. 'What in God's name do you think you were doing?' he demanded.

Jason stared at him mutinously. His face, under its streaks of mud, was very pale.

'Answer me!' Hector commanded. 'What were you thinking of? Did you plan to put him at the dyke?'

'Yes! Yes, I did! I should have known he'd refuse. He's nothing but a fat slug!'

'You may thank your stars for that! He could never have cleared such a height, even in the best conditions, and here you were asking him to take off from a quagmire! Use your eyes, boy! Look at that mud, it's inches deep.'

'He's a slug,' shouted Jason. 'He's a lazy fat coward and I hate him!'

'Peppercorn is not a coward; he's a small pony with the sense to know what's beyond his powers – which is more than can be said for you. And as we're discussing cowardice, let me tell you that it's the mark of a coward to strike those who can't strike back!'

'I didn't hit him very hard.'

'I don't mean Peppercorn. I mean unfortunates like Mr Bumper. You made his life a misery, and he had to endure all your loutish behaviour because he needed the money.'

Jason's face reddened. 'B-Bumper was a t-toad. He was a tell-tale-tit, always running to Papa . . .'

'Yes, that was a mistake! He should have warmed the seat of your breeches for you, as I shall certainly do if you try any more of this impertinence.'

'Papa doesn't permit me to be beaten! If you hit me, you'll be dismissed.'

'Ah, now I understand. You prefer a fight where your opponent's hands are tied? I think I would term that cowardice.'

'I'm not a coward, I'm not!' Tears began to course down Jason's face. 'You're like all the rest, you mean to spy on me, and p-pry into my affairs, you're as great a lickspittle as Bumper!' Sobbing, Jason snatched Peppercorn's reins from Wiske, sprang to the saddle, and set off pell-mell for the farmyard gate. Wiske would have pursued him, but Hector caught him by the shoulder.

'No. Leave him be. Let him work off his tantrum. I'll talk to him later.'

'You won't tell Sir William, sir? The lad means no 'arm.'

'He might have broken the pony's neck, to say nothing of his own!'

'That's so.' Wiske was eyeing Hector shrewdly. 'But 'e did all to impress you, Mr Finch. You're a cut above them others. Niminy-piminy lot, they was. Young Jason's took a shine to you, I can tell.'

'As I recall, Wiske, he called me a lickspittle.'

'Heat o' the moment, sir. Sorry for it, the moment 'e spoke. Give 'im a chance, and 'e'll tell you so.'

They began to walk their horses towards the far gate, which Jason had omitted to close.

'He's right about one thing,' Hector said. 'Peppercorn is far too small and slow for him. He's quite capable of managing a better animal. Why does Sir William forbid it?'

Wiske sighed. 'Reckon 'e's afeared, sir.'

'Of what? We all take tumbles.'

'It's not that.' Wiske was speaking half to himself. 'It's the woman. The Admiral fears that if the lad 'as a proper 'oss, 'e'll be off to seek for 'er.'

'You mean his mother?'

But Wiske was already regretting his burst of confidence, and with a shake of the head he lapsed once more into silence.

Entering the house, Hector made his way up the back stair to his room. He stripped off his jacket and sat down to remove his boots, wishing not for the first time that he had Peck with him. There was a knock at the door and Jason appeared, looking nervous.

'Sir? May I come in, please?'

'You may.' Hector waved him forward. 'I'll take it as a kindness if you'll help me off with these damn boots.'

Jason drew off the muddied Hessians, carried them to the corridor, and returned to face Hector.

'Wiske says I owe you an apology.'

'Does he? And do you agree with him?'

Jason rubbed the side of his nose. 'Yes. I was rude, and I'm truly sorry.'

Hector smiled. 'The apology is accepted.'

'I gave Peppercorn an apple and some sugar,' Jason said.

'I'm glad to hear it. The poor fellow needs feeding up, he's nothing but skin and bone.'

Jason chuckled. 'It's not that I don't care for him, you see? It's just that . . . well . . . he ain't exactly a firecracker.'

'True. If you wish it, I'll speak to your father . . .'

'No.' Jason shook his head regretfully. 'It wouldn't serve. The rule is I'm to ride Peppercorn, and Wiske is always to accompany me.'

It was the second time in their short acquaintance that Jason had referred to his father's intractability, and Hector felt a sharp pity for the boy.

'Wiske told me this afternoon,' he said, 'that your papa's greys need exercise. Do you think he would allow us to take them out?'

Jason looked doubtful. 'I don't know. He's very particular about who handles them. Perhaps if Wiske were to agree to it . . .'

Hector nodded gravely. He was imagining the unholy glee of the members of the Four-In-Hand Club should they learn that Wycombe's skills were to be assessed by a country groom.

'We'll see what can be arranged,' he promised. 'I'll discuss it with your papa tonight.'

Neither the Admiral nor Wiske raised any objection to the scheme, and on Wednesday afternoon the greys were harnessed to the mail phaeton and Hector and Jason, with Wiske on the rear seat, set out on their first drive.

Hector kept to the back roads for a time. The greys were feeling the effects of their long spell in the stables and fought briefly for their heads; but they soon discovered that the hands guiding them were of iron, and submitted to being put through their paces.

Hector found them to be sweet-mouthed and responsive, though lacking the precision that an expert whip required. On the pike road to the south he increased the speed, slowing again as they re-entered the village. They tooled sedately past the grain-merchants' hall and St Stephen's church, and turned homeward.

It was then that he glanced down at Jason, and saw that the boy was watching him eagerly, clearly itching for a chance to handle the ribbons. Normally Hector would not have considered such a thing, but Jason's circumstances were not normal, and he said:

'Well, Diomedes? Do you care to take a turn?'

Jason nodded speechlessly. Hector stopped the carriage and transferred the reins to Jason's hands. They proceeded at a decorous pace along the lane, Hector occasionally offering a word of advice, Jason tense with concentration. They made the turn into the home driveway with commendable neatness, and drew to a halt in the stable yard. Wiske came round to the horses' heads, and Hector and Jason alighted. The boy was trembling with excitement.

'By Jove,' he said, 'that was something like!'

'You did very well,' Hector said, but Jason shook his head.

'Oh I don't mean me! I'm the veriest whipster, but you, sir, you're a reg'lar nonesuch! Drove to an inch, I swear! Will you teach me? Wiske won't mind, will you, Wiske?'

The groom shook his head, a half-smile on his face, and Jason swung back to Hector.

'Tomorrow, Mr Finch? May we go out tomorrow?'

All the way back to the house he danced like a puppy at Hector's side, reciting the various reasons why it was desirable for him to learn to handle a team, listing the many places of interest to be visited in the district, and outlining a programme that would leave scant time for schoolwork.

Jem the stable-lad, who had come from the barn to help Wiske with the greys, stared after Jason in amazement. 'Niver see'd 'im so het-up,' he said. 'What's the new cove got, to send the lad into the clouds?'

Wiske did not answer, and his expression, as he watched Mr Finch's retreating back, was extremely pensive.

At about the time that Hector and his charge were returning from their drive, Serena Osmond entered the house by the front door. Pausing only to shed her cloak, she went in search of her aunt and cousin.

She found them in the sewing room, Lady Carey setting neat stitches in a worn altar-cloth, and Laurel making perfunctory passes at a piece of embroidery. Laurel cast the work aside when she saw Serena.

'Wherever have you been?' she demanded. 'I searched high and low for you.'

'I walked to the cottages to take Mr Poulton some calves-foot jelly.'

Laurel pulled a face. 'That old humbug,' she said. 'You've been taken in by him, Serena. All he wants is to be the centre of attention.'

Her stepmama cast her a reproving look. 'That's unkind, Laurel. Mr Poulton may be a lead-swinger, but Dr Stewart says that this time his lungs are severely congested.' She turned her myopic gaze on Serena. 'My love, I wish you will not walk in the fields alone. It's not becoming in a young girl.'

'I was only alone on the outward journey,' Serena answered, sitting down and stretching her feet to the fire. 'Bess and Crosby Nettlebed walked most of the way home with me.'

'Crosby? You saw Crosby?' Laurel clasped her hands in the attitude of one hearing angelic choirs. 'Oh, do pray tell me how he does.'

'To be honest, he seemed as cross as two sticks.'

'Ah, poor Crosby. How well I understand the agony he's suffering. To be forced to endure the pangs of separation . . .'

'Come, come,' said Lady Carey briskly. 'You saw him only two days ago.'

'To those in love, two days is an eternity.'

'If you ask me,' said Serena, 'it's not love that ails Crosby, but a head cold. It seems he took it through sitting all night on a tombstone. Lord knows what possessed him to do so.'

'He hoped to catch sight of me,' Laurel answered. 'I set a lantern in my window as a token of my constancy.'

'It might have been better to provide the poor man with a shawl, or at least warn him how damp the graveyard is.'

'His mind was on higher things. He was thinking of me!'

'In a graveyard? How unflattering!'

'I mean, he was thinking of our favourite poem – Mr Gray's "Elegy Written in a Country Churchyard".' Laurel closed her eyes and began to recite:

> 'Hard by yon wood, now smiling as in Scorn,
>   Mutt'ring his wayward Fancies he wou'd rove,
>   Now drooping, woeful wan, like one forlorn,
>   Or crazed with Care, or cross'd in hopeless Love.'

'Very touching,' agreed Serena, 'but Crosby would have been wiser to homeward plod his weary way.'

'You have no soul!' flashed Laurel. 'You don't know what it is to have Love's arrow strike at your very heart!'

'It's true I'm not romantical,' said Serena cheerfully. She saw that Laurel was close to tears, and relented. 'Crosby sent you his warmest respects. I'm not sure that respects can be warm, but he spoke hand-on-heart. He also begged me to say that he looks forward to seeing you a week from tonight.'

As Laurel looked puzzled, Lady Carey smiled. 'Yes, my love, the Nettlebeds are getting up an informal party next Wednesday, to celebrate Crosby's furlough. I've prevailed upon your papa to accept, which is a great concession on his part, for you know he holds the Nettlebeds in dislike.'

Laurel sprang to her feet and embraced her stepmother in an excess of delight; but the next moment she fell into despair.

'Wednesday! Mama, whatever shall I do? I've nothing to wear! Everything I own is in shreds!'

Lady Carey ignored this gross untruth. 'Sudbury says the pedlar Piggott is in the village,' she said tranquilly. 'I shall send for him tomorrow morning. Perhaps he can produce some pretty gauze or muslin, but you must cut and sew it yourself Laurel. There's no time to fetch a dressmaker from Leicester.'

'I shan't let that bother me,' said Laurel blithely. 'I enjoy sewing, when it's for myself. There's a pattern in *La Belle Assemblée* that I've been longing to copy. I shall look it out this instant.'

She danced away, as happy as a bird. Serena laughed. 'How clever of you, Aunt – and how lucky Piggott's to hand.'

'Laurel takes after her mama,' said Lady Carey. 'Georgina had that same passion for pretty clothes.' She met Serena's eyes. 'And the same thoughtless tongue, I'm afraid. I'm sure she didn't mean to wound you. She was only twelve when you . . . when your own hopes of happiness were dashed.'

Serena shrugged. 'That's all in the past. I'm quite over Lucius, I assure you. I don't think of him at all, now – except to thank Heaven I never married him.'

Lady Carey looked distressed. 'I hope, my dear, that you won't allow a single misfortune to blight your hopes. Surely you wish to marry? A home of your own, and children . . .'

'Oh yes, I plan to marry,' said Serena calmly, 'but I shan't let romance cloud my judgement. I shall find some man with interests similar to mine, someone of blameless character and comfortable fortune, and I daresay we shall get along very well.'

Lady Carey shook her head. She wished that dear Serena could learn to be a little less outspoken in her views. To succeed in society, one had to preserve its fictions. It didn't do for a young girl to make fun of the tender emotions, or put on that hard, uncaring manner.

Serena was pretty as a picture, she was accomplished, she

was blessed with impeccable breeding and a handsome income, but all these advantages might be brought to nothing by her uncomfortably blunt tongue. Gentlemen preferred to wed soft, compliant females. Their strong-minded sisters were apt to be left on the shelf.

Her ladyship was wondering how to broach this delicate subject when Serena abruptly introduced another.

'While I was out walking,' she said, 'I saw Mr Finch and Jason, driving along the pike in Uncle William's phaeton.'

'Your uncle thought it would be good for Jason.'

'And for the greys, of course.'

'Of course.'

'I'm surprised that he allowed a stranger to drive them.'

'Wiske felt Mr Finch was competent.'

'Competent is hardly the right word,' said Miss Osmond drily. 'Mr Finch, ma'am, is a dab hand, a regular out-and-outer. One can see at a glance that he's used to handling blood-cattle.'

Lady Carey nodded. 'In the past, no doubt he has, but I fear he's fallen on evil times – indeed, he said as much, when first your uncle spoke to him. It must be galling for one of gentle birth to be forced to seek work as a tutor, but his ill-fortune serves us well. Jason likes him, and is ready to learn from him, which is something we've not seen in a long time.'

'Oh, Finch is clever – but do you trust him, Aunt?'

'Yes, I do.' Lady Carey spoke with firmness. 'Why do you ask?'

Serena frowned. 'To come here with such a Banbury tale! If he's indeed a man of breeding, one would expect him to have friends to help him through any temporary difficulty.'

'Mr Lychgate vouched for him, remember.'

'What if Mr Lychgate proves to be a man of straw?'

'I hardly think that likely. The Lychgates are everywhere respected. As to Mr Finch, what has he done – except driving to a T – to make you mistrust him?'

'Nothing,' admitted Serena.

'Then surely he must be given a chance to prove himself? That is the Christian course, my love.'

Serena said no more, for when her aunt perceived something to be her Christian duty, nothing would shift her.

That night she thought long and hard about the state of affairs at the Manor. She'd spent enough time there to know the Careys were not a happy family. The fault, she believed, lay with her uncle.

Her own father had never held any brief for the Admiral. 'These Old Salts,' he said, 'are as near as dammit to being pirates. Will Carey has always sailed close to the wind and will come to grief some day, you mark my words.'

Fond as she was of her uncle, Serena knew there was some truth in these strictures. Moderation was not in Sir William's nature, as witness his treatment of his children. He doted upon them – one had only to watch his face to see how proud he was of Laurel's beauty and Jason's bright intelligence – yet he persisted in treating them as infants, allowing them no independent opinions, and curbing their freedom at every turn.

Lady Carey ascribed this harshness to the untimely death of his first wife. 'Losing Georgina has made him as nervous as a cat about the children,' she said. 'All he wants is to protect them from harm.'

But, thought Serena, how could a man so fearful for their safety employ as tutor a person who arrived on the doorstep unheralded, ill-clad, and virtually without credentials?'

A horrid suspicion lurked in her mind that Uncle William was in trouble, and that Mr Finch was part of it; but try as she might, she could think of no way to challenge either one of them.

VIII

The next morning as the family rose from the breakfast-table, they saw an extraordinary vehicle coming up the drive. Part-wagon and part-caravan, it was drawn by a massive Clydesdale mare, and driven by Piggott the pedlar. Beside him on the box perched a little swart monkey of a man with a scarlet kerchief knotted round his head, and a gold ring dangling from his left ear.

The ladies hurried out to the gravel turnabout, to find that Piggott and his companion had already lowered one side of the wagon to form a counter on which they were arranging bolts of silk, muslin and taffeta; rolls of lace; cards of multi-coloured buttons; and all the other paraphernalia of a mercer's trade.

Serena had never before laid eyes on Piggott, and his appearance came as a shock to her, for he was an albino. His hair and eyes were almost colourless, and his pallid skin was marred by large pinkish-brown patches. His immensely tall, thin body was clad in nankeen trousers and a green cutaway coat, and on his head he wore a large straw hat of the kind affected by French peasants.

He bowed low to Lady Carey and greeted her in a voice both deep and melodious. His accent was unusual, the broad North-country vowels blurred and softened. His movements as he unrolled his fabrics and draped them over the counter were graceful, even mesmeric. Serena, who had not intended to buy anything, found herself selecting a length of embroidered silk, while Laurel chose two of muslin and one of watered taffeta. Even Lady Carey, who cared nothing for such geegaws, was beguiled into buying a collar of point lace, which she said would nicely furbish up her old blue velvet.

Presently Admiral Carey joined his womenfolk. He was in high good humour, admired their purchases, and demanded to know how much he must stump up for these fal-lals.

Piggott named a price which Serena thought very reasonable.

The Admiral paid him, and adjured him with a wink to drive his wagon round to the kitchen door.

'You'll find plenty of custom there,' he said, 'and a stoup or two of ale, I dare swear.'

Clapping Piggott on the shoulder, he led his wife and daughter back to the house; but Serena, remembering that she needed a skein of embroidery silk, turned back towards the wagon. The swarthy man was busy rolling up the bolts of material, but Piggott had moved away and was gazing up at the second storey of the mansion. Serena saw that he was watching someone at the window of the schoolroom. It was Jason, and he was making some kind of signal, first crossing his arms on his chest, then holding up three fingers of his right hand.

Piggott nodded, and raised his hand in a similar gesture. Moving back towards the wagon, he caught sight of Serena and looked somewhat disconcerted; but the next moment he smiled, and said, 'Young Master's been at me to bring him a pocket-knife. I've a fine one, Spanish-made, but it'll cost him three shillin'. A tidy sum for a young lad to find.'

Serena bought her thread and returned to the house. As she went, she glanced up once more at the schoolroom window. Jason had vanished and in his place stood Mr Finch. He made a small bow, but whether this courtesy was directed at her, or at the pedlar, Serena could not tell.

At nuncheon the talk revolved round the party to be held by the Nettlebeds. Laurel had received a morning visit from her bosom bow Melanie Preston, and was full of news of the planned festivities.

'Everyone is invited,' she said. 'The Prestons, the Hambletons, the Garbutts. The Scott-Fishers are to bring their houseparty from Waltham. Melanie says that the refreshments are to be of the first style of elegance, and the musicians are to be brought from Leicester. Imagine, for once we shan't have to listen to old Ned Clarke and his fiddle. We shall have a proper band to play mazurkas and waltzes and . . .'

'You will not do any waltzing,' interrupted the Admiral, glowering at his daughter. 'I'm astounded that Nettlebed countenances such lascivious prancing in his house.'

'Papa, that's too gothic of you! The waltz is danced at all the ton parties, nowadays. Melanie says . . .'

'Thank you, I don't need Melanie Preston to tell me how my daughter shall conduct herself! Nor do I permit such pertness as you've just shown me. One more word, Miss, and you won't go to the party at all.'

Overcome, Laurel murmured an apology and sank back in her chair; but Serena took up the cudgels.

'Perhaps,' she said innocently, 'Mr Finch can tell us whether or not the waltz is considered proper in polite circles?'

All eyes fixed upon Hector. Seeing the trap in his path, he said blandly,

'It's certainly danced in many of the great houses, Miss Osmond, but I believe that at Almack's Club the high sticklers prevail. No young lady dares to take the floor in the waltz without permission from the hostesses.'

'How interesting! Tell me, have you visited Almack's recently, Mr Finch?'

'Not for many months, ma'am.'

'I'm told it's very hard to gain admission?'

'Very.'

She sighed. 'Do you think my cousin and I will be able to procure vouchers?'

Looking at Serena's smiling face, Hector felt a strong desire to slap her. He said bluntly:

'Not by your own efforts. Newcomers to London are well advised to find a sponsor, preferably one who's on friendly terms with Lady Sefton or Lady Jersey. They're held to be the most amiable of the patronesses.'

'Indeed? Are you acquainted with these ladies, Mr Finch? Perhaps you can put in a good word for us?'

Seeing a spark kindle in Hector's eye, Lady Carey said quietly, 'We must leave such problems, Serena, until we reach Town.' She then moved the conversation to safer ground, but later, when she and Serena were strolling in the garden together, she said gently, 'It was wrong in you, my dear, to speak to Mr Finch as you did. One should never remind a man that he's come down in the world.'

'But has he, Aunt? Was he ever as high as he'd like us to believe? He admits he hasn't set foot in Almack's for months. I

64

wonder if he was ever there. As for his talk of "great houses", and "amiable patronesses", I confess I find such name-dropping contemptible.'

'It's true, none the less, that Lady Jersey and Lady Sefton are more approachable than the rest of those gorgons. As a matter of fact, I plan to ask Lady Sefton for vouchers to one of the Assemblies.'

Serena gazed at her aunt. 'Do you know her, ma'am?'

'Why, yes. She's the second cousin once removed of my own dear mother, and has always treated me with the greatest affability.'

Serena burst out laughing. 'Dear Aunt, you never cease to amaze me! How sly of you, to conceal these lofty connections.'

Lady Carey smiled tranquilly. 'I wouldn't wish to be accused of name-dropping,' she said.

IX

It was Lady Carey's custom to lead Laurel and Jason in Bible study, on Thursday afternoons between the hours of four and half past. Hector, finding himself with no duties to perform, decided to stroll down to the village, in the hopes that fresh air and exercise would improve his temper. He had found Miss Osmond's scornful remarks infuriating, and only his determination to remain at the Manor had prevented him from giving her a sharp set-down.

It was no longer simply a question of winning his bet with Hubert. More and more he was convinced that there was something very smoky going on, and that young Jason Carey stood in desperate need of a friend.

Like Miss Osmond, he had witnessed the interchange between Jason and the pedlar Piggott; and, like her, he had deduced that the two were closing some bargain. What it might be, he couldn't imagine.

He had watched Piggott from the schoolroom window that morning and thought him oily and insinuating, not at all the sort of man who would put himself out to please a child. Piggott, moreover, was no ordinary hawker. The silks and satins he displayed were of superior quality, and to Hector's practised eye bore the stamp of Paris. Yet the Carey ladies had been in raptures about the low price set on them.

Hector was inclined to think that Piggott the mercer was involved in another, less reputable trade. Very likely the fine wines at the inn in Nether Kettleby, and the superlative port, sherry and brandy that graced the Admiral's table, had come into the country without permission from His Majesty's Customs and Excise. Contraband was brought through many of the east-coast ports, to be dispersed across England by the packhorses and wagons of the Gentlemen. If smuggling was Piggott's lay and Jason knew of it, Piggott might be ready to buy the boy's silence with a favour or two.

There were questions to be asked about Piggott and his links with the Careys. Hector thought the answers might be found at the Seven Stars Inn.

He reached the inn yard soon after four, and was gratified to note that Piggott's wagon stood in the shelter of the barn. The landlord Wragge was supervising the transference of a load of hay from a wain to the loft, but of the pedlar and his henchman there was no sign.

The main taproom was almost deserted at this hour. Mrs Molly Wragge was engaged in setting a row of polished tankards on the shelf beneath the ale-barrel. She looked up and smiled as Hector approached.

'Why, if it ain't Mr Finch! Good day to ye, sir. What'll you 'ave?'

'Brandy, if you please, Molly.' Hector laid his curly-brimmed hat on the counter, and placed a coin beside it. 'Make it the best you have, and take something for yourself.'

She shot him a shrewd glance as she reached for a bottle behind her. Pouring brandy into two glasses, she said,

'What's the toast then, m'dear?'

Hector raised his glass. 'Fortune,' he said. 'That fickle jade who permits me, on all too rare occasions, to indulge my taste for good liquor.' He wafted the glass under his nose, sipped delicately, and sighed. 'Very tolerable,' he murmured. 'A full-bodied Armagnac, well-matured.'

Molly nodded. 'Seven year in the cask, that were.'

'Very tolerable,' repeated Hector. 'Not, mind you, as good as I've been privileged to enjoy these past few days at the Manor. Sir William Carey is a connoisseur, ma'am, and he's also the most generous of men. Not many employers will condescend to offer a dram to a mere pedagogue. Tutors, alas, need not hope to enjoy the finer things of life. Erudition and moral virtue will not buy a man a noble cognac, my dear. No. It's money that talks, when all's said and done.'

Molly leaned a plump elbow on the counter. 'Aye, that's so.'

'Of course,' continued Hector, putting on a confiding air, 'I'm the first to concede that money can't buy a fine palate. There's many a rich man can't tell hock from hogwash, Mrs Wragge. Sir William Carey is an exception, a man of discrimination, a man of taste. I'd go so far as to say that Sir

67

William is a Nose. I'll wager that when it comes to choosing a bottle, he doesn't waste his blunt. Which prompts me to ask you, Molly my dear, if he buys his elixirs from your establishment?'

Molly's eyelids flickered. 'Some, 'e buys from us,' she admitted. 'Happen if Wragge comes upon a nice drop o' port or sherry, 'e'll pass the word to the Admiral. Often as not, 'e'll take a bottle or two.'

'Ah!' Hector gave a knowing wink. 'Just so, just as I thought. You have the heavenly nectar and you wish all to share it. Which prompts me to make a suggestion . . . only a suggestion, mark you . . . that might bring you in a tidy little profit.'

Molly picked up a glass and began to polish it. 'Profit, Mr Finch?'

'Profit, Mrs Wragge. Let me explain. I'm a man who has a palate, ma'am, but not the means to indulge it. I lack the dibs. I lack the ready. However, my profession takes me into houses where there is no such impediment . . . houses where the style of life is elevated, whose inhabitants desire the best of everything and are prepared to pay for it. It's been my experience that such folk are ever anxious to hear of suppliers who can procure the best quality goods. For example, this morning the good ladies of the Manor were happy to purchase several lengths of Mr Piggott's excellent silks. It occurs to me that if, in the future, I am in a position to recommend him to other members of the ton, a suitable understanding might be reached between us.'

Molly Wragge held the glass to the light and examined it critically. 'What sort of understanding, sir?'

'Why, a financial one, Mrs Wragge. Something for Piggott and his friend – I didn't catch the man's name, I'm afraid – '

'Laval.'

'Something for Laval, something for me, and of course something for you. All you need do is drop a word in Piggott's ear, the merest hint, that for a small consideration I can put him in the way of further business.'

'I don't 'ave a pull wi' Piggott.'

'Perhaps your husband does, though?'

Molly shook her head vigorously. 'Wragge'd black me eye if I was to arst 'im.'

'Then try what you can achieve, yourself. A handsome woman

like you must know how to bring a man round her thumb.' Hector took a gold coin from his pocket and slid it across the counter. 'I'll guarantee to provide the names and directions of customers in the market for silks, laces, fal-lals . . . and anything else Piggott may have to sell, if you take my meaning?'

It was clear that Molly did, for she stared at him with an expression half-greedy and half-scared. Before she could speak, voices sounded in the lobby, and Wragge and the driver of the haywain appeared in the doorway of the taproom. Molly snatched up the coin and slipped it into the bosom of her gown. 'I'll tell Piggott,' she muttered, 'but I can't promise nothing.'

She moved away to join her husband. Hector picked up his hat and sauntered out into the fading sunlight.

He was not so naive as to suppose that Piggott would take his crudely offered bait. The smuggling fraternity was far too fly to admit amateurs to its ranks. But with luck it would put Piggott on his guard, perhaps even persuade him to avoid Kettleby in future. Better that the Admiral should lose his source of supply, than that young Jason be involved with such a dangerous bunch of rogues.

He returned to the Manor satisfied that he'd done a good afternoon's work. It was a complacency soon to be rudely dispelled.

X

Hector was finding the Careys' regimen of early to bed and early to rise extremely irksome.

In Town he seldom left his bedroom before ten of the clock. His mornings were spent with his man of business, or riding with other fashionables in the Park, or paying tedious but obligatory calls on various society hostesses.

In the afternoon he might drive some reigning beauty to Richmond in his curricle, or visit Gentleman Jackson's saloon to go a few rounds with one of the champion's sparring-partners, or drop in at Tattersall's to view the bloodstock on sale.

As an acknowledged Nonpareil, and one of the most desirable *partis* in England, he was invited to innumerable balls, routs and assemblies, and for him to dine alone at his home in Berkeley Square was a rarity. Those nights when he was not engaged to attend two or three parties were occupied in squiring ladies of quality to the theatre or opera, or entertaining some bird of paradise in a rather less decorous way. Occasionally he visited Brook's Club in St James's Street, there to play baccarat, faro or whist with chosen friends.

Should the social whirl become too wearing, he could always escape to one or other of the great country houses, there to fish for trout or salmon, go out with the guns, or back his fancy at the nearest racecourse.

In short, Lord Hector Wycombe of Fontwell passed his time very pleasantly, and wasted little of it on sleep.

Mr Finch of no known address was far less fortunate. Obliged to retire to his room at nine o'clock, he found himself quite unready for bed. With Lady Carey's permission he scoured the shelves of the library, but it was swiftly apparent to him that the Admiral was not a reading man. Most of his books had been acquired in the last century, and their handsome bindings hid texts of paralysing dullness.

On that Thursday night, however, Hector struck gold. He unearthed from the farthest corner of the darkest cupboard, a volume entitled *A Brief History of The Careys of Kettleby*, by one Mr Septimus Brock.

He carried this find up to his room and settled at once to read it. To his surprise he found his attention riveted, for Mr Brock wrote with waspish candour, and was not afraid to lard his narrative with the sort of anecdote most biographers shun.

With much enjoyment Hector learned of Careys attaindered, charged with corruption, executed for high treason, or excommunicated by Mother Church. Where space was given to a virtuous member of the clan, the reader was made to understand that this was the exception that proved the rule.

Brock, like Mr Nettlebed, pooh-poohed the theory that King Charles I had visited the Manor. 'The Melancholy Monarch,' he wrote, 'never set foot in that house. Amyas Carey, the Third Baron, was no Loyalist, but a Pagan and a Lecher, addicted to riotous and adulterous living, to which end he caused a tunnel to be built from the Crypt in his garden to the Cellars of his home, thus enabling his Fellow Revellers and Concubines to pass to and fro unseen by the people of the village.

'Furthermore, to deter these same good folk from spying upon his Scandalous Orgies, he put it about that the Spectre of the King was wont to walk the grounds near the Crypt; which horrid tale persuaded all godfearing men and women to give the place a Wide Berth.

'I Thank Heaven,' concluded Mr Brock piously, 'that this tunnel is now filled in, for the very memory of it offends against Propriety, and must call a blush of shame to the cheek of any descendant of its Impious Inventor.'

Hector read this last passage through several times, then walked to the window of his bedroom and looked out at the moonlit garden. He could see plainly the path that led to the shrubbery, at the foot of which stood the Carey mausoleum.

The tunnel, if it ever existed, could have been no more than a hundred yards long. It was not uncommon for a house as old as this one to own a secret passageway. There was one at Fontwell, though it was now used for the mundane purpose of bringing ice from the icehouse by the lake to the kitchens.

If the Careys had indeed been Royalist during the Civil War, such a tunnel might have served to bring the King to sanctuary. Naseby, where the Stuart army was beaten and scattered, lay not far from Kettleby. Amyas Carey might have devised the tale of wild orgies to explain away the presence of strangers on his estate. By the same token, he might have invented the ghost to keep prying villagers at a distance.

Mr Brock averred that the tunnel had been filled, but Mr Brock could be in error. Other things than a fugitive king could be concealed in the Carey cellars – rum, brandy, crates of wine. Kettleby, situated as it was in the midriff of England, would be a convenient point from which Piggott and his cronies could disperse their wares.

Which led one to the shocking conclusion that Admiral Sir William Carey was in league with a gang of smugglers. It was a theory that explained the man's secretive ways, and his desire to keep even his children from contact with the outside world. His vaunted hatred of all things French could be a blind, meant to hide the fact that French contraband lined both his cellars and his pocket.

Hector considered his options. He had nothing to go on but suspicion. If he challenged the Admiral he would be laughed to scorn, and summarily dismissed. Yet to keep quiet would leave Jason in danger.

While he stood debating with himself, Fate jogged his elbow. Across the tranquil fields came the muffled note of the clock in the tower of St Stephen's, striking half past two. Suddenly the import of Jason's signal to Piggott became clear.

Quickly Hector pulled on his dark overcoat, buttoning its collar high to hide any trace of white shirt. Slipping his watch and flint-box into a pocket, he extinguished the candles in their sconces, and moved quietly to the door of his room.

The corridor outside was in darkness, the doors of Jason's bedroom and the schoolroom were closed. The only light was that of the moon falling through the window above the back stairway. Hector made his way down this, stepping cautiously to avoid squeaky treads.

At the foot of the stairs a passage ran north and south. Directly opposite him was a door giving access to the garden. It was not locked. Hector stepped through, and closed it gently after him.

Bright moonlight washed the lawn ahead of him, but by keeping in the shadow of the house, he was able to move to his right and gain the cover of the shrubbery. Here he paused briefly, listening for any sound from within the building. All was silent, and he continued along the path to the mausoleum.

On his first visit to it he had been absorbed in what Lady Carey had to say and had paid little attention to his surroundings. Now he looked about him with more care.

On three sides of the crypt were thick banks of pin oak, yew and laburnum, but on the fourth side a broad turfed ride led down a gentle slope to the river. A little to his left was the distant spire of the church.

He advanced to study the door of the crypt. It was secured by a heavy padlock, which looked new. The hinges of the door bore traces of oil.

Hector turned to consider the slope of turf. No human figure moved upon it. It shone grey-white, deserted, undisturbed by so much as a hunting dog.

He moved from the clearing to the deep shadow of an ancient yew. A glance at his watch showed him that it still lacked fifteen minutes of the hour. He sat down on the ground with his back against a tree-stump, and composed himself to wait.

The circumstance of having to care for an invalidish mama had made Serena a light sleeper.

Tonight she started awake in the conviction that she'd heard some sound in the bedroom above hers – a footfall, or the gentle closing of a door. She listened. The sound was not repeated, but she could not rid herself of the feeling that she ought to investigate.

Sliding out of bed, she tiptoed to her door, opened it a little, and peered through the crack. She was in time to see a figure dart across the bar of moonlight at the end of the passage. It was Jason, fully clad and moving in what could only be described as a very furtive manner.

Serena's first impulse was to rouse her uncle, who would certainly not condone such a midnight sortie; but a moment's thought made her change her mind. Jason's load was too heavy already. She'd no wish to increase it.

She wrapped her warmest cloak about her, slipped her feet into stout shoes, and made for the stairs. On the way she passed a cabinet containing an array of antique weapons: poignards, a flintlock gun with silver mountings, and a massive horse-pistol. She lifted the pistol from its case, and hid it in the folds of her cloak. Then, moving as quietly as she could, she set out after Jason.

XI

Piggott made his appearance just before the clock struck three.

From the shelter of the shrubbery, Hector saw him approach; a spectral figure astride a white horse, white cloak billowing, wide straw hat on head. Any villager abroad at this hour must have taken him for the ghost of some long-dead cavalier, for his face too shone with pale translucency under the moon, and his eyes had the flat, cold glitter of ice.

He checked his horse at the top of the turfed ride, and sat staring up at the house, whose upper storeys must be plainly in his view. After a moment, he raised his arm in salute, then advanced to the clearing and dismounted.

Hector sat motionless. He had to be sure that the man's assignation was with Jason Carey.

He had not long to wait. Within minutes he heard running footsteps on the path, and Jason burst from the cover of the bushes, making straight for the pedlar.

'Do you have it?' He caught hold of Piggott's wrist. 'Give it to me!'

Piggott laughed, showing yellowish teeth. 'In a hurry, aren't you, lad? Let's see the colour of your money, first.'

Jason dived a hand into the pocket of his breeches, pulled out a purse, and dumped it on Piggott's outstretched palm. The pedlar took his time about counting the collection of coins it held.

'Four guineas and some pence,' he said at last. 'T'ain't much, for all I've done.'

'It's all I have.' Jason danced in a fever of impatience. 'You promised, Piggott! You promised!'

As Piggott continued to smile down at him, Jason aimed a kick at his shins.

'Damn your eyes, give me the parcel, or I'll tell Papa!'

Instantly, as quick as a snake striking, Piggott's arm shot out, caught Jason by the throat, and half-lifted him from the ground.

'Sithee, lad, I've warned 'ee not to talk so.'

Jason flailed legs and arms. 'Let me go! I don't fear you, you lily-livered scum! Let me go!'

Piggott lowered the boy, but kept his grip on his throat. 'Now you listen to me, me fine young cockerel! 'T'aint me that's to be feared, 'tis the Frenchies. If they find tha's blabbed, they'll gut 'ee like a 'erring, same as they've done others. So remember, we've a pact, tha an' I. We'll go along nice an' easy, just so long as tha holds tha liddy tongue. *Comprenez?*'

He released Jason, who staggered back a pace, rubbing his throat.

'Understand?' repeated Piggott softly.

Jason nodded, and held out his hand. 'Give it to me now,' he said.

Slowly, as if he savoured the delay, Piggott reached into an inner pocket and drew out a small parcel. He held it high over Jason's head, laughing as the boy sprang and tried to snatch it.

'Eh, now, where's tha manners, lad? Don't I get a "please"?'

'Please. Please Piggott.'

'Please Mr Piggott.'

'Please Mr Piggott.'

Piggott started to lower his arm, the package dangling from his fingers. As Jason leaped for it, Hector rose to his feet and shouted:

'Piggott! *Fiche le camp! Quelqu'un vient!*'

Piggott spun round, his pale eyes scanning the shrubbery. Then with an oath he swung himself to the saddle and wheeled his horse.

'Piggott,' screamed Jason. 'My parcel!'

The pedlar's arm jerked and the package flew in an arc to land at the edge of the clearing. Before it hit the ground, horse and rider were plunging away down the slope.

Hector reached the package a fraction of a second before Jason. As he picked it up the boy lunged at him, kicking and punching, shouting in rising hysteria, 'Give it me, it's mine, it's mine!'

Hector caught his arms and pinioned them. 'Jason, hold still, you little fool! Do you want to wake the house?'

Jason checked, seeming to recognise Hector for the first time. With a great sob he twisted free and rushed headlong away, crashing through the thicket as if the devil were after him. Hector thrust the package into his pocket and was about to follow when a new voice spoke.

'Stand still, Mr Finch, or I'll shoot.'

Hector slowly turned his head.

Standing on the path not five paces from him, was Miss Osmond. Her hair was in wild disorder. She wore a cloak over her nightgown, and clutched in her upraised hands a large and somewhat rusty horse-pistol.

Serena took a step forward.

'Give me that parcel, if you please!' As Hector stood motionless, she stamped her foot. 'At once, or I shall shoot!'

Hector sighed. 'I wouldn't advise it, ma'am. For one thing, the pistol is probably not loaded, and for another, if it is loaded and you fire it, it will very likely explode and blow your hand off. It must be all of fifty years old.'

Serena lowered the pistol a little.

'What are you doing here?' she demanded.

'I came to discover why Jason planned to meet Piggott.'

'How do you know they planned to meet?'

'This morning I saw Jason signal to Piggott. First, he crossed his arms on his chest, to indicate this mausoleum, then he held up three fingers to signify the hour of three.'

'I don't know what you're talking about.'

'The statues at the crypt,' said Hector patiently. 'You'll observe they have their arms crossed in just such a way. What brought you here, Miss Osmond?'

Her chin jerked up, as if she wished to rebuke him, but after a moment she said, 'I heard Jason leave his room, and saw him sneak down the back stair. I followed him, but by the time I reached the garden, he'd disappeared. Luckily I heard voices in the shrubbery.' She paused. 'What was Piggott about?'

'I think he came to deliver something Jason had purchased.'

She relaxed a little. 'A pocket-knife,' she said. 'Piggott told me Jason wanted a pocket-knife. You may give it to me now, Mr Finch. I will see that Jason receives it.'

'Miss Osmond, do you really believe that a man like Piggott would leave his bed at three in the morning to deliver a penknife to a schoolboy?'

She made an impatient movement. 'I don't pretend to know

what Piggott will or won't do. Since you seem to have superior knowledge of the man, I beg you will enlighten me.'

'I think,' Hector said calmly, 'that Piggott is a smuggler, that he brings in contraband from France and sells it to customers in England. I suspect Sir William buys from him.'

Serena's eyes flashed. 'You go beyond what is permissible, sir!'

Hector shrugged. 'Many respectable folk take no shame in buying smuggled goods,' he said. 'I mention it only because I believe Jason has rumbled Piggott's lay, and is putting pressure on him to secure things he wants.'

'What sort of things?'

'That's easily discovered.' Hector began to reach towards the pocket where he'd placed the package, but at once Serena raised the pistol. 'Don't move,' she warned, 'or I'll shoot and . . . and scream my head off.'

'I propose only to examine the contents of the parcel, ma'am.'

She considered. 'Very well, do so, but remember what I said.'

He extricated the parcel, held it up briefly for her to see, then broke the string that bound it. Under the paper wrapping he found a small leather pouch, much worn. Lifting its flap, he drew out an oval object that fitted easily into the palm of his hand.

It was a locket of white enamel, ornamented with a bow of pearls and rubies. He opened it with a flick of his thumb, and stared at the picture it contained.

Serena edged closer. 'What is it?'

'A portrait of, I think, Georgina, the first Lady Carey.'

'Give that to me.'

Hector did not answer. He had noticed a small piece of paper tucked under the right-hand frame of the locket. Lifting it out, he unfolded it.

Its message was written in an elegant, sloping hand.

'My darling son, I will be with you soon. Your loving Mama.' The date beneath the signature was March 3rd, 1822. Last week's date.

Hector looked up to see Miss Osmond standing with hand imperiously outstretched.

'If you please, Mr Finch.'

He handed her the locket, watched her study first the portrait, then the note. Her face was very pale.

'It's not possible,' she said.

'Is it a likeness of Georgina Carey?'

'Yes.' Serena seemed too shocked to remember her earlier rage. She turned the note so that the moonlight shone full upon it, and said again, 'It's not possible.'

'You recognise the handwriting?'

She looked up sharply. 'It must be a forgery. This is some kind of wicked prank. How could that creature Piggott have come by this?'

'It belonged to Georgina Carey?'

'Yes. Yes, I saw it about her neck many times.' She folded the note, replaced it and snapped the locket shut. 'I shall give it to my uncle. I shall go to him tomorrow . . .'

'No!' said Hector urgently, and as she stared at him, he took a step towards her. 'Only think, ma'am, what it will mean to him and to Lady Carey. If Georgina Carey is alive, this second marriage is bigamous.'

'She's not alive! I tell you this is a lie, an infamous trick.' But doubt flickered in her eyes, and Hector said quietly:

'If you will allow me a little time, I may be able to find what's at the root of it.'

'You? What can you do?'

'I'm not without friends. Records are kept of deaths, you know, even in time of war. If Georgina Carey died, then it will be possible to verify the time and place of her death.'

Serena seemed hardly to hear him. 'Who are you?' she said flatly. 'Where are you from, what's your true name?'

'I am truly Hector Finch. I beg you will not say a word to Sir William until I've had time to pursue my enquiries.' He held out his hand. 'Give me the locket. It's Jason's property, after all. If I return it to him, I may persuade him to confide in me.'

As she still hesitated, he said, 'Miss Osmond, at least let us spare Lady Carey great anguish of mind!'

'Very well,' she said slowly. 'Take it. But remember, Mr Finch, I shall be watching you. If I find you've lied to me, I shall go to my uncle at once.'

Hector took locket and note, and slipped them into his pocket.

'Thank you. Now I suggest you go indoors. I'll follow in due course.'

She turned away without a word and walked off along the path. Hector waited for some ten minutes, then made his way back to the house.

XII

Serena arrived back in her room with her mind in turmoil.

She was not easily shocked. It troubled her not at all that Piggott might be a freebooter supplying her uncle with smuggled goods. She could condone Jason's making capital of the situation. Boys throve on adventure, and there was little enough of that in his dreary life.

What did disturb her deeply was the locket and letter. The former was without doubt genuine, but the latter must be – had to be – a forgery.

Mr Finch maintained that Jason had found out about the smuggling, and was using his knowledge to 'put pressure on Piggott'. Piggott might well secure the boy's silence by bringing him a memento of his dead mama.

But a far more terrifying thought loomed in Serena's mind. Was it possible that Georgina Carey was indeed still living? One thing was sure, she could not approach her uncle with such an accusation. A fine reward it would be for all his kindness, if she were to announce without a shred of proof that his first wife was alive, and his present marriage unlawful!

Serena paced restlessly about her room. The unpleasant fact was that the letter had sown doubt in her mind. Could it be that Georgina Carey still lived? Could there have been some hideous mistake, could she somehow have survived the fever, could some other female – the abigail perhaps – have succumbed and been buried in Georgina's name?

Another thought occurred to her. She had only Finch's word for it that the parcel he took from his pocket was the one Piggott had brought. What if he had staged the whole drama? What if he had somehow chanced upon the locket, and was planning to use it to blackmail her uncle?

The more she considered events, the more sure she became that Finch was a villain. That Banbury tale about wishing to learn why Jason was meeting Piggott! A conscientious tutor would have taken his suspicions straight to his employer, not indulged in this moonlight escapade. Very likely Finch was in league with Piggott, and had come to the Manor with the sole purpose of gaining the Careys' confidence, the better to extort money from them when the time was ripe.

Finch was an impostor, not a doubt of it. He was using a false name. She had heard him shout a warning to Piggott – in French, what was more – and now here he was cozening her into remaining silent while Piggott made his escape from Kettleby.

Round and round went Serena's labouring mind. Should she go to the nearest Justice of the Peace, and demand Piggott's arrest? Should she go to her aunt and uncle and unmask Finch's duplicity? Should she challenge Jason to explain his conduct?

Try as she might she could come to no conclusion, for every course seemed to lead to the same result – pain and disgrace for the people she loved.

At last, as light began to gleam along the crests of the eastern hill, she climbed wearily into bed, to fall into a dream-bedevilled sleep.

On regaining the house, Hector went straight to tap on Jason's door, for he feared that in his present desperate mood the boy might have run off to Piggott.

At first there was no response to his knock. Then a muffled voice called, 'Go away! Leave me alone!' Knowing it was futile to argue through a locked door, Hector went to his own room, lit a branch of candles, and settled down to ponder his next move.

He was convinced that Piggott was a dangerous rascal, who must be exposed and brought to justice as quickly as possible. The question was, how to achieve that.

One must accept that the locket had belonged to the late Georgina Carey. Miss Osmond testified to it, and there was no reason to doubt her word.

The letter was another matter. Close examination showed that it had been folded several times; but it was not cracked or discoloured. There was no way of telling if it were new, or several years old.

The writing on it was firm and distinctive, the ink unfaded. It should be possible to compare it with other material from Georgina Carey's hand. Somewhere in this rambling mansion there must be letters, a journal, even a recipe book that contained her writing.

Hector remembered the bookshelves beside the hearth, and crossing to them began to examine the fly leaves of the books. In a battered copy of *Gulliver's Travels* he found what he sought.

'To my dearest Laurel,' the inscription ran, 'on the occasion of her tenth birthday, from her devoted Mama.'

The writing matched that of the note. If the letter was a forgery, it was a clever one.

Hector studied it again.

'My darling son, I will be with you soon. Your loving Mama.'

It was possible that the note had been penned six years ago, and the date added last week. If that were the case, then the sender must be a person who had access to past letters of Georgina Carey.

Frowning, Hector tried to recall what Lady Carey had told him about the dead woman's last days.

The fever epidemic had struck Marseilles in 1816. Georgina's abigail had taken the infection and passed it on to her mistress and five-year-old Jason. It was not unlikely that Georgina, gravely ill and dreading separation from her son, had written him that brief line of comfort, and placed it in the locket for him to keep. Not impossible, either, that in the move to the hospice, locket and letter had gone astray, or been purloined by the abigail or some other person.

There was no way of guessing how it had come to fall into Piggott's hands.

In his conversation with Jason tonight, Piggott had let fall that he was not the kingpin in the smuggling operation. He had spoken of the 'Frenchies', people who were evil enough to commit murder to protect their illicit trade.

Had Piggott obtained the locket from these people, or from some other source? There was no way of finding out.

As for the Admiral, he had probably connived at smuggling. There was also the chance that he had deliberately committed bigamy. If so, he must live in constant dread of discovery. It would explain his dislike of those who had connections with France, and his excessive strictness with his children.

The only way out of the dilemma, Hector decided, was to establish beyond any shadow of doubt that Georgina Carey was dead. If her death could be proven, then the shadow of bigamy vanished, and one would be free to consider how best to deal with Piggott.

After some deliberation, he found pen and paper and sat down to write to Frederic Lychgate.

Kettleby Manor
Great Kettleby
Leics

March 10th, 1822

My dear Frederic,

As you so rightly predicted, I have fallen into all manner of trouble since entering upon my career as a tutor. I lack the time to recount the whole, and write to beg a favour of you. It is, quite literally, a matter of life and death.

My employer, Admiral Sir William Carey, was at one time married to the former Miss Georgina Marriott, who I collect was the then toast of London. (The year, I imagine, would be about 1804.) In 1816, while in Marseilles with her husband, the lady succumbed to an attack of enteric fever. It is her death that I wish you to verify.

I am asking you (and I know it to be a wholly unreasonable request) to quit your home and go to London, there to discover if you can the exact date, place and circumstances of Georgina Carey's demise. I suggest that the man to guide you to this information is Mr Robert Shipton of the firm Shipton and Howat in Lincoln's Inn. Mention my name and I'm sure Shipton will receive you kindly. He's a most knowledgeable person and will know how to lay hand on the records in question.

It occurs to me that a second line of enquiry may lie through the Marriott family. It shouldn't be beyond a man of your resourcefulness to identify the kin of the Georgina Marriott who set the Town afire and married an Admiral of the Fleet. Ask your Mama. I've never known her to be at a loss for a name, and she might well recall so tragic a death as this.

If you will carry out this task, I shall be forever in your

debt. The matter is urgent, or I wouldn't lay it on your guiltless head.

If you meet with success, pray write to me at this address, or better still determine a place where we may meet and talk in private. Perhaps the race-meeting to be held ten days from now at Melton Mowbray will afford such an opportunity? Admiral Carey plans to attend it, and I'm to be included in the party, to bear-lead young Jason. I shall keep an eye out for you.

Again, my apologies for burdening you in this way, and my thanks for your forbearance.

I remain

yr obedient servant,

Hector Finch

Having sealed this missive, and remembered in the nick of time not to frank it himself, he set it aside to give to Sudbury for posting.

There remained the thorny problem of Miss Serena Osmond. Thinking of her, Hector grinned ruefully. What other female of his acquaintance would sally out at dead of night to confront a ruthless impostor? – for that was certainly what she took him to be. An original, Miss Osmond, though an infuriating one.

The question was, would she carry tales to Sir William, or would she hold her tongue? He was inclined to think the latter. He'd have to mind his step, though, or he'd find himself hauled before the magistrate at gunpoint.

At least, he mused, as he climbed wearily into bed, Hubert could not accuse him of having spent the past few days in idleness.

XIII

Jason arrived at the breakfast table looking blear-eyed and defiant. Hector bade him good morning, but said no more until the footman had finished setting out beef, ham, baked eggs and devilled kidneys on the sideboard. When the man had left the room, he handed Jason the pouch containing the locket.

Jason gazed at it for a moment, then said accusingly, 'You opened my parcel!'

'Yes, I did.'

'You had no right! It's my private property!'

'Let's not discuss rights, at present. Tell me rather how Piggott came by a locket containing a picture of your mama.'

Jason thrust the pouch aside. 'I suppose you'll run to Papa?'

'Not unless you force me to, Jason.' Hector rose and began to help himself from the chafing-dishes. 'Of course, I can't vouch for Miss Osmond.'

'What's Serena got to do with it?'

'She heard you go downstairs, last night, and followed you. She may feel it her duty to report your conduct.'

'It's not her business what I do!' Nor yours, Jason's tone implied.

'It's the business of anyone who cares for your welfare,' said Hector calmly. 'Come, have some breakfast while it's hot.'

'I'm not hungry.'

'You should eat, none the less. Fasting won't help you to solve your problems.'

Jason stayed where he was. Suspecting that he was fighting tears, Hector spoke to cover the awkwardness.

'How long has Piggott been fleecing you of your pocket money?' he enquired.

Jason's chin jerked up. 'It's not fleecing. He gives . . . he gives . . .'

'Value for money?'

'Yes! It's my money, I can spend it as I please.'

'To be sure you can, but there must be an easier way to come by a portrait of your mother. Your father must have . . .'

'Papa does not wish to be reminded of Mama. It is . . . it is too painful for him to remember her.'

Hector carried his plate back to the table. 'One can see that her death must have been as cruel a blow to him as it was to you.'

Jason sat mute. His hands clutched the pouch tightly, as if he drew strength from it. Hector knew that somehow he must break the boy's silence.

'It would be a very wicked thing,' he said deliberately, 'if someone tried to deceive you into thinking your mother was alive. How long have you known Piggott was a smuggler?'

Jason blinked. 'About . . . about two years. I saw him putting crates of wine in the mausoleum.'

'You realise he's been stringing you along, Jason, just to keep your mouth shut?' He saw Jason begin to rise from his seat, and leaned across to grasp his shoulder. 'No! Sit still! We have to talk about this. Your stepmama told me, when first I came here, that she feared you believed your mother to be alive. There's no sense in such day-dreaming, Jason. It can bring you nothing but misery, in the end.'

'Mama is alive!' The words seemed to burst from Jason's heart. 'I know she is. I know.'

'How can you possibly know such a thing?' As Jason tried to struggle free of his grip, Hector said fiercely, 'Answer me, boy! What makes you say your mother is alive?'

Jason shook his head violently. 'No. You don't want to help me. You're like all the rest, you mean to spy on me and prevent me from . . .'

'I want to help you. I've said nothing of this escapade to your father, nor will I, provided you tell me the truth. Why do you think your mother is alive?'

Jason gave a half-sob. He was trembling.

'I know. I have proof. She sends me presents.'

'And letters?'

Jason nodded, and Hector released him.

'Have you never thought,' he said gently, 'that those letters could be forgeries?'

'They're not. They're real. I know her writing.'

'How many have you had?'

'Four.' Jason's defiance was crumbling, giving way to a misery that was pitiful to see. 'She's alive, whatever anyone says. She'll come back.'

'Did she write to tell you so?'

'Yes, when I was six. She wrote a whole page. She said she thought of me all the time, and one day she'd come back for me.'

'Do you still have the letter?'

Jason shook his head. Tears poured down his face. 'I showed it to Papa. He said it was all lies. He burned it.'

'I see. I expect he wished to protect you, Jason.'

'It was mine,' Jason whispered. 'It was mine.'

'He must know she's dead, you see? He must be quite sure she's dead. There are formalities when someone dies, papers to be signed, a funeral . . .'

'But Piggott has seen her!'

It was Hector's turn to stare. 'Where?' he demanded.

'In France! In Paris, two years ago!'

'I'm afraid Piggott is a liar.'

'Why should he lie to me? He's my friend. He helps me.'

'How long has he been helping you?'

'Since he saw her.'

'Let me get this clear. You received a letter from your mama – the one your father burned – when you were six. That's five years ago. How long after that did Piggott tell you he'd seen your mother?'

'It was three years after. He brought me a present from her, with a note.'

'In short, two years ago you learned Piggott was a smuggler; you told him so, and he began to bring you presents and letters from your mama, to buy your silence. Did you tell your father of it?'

'No. I knew he wouldn't let me keep anything.'

'And your sister? Did you not think of telling her?'

'No. Laurel can't keep a secret, she'd have blabbed and Papa would've given Piggott his marching orders.'

'What was in the second letter?'

'It was only a few words. Mama wrote that she loved me, and missed me a great deal.'

'Did you pay Piggott for delivering the note to you?'

'Not the first one. Afterwards, I gave him what I could. I saved my pocket money.' Seeing the anger in Hector's eyes, Jason mistook its cause and said passionately, 'It was my money and I wished to spend it for Mama. If I was rich, I'd go to France and find her and bring her home again.'

Hector said carefully, 'Jason, you're staking everything on Piggott's word. I want you to let me test his claim to have seen your mother.'

'No!' Jason turned quite pale with panic. 'You mustn't! He'll go away and never come back. I'll have no one . . .'

'Piggott shan't know what I'm doing, I promise. Will you permit me to make discreet enquiries?'

'How can you do so?'

Hector smiled. 'I've friends in high places, believe it or not. I'll test Piggott's story, and none shall know why, save you and I.' He stretched out his hand. 'Come, will you seal the bargain?'

For a long moment Jason hesitated. Then he reached out to shake Hector's hand.

XIV

Mr Lychgate read Hector's letter, which reached him on Monday, with considerable alarm.

From the outset he'd regarded Hector's latest start as verging on lunacy. The sporting bloods of society might look on it as a joke, but the high sticklers, and in particular His Grace of Wycombe, would condemn it as a shocking breach of good taste.

As if that were not enough, here was Hector talking of having fallen into 'all manner of trouble', and showing every sign of wanting to plunge still deeper into the morass. Frederic was half-minded to post off to Kettleby, and remove his lordship bodily before he became an embarrassment to everyone.

After some reflection, he decided to consult his mother. He wouldn't tell her the whole, of course. That would be to betray Hector's trust. He would merely ask a few questions about the mysterious female Hector sought to bring back from the grave.

He found his mama in the conservatory, engaged in packing peat moss into a silver epergne.

'Had a letter from Wycombe,' he told her, dropping a kiss on her cheek. 'Stayin' with some devilish dull folk, poor fellow. Bored to distraction, by the sound of things. Forced to amuse himself with readin' and the like. Came across this dead female and begs I'll assist him to trace her. Thinks you may be able to help.'

Lady Lychgate drew off her gardening gloves and regarded her son dispassionately.

'What female?' she said.

'Name of Marriott. Georgina Marriott.' Frederic was always thrown off balance by his mother's directness. 'Shouldn't think you'd know her. Don't know any Marriotts, m'self. Just another of Hector's hums, I expect.'

Seating herself on a bench, Lady Lychgate patted the vacant space beside her.

'Sit down, my dear, and try to speak rationally.'

Frederic did as he was bid. 'Stupid of me,' he said, 'to ask if you know a dead woman. Wild goose chase, I see that now. I'll write and tell Wycombe . . .'

'But I do know her,' said Lady Lychgate calmly. 'Or rather, I knew a Georgina Marriott many years ago. She was the most enchanting creature. My brother Richard was quite besotted with her and hoped to marry her, but she'd have none of him.'

'Toast of the Town, accordin' to Hector?'

'Yes, indeed. She was small and angelically fair, with violet-blue eyes. She received a great many flattering offers – the Duke of Pevensey, the Earl of Avonmore – but in the end she married a mere baronet named William Carey. Richard always swore it was the uniform that turned the trick.'

'Uniform?'

'Why yes. Carey was one of Nelson's captains. He made himself a reputation as a brilliant seaman and a dashing hero, spent three years in the West Indies and came back with a hold full of booty for The Crown. I believe Georgina Carey liked the reckless streak in him. Her own grandpapa made his fortune from Jamaica rum, so perhaps that gave them something in common. Whatever the reason, she married him, bore him two children, followed him to France at the end of the war, and died there of fever.'

'When was that?'

'Oh . . . 1816, I think. I recall that we learned of her death in February, just before we were due to remove to London. Richard was staying with us. He took the news very hard. Flighty and wilful as she was, Georgina had the gift of inspiring lasting devotion. Why is Hector interested in her?'

Once again Frederic was taken off guard, and stared confusedly at his mother, who watched him pensively.

'Lord, Mama, how should I know? Taken some notion into his head, I suppose.'

'There was a daughter,' mused Lady Lychgate. 'She'd be about sixteen years old, now. If she's anything like her mama, one could understand Hector's being bowled over. Perhaps he wishes to know more of her background, before fixing his interest with her.'

'No question of that,' said Frederic in panic. 'Not possible for him to fix his interest.'

'My dear boy, whatever do you mean?'

91

'Couldn't hope to succeed. Not at present. Above his touch.'

His mother stared. 'Frederic, are you quite well? In no sense can a Carey be rated above a Wycombe's touch!'

'Made a mistake,' said Frederic, floundering. 'Meant to say that Hector ain't in the market for a wife. Not for a sixteen-year-old, that is. Not his style. Prefers women of the world.'

'A gentleman may like to spend his bachelor days among opera-dancers and the like,' said Lady Lychgate bluntly, 'but he doesn't choose a wife from such company. As to his marrying a Carey . . . one couldn't call it a splendid match . . . Hector could do much better for himself, but the Carey line is ancient enough.'

'Hector ain't on the catch,' repeated Frederic. 'His interest is disinterested. That's to say, it's academic. Dash it all, Mama, it's the dead woman he's after, not the living.'

Lady Lychgate had raised four sons and three daughters, and had no illusions about any of them. She was aware that Frederic was not telling her the whole truth. On the other hand, she knew him to be scrupulous, kind and loyal to those he loved. If he was withholding facts from her, he must have a good reason. Deciding it would be unfair to tease him further, she said mildly, 'I fear I can't tell you much about Georgina Marriott, but Richard might help you. I can speak to him, if you like?'

'No, no. Pray don't mention this to anyone, Mama. Hector wouldn't care to have his affairs made public property.'

She nodded. 'Just as you wish. What do you propose to do?'

'I shall go to London,' Frederic answered, 'to consult a lawyer. He'll tell me where to find the relevant records.'

'Of course,' agreed Lady Lychgate, as if this errand were the most natural in the world. 'When will you set out?'

'At once.' Frederic bent to plant a kiss on her forehead. 'Thank you, dearest. I can always count on you to give me the right advice. I'll be in Town for some few days, but I'll return by Friday at the latest.'

'Friday,' repeated Lady Lychgate dutifully, but she could not resist asking, 'Why Friday?'

'Races at Melton Mowbray,' said Frederic. With a cheerful smile and a wave of the hand he departed, leaving his mama a prey to consuming curiosity.

XV

Hector quickly became aware of Miss Osmond's determination to keep an eye on him. At meals she watched him unblinkingly. If he walked in the garden with Jason, she observed their progress from the windows of the house. She sat directly behind them in church on Sunday, and on Monday when they arrived at the stables, she was already there, dressed in her riding-habit and wearing a look of grim resolution.

'I intend to ride with you, Mr Finch,' she announced, in answer to Hector's enquiring glance. 'Sultan needs a gallop.'

'He won't get it with us, ma'am,' Hector said. 'Our pace is set by Peppercorn.'

'No matter,' she said coldly. 'I'm ready to leave when you are.'

The group moved off a few minutes later. Hector thought it must present a very odd appearance. In front rode Jason, exerting every effort to coax Peppercorn into a sluggish trot. Next came Wiske, taciturn as ever. Hector followed, his ill-fitting jacket ballooning in the breeze, and in the rear was Miss Osmond on her splendid black horse.

Hector's attempts to strike up a conversation with his companions were met by gloomy silence, and he soon desisted. They took a different route from that they'd last taken; crossed the river by an ancient stone bridge, left the road and climbed slowly through a hazel wood. Emerging at last from the trees, they reached a long upland valley with steep, rock-strewn sides. Here they were able to enjoy a canter, even Peppercorn hitting his best stride. At the head of the valley they checked, and were debating which course to take from there, when they heard a wild halloo above them and saw a horseman galloping along the northern ridge, arm upraised.

As they watched he reached a point level with them and wheeled his horse, careering down the steep slope, by some miracle avoiding its cracks and boulders, and arriving at their side in a great slither of stones and dirt.

The rider was a young man of about twenty-five, of slender but wiry build. His features were regular, the nose aquiline and the jaw aggressively out-thrust. He was dressed in the height of fashion. His coat, which Hector judged to be from the hand of Schultz, was cut in the Cossack style and buttoned high to the throat. Instead of a cravat he wore a plain white stock, and his gleaming boots were fitted with silver spurs. This military effect was heightened by dark hair slickly pomaded, and a fine show of black moustachios. The young man's expression suggested that he was very well pleased with the effect he created. His horse, a big bay, was still trembling and sweating after its breakneck descent of the hill. Hector was inclined to think that of the two handsome animals before him, the horse was the more intelligent.

'Miss Osmond,' cried the newcomer in a high, affected voice. 'Your humble servant, ma'am! 'Pon my soul, I never thought to see you in company with such a bunch of slow-tops!'

This greeting was not well-received by any member of the party. Jason scowled ferociously, Wiske gazed impassively away across the valley, and Serena said stiffly,

'Good afternoon, Mr Nettlebed. I think you have not met Mr Hector Finch, Jason's new tutor. Mr Finch, may I present Ensign Crosby Nettlebed of the Eleventh Hussars?'

Hector bowed politely, but Crosby ignored him, leaning closer to Serena.

'Come, Miss Osmond, will you not abandon this camel train and ride with me? I've long wished to try my Rubicon against your Sultan.'

Serena shook her head. 'I regret, sir, but we're about to turn for home.'

'But it's such a capital day for a race! Do, I beg, reconsider.'

'I'm sorry,' said Serena tersely, and began to wheel her horse; at which point the devil entered Hector.

'Miss Osmond,' he said, smiling affably at her, 'pray don't forgo your pleasure on our account. Wiske and I will see Jason safe home.'

Miss Osmond regarded him with dislike. 'Thank you,' she said, 'but I promised my aunt we'd not be late. Mr Nettlebed, I'm sure you will excuse me? Perhaps we may stage our contest some other time?'

'By all means, by all means. My compliments, if you please, to your aunt and uncle. I look forward to seeing you all on Wednesday evening.'

So saying he galloped away, pausing at the neck of the ridge to raise his arm in dramatic salute, while his horse executed a spectacular caracole.

'Popinjay!' said Jason loudly.

No one contradicted him. Miss Osmond's faintly contemptuous smile indicated that she thought as little of Ensign Nettlebed and his antics as she did of Mr Finch.

XVI

Hector would have been amused to know that his employers had debated at some length whether or not he should be allowed to attend the Nettlebeds' party.

Sir William spoke for his inclusion. 'The invitation was to the members of my household,' he said. 'That includes Finch.'

Lady Carey, kind-hearted though she was, felt that he must be left at home. 'After all, my love,' she said, 'though the Nettlebeds might raise no objection, there are others who will. The Prestons, you know, are very high in the instep, and never allow their governess to sit down with them. One wouldn't care to expose Mr Finch to a snub.'

'Finch,' said the Admiral roundly, 'is far more the gentleman than Mr Johnny-come-lately Preston. He's a man of education, and his manners and bearing are all one could desire. Besides, if he don't come, then who's to keep an eye on Jason, may I ask?'

'I hardly think that will be necessary at Longacres. There'll be plenty of young people to bear Jason company.'

'All the more reason to take Finch. He can keep tabs on the whole boiling of 'em, and knock their heads together if they get out of hand.'

'Do but consider the difficulties,' persisted Lady Carey. 'It's one thing for Mr Finch to sit down to dinner when there'll be only our two families present; but afterwards, when the other guests arrive, and there's dancing? Will he be expected to join us, or will he be condemned to stand on the sidelines like an outcast?'

'That decision may be left to Phoebe Nettlebed,' returned the Admiral. 'If she don't wish him to take the floor, she'll make it plain to him, but I never yet met a hostess who wasn't glad of an extra man at her party. Finch can give the wallflowers a whirl. Good for his soul!' and he broke into rumbling chuckles, as if he'd made a very good joke.

When Hector learned he was to accompany the Careys to Longacres, it gave him pause for thought.

So far, he'd been lucky in that no one had guessed his true identity, but his luck might not hold for long. Not only was Miss Osmond poised to denounce him at the first opportunity, but there might well be guests at the Nettlebeds' hop who were familiar with the London scene, and could recognise so notable a pink of the ton as Lord Hector Wycombe.

One way or another, his days as a tutor were numbered. Two courses lay open to him. He could go to the Admiral, admit his deception, and tender his resignation; or he could await the inevitable and ignominious exposure.

Either way, he would have to quit the Manor. The old mode of life would resume there. Jason would be landed with another inept bear-leader, and remain a prey to Piggott's intrigue.

That must not be allowed to happen.

Slowly a third option began to form in Hector's mind. Somehow he must contrive to stay at his post until the Careys removed to London at the end of March. He could not do so as plain Mr Finch, nor as Lord Hector, but was there not a middle course? Could not mystery serve him, where honesty would not? Perhaps he could put the snobbery and pretension of the local gentry to good use.

On Wednesday evening he dressed with particular care, discarding Hubert's unshapely garments in favour of his own. He donned dove-grey pantaloons that admirably displayed his well-muscled thighs; a waistcoat of watered silk with onyx buttons; a coat of dark-blue superfine with high rolled collar and wide lapels, that Weston had delivered to him only five weeks since; a cravat tied in the style known as trône d'amour; and shoes that gleamed with the bootboy's best efforts.

Studying his appearance in the looking-glass he decided that while it might not come up to Peck's exacting standards, it was well enough.

He was attaching his watch to his fob-chain when Jason appeared in the doorway, dressed in knee-breeches, frilled shirt, stockings and shoes, and clutching in one hand a mangled length of muslin. Catching sight of Hector, he stopped dead in his tracks and exclaimed, 'Sir! How fine you look!'

Hector smiled. 'Thank you, Jason, but I see you're set to take the shine out of me tonight.'

97

Jason scowled darkly. 'I hate parties,' he declared. 'Dressin' up is for girls, and I can't tie my neckcloth.'

'No one could tie such a draggled object,' Hector said. 'Take one of mine and try again.'

After three attempts Jason succeeded in making a knot that passed muster, and Hector nodded.

'You'll do. Put on your coat and we'll go downstairs. The carriages are ordered for six.'

They were the first to reach the lower hall, and so were able to watch the other members of the party descend the stairs. The Admiral, like his son, was attired in old-fashioned knee-breeches, black stockings, and shoes with silver buckles. His waistcoat was of velvet, and his cutaway coat had long swallow-tails. A fine diamond pin was stuck in the folds of lace at his throat. He carried in his right hand a *chapeau bras*, and in his left a tall black cane. Hector thought that to complete the picture he needed a single gold earring, and a parrot on his shoulder. The old man was in tearing spirits, tossing off quips and laughing at them immoderately.

Lady Carey looked handsome in a gown of raspberry silk, with a Madeira shawl about her shoulders and garnets at her throat and wrists. Miss Osmond was elegant in pale primrose crêpe, with a cloak of darker taffeta, stiffened and ruched at the hem. But the prize, thought Hector, must go to Laurel Carey. She came running downstairs in her new white gown, her shining hair dressed high and crowned with a garland of small white roses. She was going to cause a stir among the bored London bucks – perhaps might even be as great a toast as her acclaimed mama.

At ten minutes past six they set out; Sir William and Lady Carey with Laurel and Serena in the closed carriage, and Hector, Jason and Wiske following in the phaeton.

Longacres stood in its own park, a well-proportioned building with tall sash windows, and a piecrust balustrade along its roof. Hector brought the phaeton to a halt under the portico, handed the reins to Wiske, and with Jason at his side mounted the steps to the open front door.

As soon as he crossed the threshold, he saw that his hosts affected the grand style. The hallway was two storeys deep, with a painted ceiling supported by four columns of green Italian marble. Two Aubusson carpets covered the floor, and a fire blazed in the ornamental fireplace, keeping the air comfortably warm.

Flunkeys in livery were stationed to left and right of the entrance, and a butler in black velvet with a silver chain about his neck relieved Hector and his charge of their driving-coats, and led them to where the Nettlebeds waited in the Rose Room.

This was a capacious salon hung with pink brocade. The pictures on the walls, the crystal candle sconces, the delicate white and gold furniture proclaimed the wealth and good taste of the owner. The Admiral's objections to Ensign Nettlebed could have nothing to do with the young man's financial expectations.

Mr and Mrs Nettlebed now approached, and Hector studied them with some interest. They were both of small stature. Henry Nettlebed was plump and sleek, and had the pursy mouth and complacent air of one who knows himself to be at home to a pin upon any subject. He greeted Hector with an affable nod, and dealt Jason a friendly clap on the shoulder.

Mrs Phoebe Nettlebed's reception was more guarded. She was a thin woman, with a high colour and glossy black hair. Her dress was rich and her jewels of superb quality, but she seemed to derive no satisfaction from her finery, for her expression was both restless and petulant. Her small dark eyes surveyed Hector from head to foot, and he guessed she was making a lightning inventory of his material worth.

As he bowed over the three fingers she extended to him, she said with a slight tilt of the head, 'Mr Finch, have we not met before?'

'I think not, ma'am. This is my first visit to Kettleby.'

'But in London? Have we not met in London?'

'I believe I've not had that pleasure.'

She stared hard at him for a moment, then gave a faint shrug and introduced him in a perfunctory way to the other members of her family.

Jason was quickly absorbed into the group of young people and Hector, left to his own devices, secured a glass of Madeira from a footman and moved to stand quietly in a corner from where he could observe the company. There were three Nettlebed daughters, all small and plump like their papa, and two sons younger than Crosby. The boys ignored Hector, but the girls seemed very much aware of him, and looked at him slantwise under their lashes.

Crosby himself was splendid in the dress uniform of his regiment. He lost no time in cutting Laurel Carey from the herd, and drew her over to the window where he began to flirt with her in a heavy manner, clasping her fingertips, sending her arch looks, and indulging in frequent bursts of loud, braying laughter. Strangely enough, Miss Carey seemed enchanted with this behaviour, and gazed at Crosby in such open admiration that Lady Carey soon felt obliged to intervene and carried Laurel off to talk to Mrs Nettlebed.

Thwarted, Crosby went to join his father, demanding to know what his mama could have been thinking of to invite Jason Carey's bear-leader to the party.

'If you mean Mr Finch,' returned Mr Nettlebed equably, 'Will Carey chose to bring him. We could hardly refuse him the door.'

'Fellow don't know his place,' grumbled Crosby. 'Tricked out as fine as fivepence! A man-milliner, if ever I saw one!'

Mr Nettlebed directed a sly smile at his son. 'Your mama fancies she's seen him before. Suspects he's using a *nom de guerre*. Says he has a marked air of distinction.'

Crosby snorted. 'He's a tutor, ain't he? There's no distinction in that!'

'"The rank",' mused Mr Nettlebed, '"is but the guinea's stamp, a man's a man for a' that."' Seeing Crosby's blank stare, he chuckled. 'I quote from the poet Burns.'

'Never heard of him, but he must be a dashed commoner to write such stuff!' Crosby became aware that Serena was standing beside him. 'What's your opinion, Miss Osmond?' he demanded. 'Is Finch a gentleman, or not?'

Serena was saved from having to reply by the entry of the butler, to announce that dinner was served.

As this was a gathering of old friends, Mrs Nettlebed made no attempt to seat her guests according to protocol, but simply divided them by age, placing Jason and her younger children at the foot of the board, and the seniors at its head. Hector found he had Laurel Carey on his right, and Miss Eliza Nettlebed, a tongue-tied fourteen-year-old, on his left. Opposite him was Miss

Osmond, with Crosby Nettlebed on her left and James Nettlebed, down from Oxford to recover from an attack of scarlet fever, on her right.

The meal was conducted without formality, the guests conversing across the table as well as with their immediate neighbours; and when the main course had been removed and the dessert brought on, Lady Carey caught the attention of all present by mentioning the 'Treasure of Merlin's Cave'.

'The story runs,' she said, 'that before falling victim to sorceress Morgan le Fey, the enchanter Merlin stored certain treasures in a cave not far from here. To protect the hiding-place he laid a spell on it. Anyone who dares to lay hands on the hoard arouses a troop of demons. Their voices can be heard whistling and moaning and laughing all around, and the would-be thief runs mad and never returns to the ordinary world.'

Mr Nettlebed smiled benignly on Lady Carey. 'The legend of Merlin's Cave is widespread,' he said. 'Indeed it exists all over England, wherever there are underground caverns. I have in my library a book by the Reverend John Hutton, who in 1780 explored the caves near Ingleton and Settle in the Lake District. He gives a vivid description of the roar of subterranean rivers and waterfalls. Probably that is the source of your demon voices.'

'All the same,' said Crosby unexpectedly, 'Merlin's Cave exists. I know, for I've entered it myself.'

All eyes swivelled towards him, and he smiled and preened his moustache with a knowing air.

'I daresay you're speaking of Merlin's Pot,' said Mr Nettlebed, selecting a peach from the dish in front of him and beginning to peel it with delicate care.

'What's Merlin's Pot?' asked Laurel. 'I never heard of it till now.'

'It's part of a system of interlinked caves,' Mr Nettlebed answered, 'that stretches from Derbyshire down to Stubleigh Village, a few miles north of here. The rock, you know, is limestone, which is easily eroded by rivers and streams to leave a series of potholes, tunnels and caves. But the underground systems existed long before the time of Merlin. They're a natural phenomenon and the only treasures to be found in them are those created by Mother Nature.'

Laurel turned to Crosby with shining eyes. 'I think it the most romantic thing I ever heard,' she breathed. 'Do, pray, tell us about it.'

Crosby hesitated, but other voices were joined to Laurel's, and with a shrug of his shoulders, he obliged.

'It was years ago, when I was a mere boy,' he said. 'A few of us had been discussing the old tale, and some wag dared me to go into the caves – alone, of course – and see if I could find the treasure. I didn't much like the idea, but I felt bound to accept the challenge, so I equipped myself with candles and flints, and a length of stout rope, and rode off at daybreak to Stubleigh.

'The cave lies about a mile from the road, on the southern side of the village. The local peasantry know it well, though none of 'em will go near it. They call it the Mouth of Hell.'

Crosby paused to allow his hearers to enjoy a frisson of horror, then continued in a low, dramatic tone.

'It is in truth a very fearsome place. The mouth of the cave is fully seventy foot wide and fifty high, and out of it tumbles a stream as green and cold as if it came from the land of lost souls. I entered, and found the floor to be smooth and sandy; but as I progressed the roof sloped steeply down, and the walls drew together until all that was left was a rounded tunnel about the height of a tall man. Through this the stream emerged in a steady torrent.

'There was no light at that point, and I lit a candle and held it high. I waded along the course of the stream for some way, stumbling and groping for foot and hand holds, until I found my way barred by a rock wall, over which the water tumbled in a white and foaming fall. The roaring of it near deafened me, and I can tell you I was ready to give up the venture; but I thought of my wager and pressed on. I managed somehow to scramble up the rocky face and floundered on a short way. Then to my amazement the channel broadened, and the light of my candle showed that I stood in an immense cavern so high and broad that I could not gauge its limits. I stood immobile, afraid to move. It was then that I heard the voices.'

Crosby leaned forward, fixing his gaze on the children listening goggle-eyed at the foot of the table.

'At first it was only a murmur,' he said, 'but then the sound grew and seemed to come nearer and nearer, muttering and chuckling and crying out words that I could not quite understand. It was all about me, dinning in my ears, numbing my senses. I knew if I remained, the demons would seize me and drag me down to the depths of the earth. I broke and ran, stumbled back to the waterfall, plunged down its slippery rocks, floundered along the tunnel until I reached the outer cave and the blessed gleam of daylight. I did not wait to rest, but sprang on to my horse and galloped back to Kettleby as if Merlin himself were after me.'

'And the treasure?' cried Laurel. 'Did you see the treasure?'

'There was none,' Crosby answered. 'There was nothing in the inner cave but darkness and mud and terror. All I gained from my wager was half a crown, a pair of grazed knees and a heavy cold. From that time on I've made sure that if I risk my neck, it's above ground, and against an enemy I know to be human.'

Mrs Nettlebed, judging that the children had been frightened quite enough, now brought the meal to an end. Half an hour later the company gathered in the ballroom and the musicians brought from Leicester settled in the gallery and struck up a lively tune. Very soon the carriages began to roll up the driveway, and the Nettlebeds' guests came streaming into the house.

XVII

True to the Admiral's prediction, Mrs Nettlebed positively encouraged Mr Finch to take part in the ball.

It was not kindness that prompted her, but self-interest. She was convinced she had met Mr Finch before, though she could not recall where. She watched him covertly during dinner. His manners marked him as a gentleman, his clothes as a man of means. Certainly he was no tutor. It must be that he was engaged in some private charade.

Observing the thoughtful gaze he bestowed on Crosby, and the very warm looks he gave Laurel Carey, Mrs Nettlebed formed a theory. Mr Finch was masquerading as a tutor because he had fallen in love with Laurel and could find no other way of breaking the barriers the Admiral set about her. His presence at the Manor gave him a distinct advantage over other suitors. He had good looks, money, and address. One could predict a successful outcome to his courtship . . . perhaps even a runaway marriage.

Any woman less selfish than Phoebe Nettlebed would have been deeply shocked by such a notion; but she felt it would suit her purpose very well if Finch carried the girl off to Gretna Green. She disliked the friendship between her son and Laurel quite as much as did the Admiral. Crosby, she believed, was far too young to burden himself with a wife, particularly one as feather-brained as Laurel. A soldier's wife must perforce travel the world with her husband, and manage her household in strange and often hostile surroundings. Crosby would be well-advised to put aside all thought of marriage until he had at least won his captaincy. If in the mean time there were rival claimants to Miss Carey's hand, so much the better.

So it was that Mrs Nettlebed urged Mr Finch to join one of the sets for the first country dance; and when her bosom friend Mrs Preston questioned the propriety of allowing an employee to partner their girls, Mrs Nettlebed informed her with an air of dark mystery that she had reason to suppose that Finch was not the gentleman's true name, but that he was in fact the scion of a wealthy and distinguished family, whom it would be unwise to offend in any way.

Mrs Preston, contemplating Mr Finch's immaculate tailoring, and watching him lead her awkward Harriet with impeccable grace through the steps of the grand bourrée, was inclined to agree that this was no ordinary pedagogue; and though she scorned romance as much as she disliked mysteries, she decided that it might be safer for the moment to give Mr Finch the benefit of the doubt.

Hector, for his part, was enjoying himself hugely. For the first time since he turned eighteen, he was being judged on his own merits. It was pleasant to be free of the toad-eaters and match-makers who dogged his footsteps in London. It was amusing to take the shine out of the arrogant Ensign Nettlebed. And though the mamas present might regard him with constraint, their daughters welcomed him with enthusiasm.

He performed his duty dances with his hostess and Lady Carey, led Laurel through a vigorous polka, and was sitting chatting to Sir William when the band struck up the robust strains of 'Ah, du Lieber Augustin'. The Admiral jerked upright in his chair.

'What's that damned tune, eh?'

'Apparently,' said Hector with a smile, 'our hosts have given their sanction to the waltz.'

'More fool they,' grunted Sir William. 'Well, Laurel knows she's not to indulge in such vulgar prancing.' He turned to glare at Hector. 'As for you, you may do as you choose, I suppose.'

'You're my employer, sir. I'm bound to respect your wishes.'

'Are you, indeed?' The Admiral's gaze became sardonic. 'And how long will this dutiful subservience last, may I ask? How long may we expect to enjoy the services of Mr Finch?'

'I believe,' replied Hector calmly, 'that it would be good for Jason if I remained in my post until such time as you take your family to London.'

The Admiral stared at him challengingly for a moment, then gave a dry chuckle. 'Ay, that may be. But hark'ee, Finch, don't take me for a jobbernoll, for that I'm not.' As Hector began to speak, the older man waved an impatient hand.

'Not now, not now. Go and dance, man. I couldn't prevent you, even if I would.'

Hector stood up and surveyed the room. Most of the younger set had followed Crosby Nettlebed's example, and were twirling merrily about the ballroom. Lady Carey, with Miss Osmond and a disconsolate Laurel, stood watching the dancers from a doorway. Hector made his way over to them, bowed, and said,

'Miss Osmond, will you do me the honour to waltz with me?'

Serena studied him coolly. The import of his changed appearance, indeed of his whole behaviour tonight, had not been lost on her. For some reason, 'Mr Finch' had chosen to allow the company a glimpse of his true self. It infuriated her that Mrs Nettlebed and the other matrons had allowed him to get away with it. Could they not see that he was gulling them?

She would have liked to refuse to dance with him, but she knew that would leave him in possession of the field. Laying aside the fan she was holding, she placed her fingers on his extended arm, and allowed him to lead her on to the floor.

Serena had attended enough balls to know good partners from bad, and she had to admit at once that Mr Finch was an expert. He guided her with a touch so light, yet so sure, that she felt herself to be flying. He neither plagued her with commonplace remarks, nor pretended a fashionable indifference. And when she cast a quick look at his face, she saw he was watching her with amused appreciation.

She at once assumed a severe and distant expression. To her annoyance this only made him smile more broadly.

'You are in great beauty tonight, Miss Osmond.'

She frowned. 'You may spare me empty compliments, Mr Finch. I find them distasteful.'

'They're not empty, I assure you; they're truthful.'

'Indeed sir, I had not thought you to be an exponent of the truth!'

'I can't recall having lied to you at any time.'

'Have you not? Then I take leave to tell you that if you are indeed Mr Finch, you have overstepped the bounds of what is permissible in a tutor, and if you are not Mr Finch then you have practised a most despicable fraud.'

'I am indeed Hector Finch, Miss Osmond, and ... for the present, Jason's teacher. I see, however, that I've presumed too much. Being permitted to mingle with my betters has quite gone to my head. It will pass quickly, I assure you. When midnight strikes, I shall become a tutor again.'

'It is not a question of your presumption,' said Serena hotly. 'It's a question of deceiving those who take you in good faith. Why are you indulging in this . . . this mummery? What have we done to deserve such an invasion of our privacy?'

Hector considered her gravely. 'If I were indeed committing a fraud,' he said, 'there could be only two reasons for it: one, that I was a criminal out to profit by my stay at the Manor; the other, that I wish to protect its inmates from a true criminal.'

Before Serena could reply, the music soared to a triumphant end, and the dancers checked and broke into polite applause. Hector met her angry gaze.

'This is the supper dance, I believe,' he said. 'May I take you in?'

'You may not,' said Serena through her teeth. 'You may not take me in to supper or in any other sense! It's my earnest hope, Mr Finch, that you are taken up by the Law, and sent where you can't play tricks on respectable people!'

She gathered up her skirts and hurried away to join Lady Carey. Hector was obliged to escort the plump and perspiring Eliza Nettlebed to the supper room.

The Nettlebeds' ball occasioned a good deal of talk among those who had attended it, their interest being centred on the mysterious Mr Finch.

As Mrs Scott-Fisher said to Mrs Preston, with whom she took tea on Thursday afternoon, there was something decidedly smoky about a man of distinguished bearing who took a post as a tutor.

'I don't swallow Phoebe Nettlebed's tale that he's after Laurel Carey,' she said. 'If that was his purpose, why didn't he wait until the Careys reached London, where a man may devise a hundred ways of meeting a girl? No, Almira, the explanation is far more simple. Finch is hiding from his creditors. He's run himself into dun territory, mark my words, and has gone to ground until he's found a way to meet his debts. After all, who would think of looking for a member of the ton in Kettleby?'

'That doesn't explain why he applied for the post,' demurred

Mrs Preston. 'He'd only to put up at the Seven Stars, when all's said and done.'

'Too much gossip in a public inn,' said her friend with a knowing shake of the head. 'What's more, I strongly suspect that that old rogue Will Carey knows precisely who Mr Finch is. How else would he let the man near his children? You know how he guards them against all comers, for all the world as if he expected someone to spirit them away. I tell you, Finch is known to the Admiral. They're playing some little game, and romance doesn't come into it.'

'I'll grant you Will Carey likes to play tricks,' said Mrs Preston. 'He's like his father and grandfather before him. No proper sense of right and wrong, which is no doubt very useful when one has had to deal with monsters like Bonaparte, but not at all desirable when the country's at peace. I for one will be heartily glad to leave for London next week. I want Amanda and Caroline out of harm's way, if you understand me?'

Mrs Scott-Fisher understood perfectly. Mothers of nubile daughters desired them to consort with gentlemen of good family, sound reputation and solid fortune. It was doubtful if Mr Finch met any of these qualifications, and it would be best to keep him at a safe distance.

The Careys too recognised the Nettlebeds' party as a watershed event. Lady Carey knew that Serena disliked Mr Finch, and the knowledge troubled her; but when she tried to discuss the matter with her husband, he was unusually brusque with her.

'Leave Finch alone,' he commanded. 'If you meddle, Amelia, the consequences might be unpleasant for all of us.'

'My dearest, if there's any suspicion in your mind that he's not what he claims to be, surely it would be wiser to . . .'

'I said, leave him be! I have his measure. I know what I'm about. Just go on as usual, if you please, and bid Serena do the same. I don't want any hysterical starts from any of you, understand?'

To Laurel, the party had been a high point in her life. She was more than ever convinced that Crosby Nettlebed was the man for her. His dramatic account of the exploration of Merlin's Pot had enhanced her opinion of his courage and daring. However, she was astute enough to know that if she wanted to meet Crosby in London, she must obey her papa's wishes in all things. She was at pains to please him, fetched his pipe and tobacco for him after dinner, read to him from what she thought to be an excessively dull book on marine history, and embroidered a pair of slippers for his forthcoming birthday.

Jason offered no comment on the ball except to say that the pastries had been bang up to the mark. He seemed listless, and disinclined to go out for his afternoon ride, which led Lady Carey to ask if he had the headache, or felt a tickle in his throat.

Jason answered that he thought perhaps he had caught cold, and asked to be allowed to sit by the fire in the library, and read his book, a suggestion that Sir William readily agreed to.

'Best thing for him, if he's below par,' he said, and he directed his wife to see that Jason drank plenty of ale, soup and lemon-barley-water. 'Flush out the system, that's my motto,' he said. 'Keep a man's bowels and bladder working, and he'll have no need of any new-fangled quackery.'

XVIII

Jason's malaise was fleeting, and by the end of the week he was well enough for his father to fulfil a long-standing promise to take him to a point-to-point at Melton Mowbray. The expedition was designed to kill two birds with one stone, the men of the household going to the races, while Serena and Laurel accompanied Lady Carey on a visit to her papa, Bishop Harley, who lived in the town.

It would have been a tight squeeze in the carriage for six passengers, but luckily the day was so fine that Jason was able to ride on the box with Coachman Tilley. They drove straight to Melton Mowbray, and set down the ladies at the Bishop's door, departing under a strict injunction to return at four so that they might share in a light meal before journeying home to Kettleby.

The races were to start from the Silver Penny Inn, and the field next to it was already crowded with carriages, curricles, gigs, carts and looseboxes, for the meeting was a popular one. There were also a number of gipsy caravans drawn up along the edge of a neighbouring wood. Jason scanned them eagerly and Hector guessed he was looking for Piggott's wagon, but there was no sign of the pedlar or his sidekick Laval. Nor was Frederic Lychgate anywhere to be seen, which made Hector think his enquiries had met with failure.

Sir William declared that he was not a betting man, but he gave Jason two guineas, and bade him make his fortune if he could. Jason spent the next half-hour in close scrutiny of the entrants for the first race, and begged Hector and Wiske to tell him which was the best prospect.

Wiske said bluntly that Jason should save his money. 'Them's novices, Master Jason. Still be runnin' come Lammas Tide! You'd best wait for the two-o-clock.'

Jason was not to be put off. 'I feel I shall be lucky,' he said. 'I must win, I need to win.'

'You an' all the other Chase-me-Charlies,' Wiske said. 'Luck won't lift an 'oss over a fence, lad, an' that's a fact.'

He was right. Jason backed a wild-eyed chestnut that fell at the second fence and was seen no more. This filled him with a resolve to recoup his losses on the next race, and he dragged Wiske away to see if any pearls of wisdom could be garnered among the grooms and ostlers gathered in a group near the start.

The Admiral had found a crony and was deep in conversation with him, so Hector made his way back to where the vehicles were parked, arriving just in time to see Mr Lychgate drive through the gate. He spotted Hector and beckoned him over with a flourish of his whip. Handing the reins to his tiger, he sprang down and approached Hector with hand outstretched.

'Nearly missed you,' he declared. 'Didn't recognise you in that gear. You look like a crooked horse-coper. I wouldn't buy a tit from you, at any price.'

'A working man,' said Hector with dignity, 'can't be expected to be a fashionplate. Did you do as I asked?'

'I did.' Mr Lychgate settled his rump on a convenient stone wall, and stared at Hector accusingly. 'A fine old chase I had of it! The lawyer Shipton – I never met such a wordy fellow! Pounded my ear for hours on end, and dragged me through God knows how many dusty archives and worm-eaten libraries! I swear I was ready to throw in my hand.'

'What about Georgina Carey? Did you confirm the date of her death?'

Mr Lychgate rubbed his nose. 'I did and I didn't.'

'What do you mean?'

'Georgina Carey,' said Frederic with the air of a conjuror producing a rabbit from thin air, 'didn't die in Marseilles in 1816. It was the abigail that stuck her spoon in the wall. It's all there in black and white. Read it with my own eyes. Shipton discovered some pen-pusher at the French Embassy who had it all down pat. Seems that Lady G and her maid and the little boy with the Greek name . . .'

'. . . Jason.'

'. . . that's him. They all went down with the fever – wicked sort of thing that rots the guts – and were whisked off to this nunnery. The abigail died and was buried in the cemetery there. Lady G and the boy recovered.'

This was so far from what Hector had anticipated that for a

moment he stared at his friend in disbelief. Then he said, 'Did you learn what became of Georgina Carey?'

'No,' said Frederic. 'Records don't say. Seems she vanished off the face of the earth.'

Hector shook his head. 'There must have been some error in the entries to the records. Admiral Carey announced the death of his wife when he returned to England. There was never any query . . .'

'Wouldn't be, would there? Respected gentleman, officer in the King's Navy . . . no one would suspect him of doin' anything havey-cavey.'

'If Georgina Carey's still alive,' Hector said, 'it means William Carey's a bigamist and his marriage to Lady Carey is invalid. The letters Jason received may be genuine.'

'What letters?'

Hector gave a brief account of the events at Kettleby Manor, Jason's rendezvous with Piggott, and the discovery of the locket and letter. At the end of the recital Mr Lychgate sighed.

'I'll be honest with you, I can't make any sense of it.'

'No more can I, but I mean to, believe me.'

Frederic looked anxious. 'Can't interfere, Finch. None of your business, after all. Carey may have a dozen wives, for all you know. In for a penny, in for a pound.'

'It's not Will Carey I'm concerned about,' Hector said. 'It's Jason.'

'Well, I'm sorry for the lad, of course. Can't be pleasant to know one's father's behaved like a Turk. But it don't alter the boy's situation. He was born in wedlock, wasn't he?'

'In her letters, his mother hints that she intends to claim custody of him.'

'No chance of that,' Frederic said. 'If she ran away from her husband, the courts won't let her near the children.'

'Even if that husband has falsely declared her to be dead, and taken a second wife?'

Frederic ran a hand over his hair. 'That's a tricky one, I admit. The law will have to decide.'

'The law may not be given a chance. Georgina Carey may be planning to entice the boy away. He certainly believes she's alive, and is hell-bent on finding her. I shall have to warn Sir William.'

'You can't do that!' Frederic looked aghast. 'Can't go around accusin' people of bigamy, and kidnappin'. You'll be hauled off to Bedlam!'

'No, I won't.' Hector noticed that the crowd was moving towards the starting point again, and said hurriedly, 'I can't stay, Frederic. Thank you for all your efforts. I'll see you soon in London, and settle accounts. Do me one more favour – don't speak of this to anyone.'

Frederic looked uncomfortable. 'M'father knows a good deal,' he admitted. 'You told me to ask Mama about Lady G, and I did. Mama doesn't keep things from Papa, and when I returned home last night, he was lyin' in ambush. Collared me and demanded to know what I was about, where you were holed up and why. I thought I'd best make a clean breast of things. Told him about your wager with Hubert, and how we met with that loose-screw Bumper, and your signin' on as a tutor.'

'How did he take it?'

'Said it was a dashed rum go, and he'd give a monkey to see you playin' the schoolmaster. He's no spoilsport though and won't spill the beans. Mum as a funeral mute when he wants to be.' Mr Lychgate stood up. 'Goodbye, Finch. Best we're not seen together. Might set tongues waggin'.'

'No danger of that,' said Hector with a grin. 'You're my patron, remember. Here to see I'm keeping my nose to the grindstone, as Hubert stipulated.'

He shook Frederic's hand and strode away to rejoin Jason and Wiske. Mr Lychgate watched him go with trepidation. Finch had the bit between his teeth, all right. They'd be lucky to avoid the very devil of a scandal. Sighing, he returned to his curricle, and spent the journey to Leicester preparing an expurgated version of the conversation for the edification of his parents.

Shortly after half past three, the Admiral announced his intention of returning at once to the town. Jason's pleas that he be allowed to stay for the last race of the day met with a stern refusal.

'A fine thing it would be if we kept Bishop Harley waiting,' Sir William said. 'Where are your manners, boy?'

'But sir, I have this strong tip for Lightly Over, and if I back him and he wins I shall have twelve guineas!'

'You'd be throwing good money after bad! Lightly Over's a rank outsider, and if he wins you may bite me. Come now, no sulking! Gambling isn't the way to make money.' The Admiral shot a sidelong glance at Hector. 'Honest toil's the way! Ask Mr Finch.'

Hector, remembering how Lord Stavordale had won eleven thousand pounds in a single hand at hazard, thought it best not to reply.

Jason climbed into the carriage looking downcast, and not even the sight of what the Bishop was pleased to call a light repast was able to lift his spirits. He barely touched the ham and roast capons, the raised pie and vegetables, the fresh bread and Stilton cheese, and the blancmange pudding with cream that were set out on the long refectory table.

Hector guessed that he had hoped to win enough at the races to finance his plan to find his mother. It was a disturbing thought, and increased Hector's determination to speak to the Admiral as soon as possible.

Bishop Harley was a good host, and once the meal was over, made it his business to converse with each one of his guests. When Hector's turn came, the old man chatted inconsequentially for a few minutes, then suddenly asked whether Mr Finch had any relatives living in Leicestershire.

'For I must tell you,' he said, 'that you put me strongly in mind of a long-time acquaintance, Julian Wycombe. We were at Eton together, and later Oxford, but after that our paths diverged. We still correspond from time to time. You have very much the look of him, the same cast of countenance and the same build.'

'To my knowledge,' Hector answered, 'I've no relations in this county.'

The Bishop seemed about to enquire further but, seeing the closed expression on Hector's face, he desisted, and switched to the vexed topic of Catholic Emancipation.

When he moved away from Hector, he found himself face to face with Miss Osmond, who wore a distinctly challenging look.

'Uncle Sebastian,' she said forthrightly, 'I couldn't help overhearing your conversation with Mr Finch, and I wish to know your opinion of his statements.'

'On Catholic Emancipation?' said the Bishop, puzzled.

'No, no. I mean what he said about having no relatives in Leicestershire. Do you believe him?'

'I've no reason not to, my dear.'

'You spoke of a Mr Julian Wycombe, whom you once knew . . .'

'Not Mr Wycombe. The Marquess, as he was then, and now the Duke of Wycombe.'

'Whom Mr Finch strongly resembles?'

'In feature, yes.'

Serena looked triumphant. 'It's just as I thought. The man's an impostor!'

Bishop Harley regarded her shrewdly. He was extremely fond of her, and respected her strength of purpose, but he was aware that it sometimes carried her past the bounds of propriety. Himself a member of an older and far from mealy-mouthed generation, he decided to speak frankly.

'There's no call, Serena, for you to doubt Mr Finch's veracity. Julian Wycombe, alas, was a notorious rake in his youth, and the Wycombes stamp their get. There are many bastards who prefer not to proclaim their bastardy.'

Serena coloured. 'I hadn't thought of that,' she admitted. 'I suppose he may be what he claims to be.'

'Quite so,' said the Bishop.

Serena was then called away by Lady Carey to see a portrait of her own mama, done at the age of sixteen. Watching her go, the Bishop hoped he had managed to blunt her curiosity about Hector Finch. He himself was sure this was Julian's son. The physical likeness was too strong to be missed, and every Wycombe carried the traditional name of Finch. But Serena would burn her pretty little fingers if she attempted to rake out the Wycombe coals. The family was large and very powerful. To displease them could put an end to the girl's hopes of a place in society, and spoil her prospects of making an advantageous marriage.

It was certainly puzzling that any Wycombe, legitimate or not, should take a post as a tutor; but then, the whole of life was a puzzle to which only God knew the answer.

Putting aside thoughts of genealogy, the old man called Jason to him, and tried to cheer him up with the promise of a fishing expedition to the banks of the Dove, as soon as the weather should be warm enough.

XIX

As it turned out, neither Serena nor Hector found a chance to talk privately to Sir William, for as soon as they reached home he announced that he was worn to a frazzle, and retired to bed.

The following morning dawned cold, with heavy rain blanketing the countryside. Hector rose early, hoping to waylay the Admiral before breakfast; but Sudbury informed him that the Master had left already for Leicester.

Lady Carey explained later that her husband had chosen to travel on Sunday in order that he might be in his solicitor's office first thing on Monday morning. 'He'll spend the forenoon with Mr Taggart, and the afternoon buying equipment for the dairy,' she said. 'He won't be home until tomorrow night, or perhaps even Tuesday.'

'He never told me he was going,' said Jason pettishly. Lady Carey gave him a severe look.

'That hardly signifies, Jason. We need none of us question your father's decisions. Church is at eleven o'clock. I've ordered the carriage for half past ten, so please be ready in good time.'

'I don't wish to go to church,' whined Jason. 'I feel sick!'

Lady Carey placed a hand on his forehead. 'You're quite cool.'

'It's my stomach,' Jason said, clutching his midriff. 'If you make me go, I'll very likely cast up my accounts in the aisle.'

Her ladyship sighed. She had a strong suspicion that Jason was malingering, but she knew he was subject to bilious attacks, and that yesterday's jaunting and rich food might have set one off.

'Very well,' she said, 'you may stay at home, but you're to go to bed, keep warm and rest. I'll tell Ellen to look in on you now and then, and you must drink plenty of lemon-barley-water.'

Jason trailed off to his bedroom, and at half past ten the family and staff, with the exception of Ellen and Mrs Hodge the cook, set out for church.

The visiting clergyman was of the fire-and-brimstone school.

He preached a sermon that lasted nearly three hours, and it was after two o'clock when the Careys re-entered the Manor. Their ears were at once assailed by a battery of muffled thumps and shouts, which were quickly traced to the bootroom next to the kitchens. Lady Carey unlocked the door and released the near-hysterical Cook and Ellen.

'That wicked boy,' cried Cook. ''E shut us in, ma'am! 'E called us in there, and when we was in 'e sprung out, slammed the door and turned the key. We've been 'ollerin' an' cryin' for hours, with none to 'elp us!'

Hector led the rush up the stairs to Jason's room. His bed was unrumpled, and a note was pinned to the bolster.

Lady Carey snatched it up and read it, then sank down on the edge of the bed.

'He's run away,' she said faintly.

Serena leaned over and took the paper from her aunt's hand. The message was brief and to the point:

TO WHOM IT MAY CONCERN. I have gone to find
Merlin's treasure. If Crosby could go into the cave so can I.
No one is to try to prevent me, my mind is made up. I will be
home tomorrow, before Papa comes. Yr obedient servant,
JASON LUDOVIC CAREY.

'We must stop him,' said Lady Carey desperately. 'It's too dangerous in the caves . . . Wiske must go at once . . .'

'No,' said Hector. He took Lady Carey's hand and held it firmly. 'First we must discover how he travelled. If he rode Peppercorn, we've a chance of overtaking him. I'll go to the stables and find out. In the meantime, I suggest you ask Sudbury to make up a hamper of supplies. We'll need candles and flints, and a couple of those sea-lanterns from Sir William's study . . . blankets, bandages, food and brandy . . . flasks of water, one can't be sure that the water in the caves is drinkable . . . knives, spades, a hammer. And ropes. I'll ask Wiske to provide those.'

'There's no time,' cried Lady Carey.

'Yes, there is,' said Hector firmly. 'If Jason's safe and sound, a half-hour's delay can lose us nothing. If he's hurt, or in difficulty, we must be equipped to help him.'

Lady Carey and Laurel hurried off to collect the items he'd

listed, but Serena followed him out to the stables. 'It will be best if I know your plans,' she said. 'My aunt's in no state to think clearly.'

Wiske met them at the back door, looking grim.

'He took Roland,' he said. 'That numskull Jem saw 'im saddlin' up, an' never thought to ask where 'e was goin'. Wasn't even sharp enough to see which road young master took.'

'No doubt of it, he's gone to Merlin's Pot at Stubleigh,' Hector said. 'He thinks to find treasure in the caves. We must go after him, Wiske.'

'You can take Sultan,' said Serena quickly. 'He's the fastest we have.'

Hector smiled at her. 'Thank you, but we must take a carriage. We've a lot to carry, and if Jason's hurt, we can bring him back more comfortably.' He turned back to Wiske. 'Did Sir William take the greys?'

'No, sir, the bays.'

'Put the greys to the phaeton, and find me some stout ropes. You'll need warm clothes, boots. Oilskins if you have them.'

As Wiske hurried off, Serena spoke. 'May I come with you?'

'No, I need you to set up a search party. Call on the neighbours for help. It will be best if they gather at some point away from here. Lady Carey is in enough distress, without being plagued with questions and useless advice.'

'I'll ask the Nettlebeds,' Serena said. 'They'll fix it.'

Hector nodded. He was staring skywards, at the rain still teeming down from heavy clouds. 'Miss Osmond,' he said abruptly, 'I know very little about underground caves, but I do recall having heard that they're prone to flooding during heavy storms. If that happens at Stubleigh, Jason and Wiske and I may be away for . . . for some hours. I rely on you to keep things running smoothly here, to comfort Lady Carey and Laurel until Sir William is home. Can you get word to him, do you have his direction in Leicester?'

'He told Aunt Amelia he'd put up at the Golden Lion for the night. Jem can ride over and bring him back.'

'Good.' He hesitated, then said quietly, 'One more thing. In the event of a long delay in my return, will you ask Sir William to inform my friend Mr Lychgate, of Bargate House, Leicester?'

Serena met his eyes. She knew that he was warning her that

neither he, nor Jason, nor Wiske might return from the caves, and her heart grew cold at the thought, but she said calmly, 'I'll remember.'

He smiled at her again. 'Thank you. Don't fret. We'll come about. Bad pennies always turn up, you know.'

With a reassuring nod, he went off to join Wiske in the stables.

It was not until Serena was turning back into the house that she realised that she had without hesitation placed Jason's safety in the hands of the despised Mr Finch.

Within fifteen minutes, the mail phaeton with the greys inspanned had been brought to the back door, and the goods Hector had listed placed in its capacious rear section. Wiske tied an oilcloth securely over the provisions and blankets, and took his place on the rear seat. Hector raised his whip in salute to the ladies gathered in the kitchen porch, and the carriage rolled briskly out of the stable yard.

Wiske gave it as his opinion that Jason must have travelled by the side lanes; 'But we mun stick to the pike,' he said, 'heavy-loaded as we are.'

Hector agreed, and as soon as they reached the pike road, he brought the greys along as fast as he dared. It took all his skill to keep the vehicle clear of potholes and puddles, and he was thankful that the rain was driving from behind him rather than directly into his face.

They reached the village of Stubleigh shortly before four o'clock. As was natural on a pouring wet Sunday afternoon, no one was about in the street. Hector enquired at the local public house, and was told that he'd reach Merlin's Pot by taking the lane a hundred yards further along. The landlord thought fit to enter a word of warning.

'You won't want to be pokin' about in they caves today, sir. All this rain, the stream'll be risin'. There's bin folks drownded afore now, an' you don't want to be took off in your prime.'

Hector's request for men to help in the search met with a shake of the head.

'I'll pass the word for you, sir, but I doubt any of the lads will turn out, not for love nor money. Tomorrow, if the rain goes off, mebbe they'll agree.'

'Have you visited the caves yourself? Can you tell me anything about them?'

'I've bin as far as t' second cave,' said the innkeeper, 'with the other childer. We weren't no higher than toadstools, and when we heared the demons comin' we didn't bide to greet them. I'll say this much. If you get caught by t' floodwater, keep over to the right o' the second cave. Climb the Cathedral Steps, and you'll keep y' feet dray. Then when the rains are done, we'll come an' fetch you out.' Dead or alive, his expression said.

Hector caught sight of a gangling lout leaning at the entrance to the stables.

'At least send that lad with us,' he said. 'I won't ask him to set foot in the caves, just to bring the horses back to shelter.' He produced two gold coins and handed them over. The landlord pocketed the coins and shouted to George to look lively and climb aboard the phaeton, which he did without enthusiasm.

They set off once more, found the lane and followed it for just over a mile, fetching up at the foot of a towering rock face. Confronting them was a vast dark hole in the cliff, from which tumbled a foam-streaked rivulet.

Hector handed the reins to Wiske. 'Wait here,' he directed.

A short scramble took him up to the mouth of the cave. It was as Crosby Nettlebed had described it, wide and lofty, its inner reaches lost in gloom, but near its mouth an uncertain light penetrated. It allowed Hector to descry, on the clean sand of the cavern floor, a set of small footprints heading purposefully into the dark.

Hector spent some minutes casting about, but could find no set of prints to show that Jason had returned. Going back to the phaeton, he found that Wiske had already unharnessed the greys, and was instructing the nervous stable-lad on how they were to be housed, fed and groomed, and what fate he might expect if he harmed a hair of their handsome heads. The boy, only too eager to be out of what he plainly regarded as an accursed place, led the greys away at a brisk trot, and Wiske turned to gaze anxiously at Hector.

'He went in,' Hector said, 'but he hasn't come out. We'll light a couple of lanterns and see what we can find.'

It was little enough. The light of the lamps, though not strong enough to penetrate the full width and height of the cave, was sufficient to show the way Jason had taken. His footprints crossed the floor towards the point where the cave narrowed to a round tunnel in the rock, along which the rivulet ran. The formation of the tunnel was symmetrical, its walls smooth, which made Hector think that at times the flow of water must fill it entirely. He watched the stream carefully and thought that its level was rising.

Turning to Wiske, he said, 'We must get the supplies into the second cave. Come, make haste.'

They worked as fast as they could to bring the supplies into the cavern, and wrapped them into four portable bundles, each protected by an oilcloth. When it was done, Hector said, 'Wiske, there's a danger of flooding. There's no call for you to go any further. You're a family man . . .'

'I'm goin' in,' said Wiske flatly, and Hector didn't argue. Each of them strapped a brace of bundles to his back, and then, holding their lanterns high, they began to edge their way along the stream. Though the water was as yet only thigh-high, they made slow progress, for the course was uneven and pitted with deep holes. For the last few yards they were obliged to bend double as the roof sloped sharply downward. The sound of the stream was loud, and the darkness absolute. Without their lamps they would have been blind men.

Suddenly they were through the tunnel. Reaching up his free hand, Hector felt only space above him, and turning his lamp this way and that he saw that the rock face ran away at right angles on both sides. They had reached the second cave, and remembering the innkeeper's words, Hector stepped cautiously to his right and shone his light about. Wiske followed suit, and together they surveyed the expanse of Merlin's Pot.

Hector's first thought was that Crosby Nettlebed had never set foot in the place, so little did his description fit the facts.

The lamplight showed a cavern narrower than the one they had left, but far loftier. The walls nearest them soared upward like the buttresses of a gothic cathedral. To the left of the stream the roof was visible, supported by pillars of rock that gleamed as white as pearl when the light struck them.

At the back of the cave a waterfall tumbled into a broad pool from a height so great they could not see its source. A yard or two from where they stood, a massive slab of rock formed a natural bridge across the stream, and by common consent Hector and Wiske moved over it, to what must surely be the Cathedral Steps of the landlord's description. These rose from a broad shelf in a series of shallow ledges to a double rank of massive organ pipes, between which a curtain of pure white crystalline rock fell in delicate folds, as if drawn across the mouth of a sanctuary.

All about them was the continual thunder of the water. Cold, fresh air surged past them like the beat of giant wings.

Hector called Jason's name, but the cry was lost in clamorous echoes. He made his way up the steps, still calling. Reaching the organ pipes he searched for any crack or cranny where a boy might hide, and found none, nor was there any space behind the rock curtain. There was no way out of the cave on this side of the stream.

Wiske in the mean time was prowling along the back of the cave, examining the walls and peering behind the waterfall. Rejoining Hector, he shook his head. 'Nothin',' he said, and glanced down at the stream rushing past.

'She's risin',' he said. 'We'll have to find 'im fast.'

Hector nodded. Crossing to the left-hand side of the cavern, they made their way slowly along its wall. Boulders obstructed them, and shallow pools whose rims seemed encrusted with pearls. They found no sign of Jason, and Hector began to fear the child had fallen into the torrent and drowned.

They were nearing the back wall again when they became aware of a sudden turbulence in the air, a whistling wind that plucked at their garments and struck ice cold in their lungs. Hector stepped forward to shine his lamp on the rock face, and found what they sought; a horizontal fissure along the foot of the rock wall through which the windstorm came. The gap appeared to be some fifteen feet broad, but no more than a foot high.

Lying flat on their bellies, the two men shone their lanterns on the fissure. It stretched back for some three yards, and was then blocked by a slab of rock. Whether there was space to pass that by, they could not tell.

'Jason must have wriggled through,' Hector said. 'I'll take a look.'

'Let me go,' said Wiske at once, but Hector shook his head.

'There's no way for such a fine figure of a man,' he said; and

Wiske, conscious of his ample paunch and fleshy shoulders, was forced to agree. Unwinding the rope slung about his torso, he attached one end to Hector's ankle.

'If you find 'im,' he said, 'tie 'im on, and I'll pull 'im through.'

Hector nodded, and eased himself forward into the fissure. For a moment, as he felt the rock brush his back, he was seized with fear that he would stick fast; but he quickly found that by stretching one arm forward, pushing the lamp, and letting the other trail at his side, his body was flat enough to avoid contact with the roof. Groping for finger-holds, squirming and contorting, he inched ahead, and at last felt space above his shoulders, and saw the lamplight spring up the face of the nether rock. This was some two feet away, and by swivelling sideways, and sliding away from the fissure, he was able to struggle to his feet and raise the lantern over his head.

As he did so, he was wellnigh blinded by a burst of light that seemed to explode in front of him. For an instant he thought himself the victim of an hallucination, but then he saw that a little to his left, and level with his head, there was a natural alcove in the rock, and this niche was lined with crystal; crystal flowers of fantastic shape; delicate straws of crystal that hung trembling in the wind; jagged points of crystal that caught the lamplight and magnified it a thousand times so that he seemed to be staring at a vast store of jewels. And as he gazed he heard the demon voices mutter and whimper in the fastnesses of the rock above him, laughing and chattering and coming always closer, eager as hounds closing in for the kill.

Instinctively he moved towards the grotto, and was about to call Jason's name when his toe struck a softness, and lowering the lamp he saw Jason at his feet.

Kneeling, Hector examined the boy. He was breathing but unconscious. There was a deep gash on the side of his head and his hands were badly grazed. Evidently he had tried to scramble up to what he took for Merlin's treasure and had fallen and struck his head. A rapid check confirmed that his limbs were unbroken. Leaning to the fissure, Hector shouted,

'Wiske, can you hear me? I've found him. He's alive.'

Wiske's face showed, puckered with anxiety.

'Hurry, sir, the water's risin' fast.'

Hector pulled on the rope, gathering several yards of slack.

He tied the line round Jason's ankles, keeping hold of the free end. Placing the boy flat on the ground, feet towards the main cavern, he gave a sharp tug on the rope. Wiske began to pull, and Jason vanished from sight. With some difficulty, Hector managed to lie down and roll into the fissure. He extinguished the lantern, took a firm grip on the rope, and shouted:

'Wiske! Heave away, man!'

Bumping and scraping, he was dragged through the cleft, to arrive bruised and breathless at Wiske's side.

He saw that luck had favoured them. The waterfall was now a solid column of thundering water. The whirlpool at its foot was capped with foam, the stream had broken its banks and was ankle deep on this side of the cavern. Within minutes it would have flooded the fissure, and Jason lying prone on his face must have drowned.

The tunnel leading to the outside world was no longer visible, save as a sinister sucking of the tide. Of the rock bridge, only the highest point showed.

Wiske gathered Jason in his arms.

'Light the way, sir,' he said. 'I'll follow.'

Carrying the two lamps and the sodden coils of rope, Hector waded over to the bridge. He stepped across and turned to steady Wiske's progress. They climbed the steps to the broad shelf at the foot of the organ pipes.

As they laid Jason down, a strange thing happened. The demon voices that had risen to a tumult began to fade, and the turbulence of the air ceased.

Lifting his head, Wiske gave a half-fearful laugh. 'Seems the Devil can't step on 'oly ground,' he said.

Hector thought there was another reason for the respite. All the openings to the cave were now sealed by water, and the wind could no longer play through the myriad cracks and pipes of the mountain above them.

It was not a happy idea, and he suppressed it. Setting down the lantern, he said briskly,

'Unpack the supplies, will you, Wiske? I'll get this hero out of his wet clothes and into a blanket – and we'll need the basilicum ointment, and bandages for his head.'

XX

At Kettleby Manor, Lady Carey, Serena and Laurel waited in an agony of uncertainty for news. Mr Nettlebed had organised a sizable rescue party which had already set out for Stubleigh; and the news of Jason's venture having spread like wildfire through the district, the Careys found themselves the target of so many well-wishers that at last Lady Carey requested Sudbury to allow no one else past the front door, since she was quite unable to face any more kindness.

An exception was made for Mr Tonkin the Vicar, who spent half an hour at the Manor, and whose solid counsel and prayers for Jason's safety were a great comfort to his hearers.

The servants did not help matters by tiptoeing about the house as if there were already a death in the family; and when Cook set a large meal on the table and urged the ladies to keep up their strength for poor young Master's sake, Laurel burst into tears and declared she couldn't touch a morsel while her darling brother was in peril of his life.

Lady Carey tried to put on a cheerful face. 'Jason is alive,' she said firmly. 'I know it in my bones. I daresay he'll be here any minute and hungry as a lion.' She rather spoilt the effect by adding in an undertone, 'If only your father was at home.'

'We can't hope for him before midnight,' Serena said.

'I know it.' Lady Carey glanced at the clock, whose measured ticking had begun to play on her nerves. 'I wonder if he may have gone direct to Stubleigh?'

'He won't do that, Aunt. He'll surely call here first, in case . . . in case Jason has already returned.' She rose and extended her hand to Laurel. 'Come, let's all sit in the drawing room, so we'll see when his carriage turns through the gate.'

They followed her suggestion, and tried to pass the time by talking of everything but the subject that filled their minds. It was at half past eleven that Laurel, on watch at one of the windows, called out that the carriage was coming up the drive.

It swept to a halt at the front door, Sir William sprang down from it, and a moment later came striding into the room.

He flung his arms about his wife and daughter, but it was to Serena that he looked for information. She gave it as simply as she could, telling him of Jason's letter and what had transpired.

'We've no recent news,' she concluded, 'except that Mr Nettlebed sent us word at nine o'clock that Jason, Mr Finch and Wiske must all have entered the caves, for they found their footprints in the sand. It's not possible at present to go after them because the rain has . . . has caused flooding. Once that subsides . . .'

Here Laurel broke into fresh sobs, which caused the Admiral to say bracingly, 'There, there, puss, no need to kick up a rumpus! The rain's stopped here and may well have done to the north. We'll fetch Jason out safe and sound.' He dropped a kiss on Laurel's cheek. 'Be a good girl and fetch my second greatcoat from the closet. This one's wet as a spaniel. And Amelia, my love, pour me a glass of brandy to keep out the cold.'

As his womenfolk hurried away on these errands, Sir William said quietly, 'Serena, is there a doctor at Stubleigh?'

'Dr Shotton has gone over with Mr Nettlebed,' Serena answered.

'Good. I see I've found a worthy lieutenant in you, my dear.' He sighed. 'God knows what possessed the boy to do such a hare-brained thing.'

'I think he hoped to find Merlin's treasure. When Crosby spoke of it the other night, Jason was all ears.'

'That popinjay,' said the Admiral bitterly. 'If aught befalls Jason, Crosby shall answer to me for it.' Before he could say more Laurel came running into the room, followed by Lady Carey bearing a glass of brandy, and a silver hipflask, which she slipped into the pocket of the greatcoat.

'Never too much of it,' approved the Admiral. He put on the coat, drained the glass, kissed his wife and, with a cheerful wave at his daughter and niece, hurried away to the stable yard.

In Merlin's Pot, Hector consulted his watch. 'Ten past eleven,' he said.

'Mebbe it stopped,' Wiske said.

There was no way of telling time in the total blackness that surrounded their small pool of light. The night seemed interminable. The cold was intense.

Jason, his wounds dressed and bound, lay wrapped in a blanket between them. He had come to briefly, but had fallen back into delirium, tossing and turning and muttering gibberish. Sometimes he opened his eyes and stared about him, but he did not recognise his companions. He had a high fever, and Hector soaked his cravat in the icy water of the stream and placed it on the boy's forehead, which seemed to give him some ease.

'It's a concussion,' Hector said. 'He probably has the devil of a headache.'

Neither he nor Wiske felt any desire to sleep. They watched Jason, they watched the floodwater swirling past, they ate bread and cheese and drank a little wine. It warmed them somewhat, and prompted Hector to ask the question that had been troubling him.

'Wiske, why do you imagine Jason came here?'

A few hours ago Wiske would have returned some evasive answer, but now he looked directly into Hector's face and said, 'For the treasure, a' course.'

'It doesn't exist, man. It's no more than a legend.'

'Aye, we know that, but we're full grown. A lad his age believes what he wants to.'

'He told me once that if he had money, he'd bring his mama home to Kettleby.'

'His mam's dead.'

'Piggott says she's alive.'

Wiske turned his head aside and spat into the pool at his feet. 'Piggott's a liar. If I had my way, he'd not set foot in these parts again. I've told Sir William, over an' over, but he don't choose to listen. Mebbe he will, now.' Wiske paused and then said slowly, 'Happen you'll tell the Master, sir, to be rid o' Piggott? Happen he'll listen to you.'

'Few masters take advice from tutors, Wiske.'

Wiske smiled crookedly. 'Happen he'll listen to you,' he repeated.

At four in the morning, Jason opened his eyes and complained of being thirsty. Wiske gave him water from the flask in the hamper. The boy drank greedily, but was seized almost

127

immediately by a bout of vomiting. When it passed, Hector lowered him back on to the blanket.

'Lie still, Diomedes! You took a good knock.'

'Mr Finch?' Jason's puzzled gaze shifted from Hector to Wiske, then roved across the shadowy shafts of stone that surrounded them.

'We're in Merlin's Pot,' Hector said. 'Remember?'

'Yes,' whispered Jason. He frowned. 'My head hurts.'

'It will be better presently. Go to sleep.'

Jason was silent for a moment. Then he said, 'Jewels. I found them. Diamonds and rubies, but they broke when I touched them.'

'They were not real, you see. Only crystals.'

Jason struggled to sit up. 'I promised Piggott . . . Piggott asked me . . .'

'Piggott,' promised Hector, 'will get what he's asked for.'

Jason sighed. 'I want to go home.'

'Tomorrow we'll go home. Now you must rest.'

The boy's eyelids flickered, drooped. Within seconds he had fallen into an uneasy sleep.

Picking up a lighted candle, Hector went to check the level of the stream. It had dropped slightly. The rock bridge was nearly clear, the maelstrom under the waterfall had dwindled to a gentle eddy, and foam-flecked water was moving out through the tunnel.

Returning to the top of the steps, he sat down next to Wiske. 'It's subsiding, but it's still too high for us to carry Jason through. We must wait for daylight.'

Wiske squinted at the darkness above. 'What if it rains again?'

Hector shrugged. 'If you're a praying man, pray for a spell of drought.'

Later, Hector was given many accounts of the adventure as seen through the eyes of those waiting in the great entry cave to Merlin's Pot: how the rescuers had watched with dread and anguish the mounting floodwaters, convinced that by now all within the second cave must have perished; how Sir William had crouched hour after hour at the mouth of the tunnel, speaking to no one; how Mr Nettlebed and Dr Shotton had quietly discussed what must be done to recover the trapped men, alive or dead;

how when the dawn came up, and it was seen that sunlight crowned the surrounding hills, a great huzza went up from the assembled crowd; and how, as the level of the stream began to fall, it had taken the combined strength of Crosby Nettlebed and the innkeeper to restrain the Admiral from plunging headlong into the water in an attempt to reach his son.

Hector's own recollection of his escape from the cavern was confused, for rescuers and rescued met halfway along the tunnel, and there was so much shouting, and embracing, so much praising the Good Lord for his mercy and Hector and Wiske for their valour, so much congratulating Jason for merely being alive, that rational thought was impossible.

What stayed in his mind was the look on Sir William's face as he received his son into his arms. For a moment the old man could not utter a sound; but then he nodded to Wiske and Hector as they stood in their draggled state, and said quietly, 'God bless you both. We'll talk later.'

Dr Shotton, having made a brief examination of Jason and declared him to be suffering more from shock and exposure than from his injuries, hustled Sir William and the boy into his own carriage, so that he might keep an eye on his patient during the journey back to Kettleby.

Hector and Wiske were taken up by Mr Nettlebed, and Crosby was detailed to bring the Careys' phaeton home.

Hector was too tired to worry about Crosby's ability to manage the greys. Leaning his head against the leather squab of Mr Nettlebed's well-sprung coach, he abandoned himself to the comfortable anticipation of hot water, dry clothing, and a substantial meal.

XXI

Jason was put to bed in the guest chamber next to his parents' room. Hector, calling next morning to see how he did, found Lady Carey and Dr Shotton in quiet conference. Lady Carey at once stretched out both hands to him.

'Mr Finch, I am so glad to see you. I didn't thank you sufficiently last night. Mere words can't express what I feel. Sir William and I stand forever in your debt.'

As Hector began to murmur a disclaimer, an impatient voice called out from the fourposter: 'Sir? Is that you?'

Hector went to stand beside the bed. Jason was sitting propped up on his pillows. His face was very pale, but his eyes had lost their fevered look. He said in a subdued tone, 'Thank you, Mr Finch, for saving me. I was very wrong to go to that place. It was only that I hoped . . .'

'. . . to find treasure. Don't dwell upon past errors, Diomedes. Think of the rosy future.'

'But will you be here? Papa says . . .'

'We're all to remove to London very soon, I think.'

'Then I shan't see you again!'

'Why not? London isn't so vast that friends never meet.'

'Truly?'

'Truly. I intend to flaunt you, you know, as my star pupil.'

Jason chuckled, and would have taken the conversation further had not Lady Carey said firmly that he was not to tire himself.

'You won't leave without telling me?' he said anxiously, and Hector smiled down at him.

'Certainly not. Now do as your mama bids you, and try to sleep. I shall look in this afternoon to see how you go on.'

A footman now appeared to say that Dr Shotton's gig had been brought to the door. The doctor said his goodbyes, picked up his bag, and then surprised Hector by saying abruptly, 'Mr Finch, a word with you in private, if you please?'

He did not speak as they made their way downstairs, but on the driveway before the house he turned to face Hector squarely.

'I hope, Mr Finch, that you meant what you said to that boy. I hope you don't intend to disappear from his life?'

As Hector stared, the doctor repeated, 'I trust you will see him from time to time?'

'That will be for Sir William to decide, I suppose.' There was a distinct edge to Hector's voice, but the doctor was not deterred.

'Jason holds you in the highest regard,' he said. 'In fact, you're his hero. He's not a strong child. If he finds you've deceived him, it will be a grave blow to him and could affect his health. You'll forgive my plain speaking, sir. I count the Careys my friends as well as my patients.'

It was impossible to snub such sincerity, and Hector smiled. 'They're fortunate on both counts. Goodbye, Dr Shotton, and thank you for your counsel.'

The doctor departed with the air of a man who knows he has done his duty. It was in Hector's mind to go and chat to Wiske, and he was about to set off round the house when he realised that Sir William was watching him from the study window.

The old man stood as he must often have stood on the bridge of his ship; legs spread, hands clasped behind his back, eyes watching to see if the approaching craft was friend or foe.

As Hector raised a hand in greeting, this belligerence faded. Bending forward, Sir William threw up the lower frame of the window and leaned his hands on the sill.

'Good morning, Lord Hector,' he said.

XXII

'Pray sit down, my lord,' said the Admiral, when a few minutes later he ushered Hector into his den. 'You've breakfasted, have you? Good. I hope the smell of baccy doesn't trouble you. This is the only room in the house where I'm permitted to blow a cloud, and I'm afraid the smoke gets into the hangings.'

He settled himself in the chair facing Hector's and said with a wry look, 'I confess I was somewhat unsure how to bring you to this meeting. As an employer I'm free to summon Mr Finch as and when I please; as a host, I must be careful not to inconvenience so distinguished a guest as Lord Hector Wycombe of Fontwell. Luckily, chance and Dr Shotton brought you to my net.'

'Sir William,' began Hector, 'there is something I must say to you . . .'

The Admiral held up a hand. 'Let me say my piece first. Last night, Lord Hector, you saved the life of my son. Wiske has told me how you put yourself at risk to bring Jason from that death trap. Your action is one I can never repay, but I wish to thank you with all my heart. I wish you to know that if ever I can be of service to you in any way . . . any way at all . . . you have only to say the word.'

'Indeed, sir, there's no need to thank me or . . . or to feel in any way in my debt. It's I that should make reparation to you, for coming into this house under false pretences.'

'You fulfilled your contract. You were an excellent tutor to Jason.'

'That's hardly the point. It was a betrayal of your trust.'

The Admiral gave a great crack of laughter. 'What makes you think I trusted you? I'm not a man who takes anyone or anything on trust!'

'Then may I ask why you employed me?'

'Wanted to know what you were up to. I'd a suspicion you might be nosing about for the King's Customs and Excise. Of course, that was before I learned you were born to the purple and had no need to earn your keep.'

'And when did you learn that, sir?'

'Why, the very day you set foot in Kettleby. This is my bailiwick, Lord Hector. Not much goes on in these parts that I don't hear of. Jimmy Wragge sent to warn me that there was a stranger at the Seven Stars, asking for me; and when you turned up with that damned smoky tale about wanting Bumper's job, I sent Wiske out to make a few enquiries. Wiske's sister is married to the landlord of the Cap and Bells at Nether Kettleby. She told Wiske that a Lord Hector Wycombe and a Mr Frederic Lychgate had bespoken rooms at the inn, and had entertained Ebenezer Bumper to dinner. It didn't take a genius to see that Hector Wycombe and Hector Finch were one and the same.'

'Yet you said nothing! You allowed me to continue the deception!'

The Admiral shrugged. 'Why not?' he said blandly. 'Your reference was genuine, your work proved satisfactory, and Jason took a shine to you. That was a new departure, I can tell you! It pleased me to see him happy, and I admit you tickled my curiosity. I was hard put to it, not to ask you straight out why you wished to pass yourself off as Mr Finch.'

'I'm ashamed to say I did it for a wager.' Hector launched into an account of his bet with Hubert, his meeting with the lachrymose Mr Bumper, and his impulsive decision to apply for the vacant post. Sir William chuckled appreciatively, but at the end he gave Hector a shrewd look.

'By what you say, my lord, your wager was that you would earn your living for one week. That was accomplished days ago. Why didn't you leave Kettleby at once?'

Hector met the hard black gaze. 'Because,' he said, 'I'd come to believe that Jason was in danger.'

'Danger? What d'ye mean, what kind of danger?'

'The danger of being tricked into trying to find his mother.'

'Jason's mother is dead, my lord. She died in France in 1816.'

'No, Sir William. The official records show it was the abigail who died. Your wife survived the fever.'

For a moment the Admiral stared wordlessly at Hector. Then he jerked to his feet, his face scarlet.

'So you're a damned spy, after all! You came here to spy on me and to pry into things that are none of your concern. Who set you on? Answer me!'

Hector shook his head. 'If, as you say, your first wife is dead, then how is it that Piggott brings Jason letters from her?'

'You're lying, trying to gull me . . .'

'I'm trying to reach the truth, Sir William. A moment ago you said that you take no one on trust, yet you trust a treacherous rogue like Piggott . . .'

'Piggott's no traitor, he served King and Country as I did!'

'And now he serves whoever will pay him his price.'

'What of it? If he brings in a little wine, or a roll or two of silk, where's the shame in that?'

'I don't speak of contraband. What Piggott smuggles in is far more dangerous. A few days ago he tried to sell Jason a locket containing a picture of your late wife, and a note written by her. Jason told me he's received four such messages in recent years.'

'You're lying! He would have told me.'

'Would he, sir? Would he have run the chance of having you destroy the letters and drive Piggott away?'

The Admiral sank into his chair. 'It's not possible,' he muttered. 'The boy has only his pocket-money. Why would Piggott risk my good will for a few guineas?'

Hector drew a bow at a venture. 'You pay him, I take it, to keep an eye on certain people in France?'

As the old man made no answer, Hector persisted. 'Isn't that the case, that Piggott's your agent?'

'I have . . . certain interests. He watches them for me.'

'And now he's taking money from those "interests" as well as from you.'

As Sir William stared at him stony-faced, Hector said urgently, 'Don't you understand, man? Piggott's deceived you, he's tricked your son most cruelly! There's no more room for half-truths, you have to tell me the whole.'

The Admiral heaved a long sigh, letting his head fall back against the chair. At last he said:

'It's true that my wife survived the fever. I put it about that she'd died, to conceal the fact that she'd run off with a damned Frenchman . . . a cardsharp, a common ivory-turner. I couldn't let my children know their mother was no better than a whore.

'Georgina was many years younger than I. Beautiful, frivolous, used to being the darling of society. When we went to Marseilles, I was too busy to pay her the proper attention. She looked

134

elsewhere for it. The man was Comte Etien de Rennes. He'd served with distinction in Napoleon's army, but he was a wastrel. Went through his own fortune, and took to gambling and leeching on wealthy women. He became my wife's lover. They were discreet, I knew nothing of the affair. Then the fever plague struck the port. Jason and the abigail took the infection. I arranged for Georgina to accompany them to a hospice in the hills, thinking she would be safer there. De Rennes persuaded her to desert her child and go to Paris with him. The nuns sent me a letter she left. I hurried to the hospice to be with Jason. He recovered, the maid died and was buried at the nunnery. My dear Amelia, who had charge of Laurel at the time, crossed to France and brought Jason home. I followed soon after, and announced that my wife was dead. People accepted my word.'

'But your wife did not, Sir William. She wrote to Jason, saying that she loved him, and would return to him some day.'

'She wrote, yes. Jason showed me the letter. I told him it was a forgery, a trick by villains who hoped to extort money from me. I bade him forget all about it. I wrote to warn my wife that if she ever again attempted to communicate with my children, I would set the law on her. That, Lord Hector, is the whole story.'

'Not quite, sir. You've remarried. If your wife is still alive . . .'

'She's not. Georgina died in Paris in 1818. She'd endured two years of misery, forced to aid her paramour in his gaming house, living from hand to mouth, pursued by duns, shunned by decent society, and cut off from her own kith and kin. She fell into a decline, and death released her in the autumn of that year. The records will show that I speak the truth.'

'And de Rennes?'

'The scoundrel wrote to tell me of her death. He tried to get money from me – to bury her, he said. I went to Paris and met him, made him understand he'd not get a groat from me, then or ever. I gave Georgina a decent burial and returned to England.'

'Have you heard from de Rennes since?'

'No. Not that I set much store by his silence. Rogues like that never give up.'

'So you set Piggott to watch him.'

'Yes. He brought me reports whenever he came to England.' The Admiral rubbed a hand over his face. 'I never dreamed he'd cheat me. I've saved his hide more than once, in the past. Well, that's water under the bridge.' The Admiral straightened his shoulders and spoke with his old briskness. 'I'll send Piggott to the rightabout, never fear. I'll set things straight with her ladyship and the children, too.' He met Hector's eyes. 'They love me, they know I love them. They'll understand I acted for the best.'

Hector did not answer. He was thinking that while Lady Carey and Laurel might understand Sir William's motives, Jason would not easily recover from the shattering of his dream. Aloud, he said,

'At a time like this, you'll be wishing me at Jericho. I think it will be best if I leave Kettleby this afternoon. I shall take the mail coach to Leicester . . .'

'No question of that. My carriage is at your disposal.'

'Thank you. Before I leave, I'd like your permission to tell Jason who I am, and why I embarked on this hare-brained adventure. I don't want there to be any misunderstanding between us.'

'As you please.' The Admiral rose to his feet. 'I repeat, Lord Hector, that I'm indebted to you for the many services you've rendered me and my family.' His eyes twinkled suddenly. 'I hope you will forgive my deceptions, as I forgive yours.'

Hector stood up and shook the outstretched hand. 'Of course. I trust we'll meet soon, in London.'

'I doubt it. Your world and mine are very different.'

'My world,' Hector said, 'is what I choose, and I certainly don't choose to forget Kettleby or the friends I've made here.' He smiled. 'Besides, I stand in need of a reference to show my brother, a glowing one if you please, saying that Mr Hector Finch admirably fulfilled his tasks as a tutor, and is to be highly recommended to any prospective employer.'

Leaving the Admiral's study, Hector found that everyone in the household knew his true identity. Tongues had obviously been wagging in the servants' hall, and he could only hope that the whole of the fashionable world would not soon learn of the short but eventful career of Mr Finch.

Luckily most of the Careys' staff would remain at Kettleby,

and Wiske, who was to accompany them to London, quickly made it plain he was not one to gossip.

He greeted Hector with a nod of the head and a calm, 'Mornin', m'lord,' and when Hector tried to embark on explanations, cut him short with a grin.

'Lord love you, we wasn't fooled. Not as silly as we look, hereabouts.' He laid aside the piece of harness he'd been polishing, and faced Hector.

'Reckon you'll be leaving us, soon?'

'Yes, this afternoon.'

'The boy'll miss you sorely.'

'I shall see him in Town.'

Wiske considered Hector without illusion. He knew something of London, and the ways of the Quality. Not much time, in that crowded life, for a lad of eleven.

'That Piggott,' he said. 'He'll be back.'

'Sir William intends to send him packing.'

'He'll be back,' repeated Wiske.

Hector reached into his pocket for one of his calling cards, and handed it to Wiske.

'That's my direction in London. If you see or hear anything of Piggott or Laval, let me know of it at once.'

Wiske's brow cleared. 'I will, my lord, and thank 'ee.'

Later that evening, when enjoying a pint of porter at the Seven Stars, Wiske informed his fellow drinkers that Lord Hector Wycombe, besides being pluck to the backbone and a dab hand with the horses, was a gentleman who knew just how many beans made five, and could be trusted to put his money where his mouth was.

Molly Wragge and her husband, locking the tavern door when the drinkers had departed, voiced a very different opinion of his lordship.

'May the devil take that nosy parker,' said Molly viciously, as she piled tankards on a tray. 'Piggott wouldn't 'ave took off, if it wasn't for Mr Finch an' 'is meddlin'.'

Mr Wragge stared slack-jawed. 'Wotcher mean, Piggott's took off? Where?'

Molly shrugged. ''Oo knows? The Admiral told 'im never to set foot in Kettleby no more. Blazin' row they had, simly.

Piggott's took all his stuff. Proper queer 'e looked, with them white eyes burnin' like ice.'

'Don't see what Finch 'ad to do with it.'

'Well, use yer loaf, Wragge. It was 'is lordship tipped the Admiral the wink to send Piggott packin'. Knew all about Piggott's lay, 'e did, tried to get me to cut 'im in, but I saw through that, all right. I told Piggott to watch out. And now the Admiral's cut line, an' taken our profits with 'im.' A thought struck her. 'You don't reckon the old man'll go to the magistrates, do 'ee?'

'Nah! In too deep 'isself. We'll just lay low and keep a quiet tongue, and all will come right.'

'Piggott won't lay low,' said Molly with conviction. 'T'urble angered, 'e was. Stared at the Manor, an' shook 'is fist, an' swore as all debts must be paid wi' interest.' She shivered. 'I tell 'ee, Wragge, I wouldn't care to stand in Sir William's shoes, an' that's the truth!'

An hour later Hector strolled into Jason's bedroom to find him scowling at a tray of delicacies Cook had sent up to him. He did not look up as Hector approached.

'Well, Diomedes,' said Hector, 'how are you getting along?'

Jason crumbled a piece of bread. 'Papa says you're going away.'

'It's time for me to move on.'

'Because you're a lord?'

'Who told you of that?'

'Ellen, and everybody. Everybody says you came for a wager.'

'Yes, I did, but I stayed out of choice.'

'You said you'd stay till we moved to London. That's not for another week. Why do you have to leave?'

'Circumstances have changed, Jason.'

'But I haven't.' Jason's eyes filled with tears. 'I'll never change.' He looked up accusingly. 'You were teaching me to drive! You were my friend!'

'I still am, which is why you must rely on me not to toss you on the ash heap. As to driving lessons, I see no reason why those can't continue.'

Jason sat up straighter. 'Truly, sir? You're not gammoning me?'

'No. There are certain conditions attached, however.'

'What are they? I'll do whatever you say.'

'On the contrary, you're to do what your father says, and if a tutor is employed for you, you'll treat him with respect. No pranks, and no shirking. Understand?'

'Yes, I promise. When shall we begin lessons?'

'That will depend on what engagements I have already. I'll let you know.'

'But how? How will you find me?'

'At Number Twelve Bruton Street, which I collect your father has rented for the Season. It's just round the corner from where I live.' Hector ruffled Jason's hair. 'Au revoir, Jason . . . and eat your nuncheon. It takes bone and muscle to handle blood-cattle.'

He left the room, and Jason, his expression beatific, picked up his spoon and began to eat with a will.

XXIII

Hector did not encounter any of the ladies of the family that morning. He supposed they now knew the whole story of his imposture, and preferred to avoid him. He decided to leave Kettleby without formal farewells, and to write a letter of apology to Lady Carey when he reached Town.

He ate his nuncheon alone, and soon after was informed by Sudbury that the carriage awaited him at the front door. As he left the house he was surprised to find Miss Osmond standing on the front steps, her demeanour that of one facing a firing squad. She made Hector a small curtsey and offered him a package wrapped in paper.

'My uncle asked me to give you this,' she said. 'He begs you will pardon his not being here himself. He's with Jason at present.'

'I understand.' Hector slipped the parcel into the pocket of his driving-coat and held out his hand. 'Goodbye, Miss Osmond. I hope we shall meet again in London.'

Serena looked directly at him. 'I will not be going to London, Lord Hector.'

'Oh? Why is that? I understood you were to make your come-out with Miss Carey?'

She shook her head. 'My plans are changed. I received a letter from my mother last week. She's formed a dislike of foreign watering-places, and is returning to England. She desires me to go with her to Brighton.'

'A pity,' he smiled. 'Your presence would have added sparkle to our humdrum round.'

Miss Osmond did not respond to the compliment. Dropping another stiff curtsey, she turned and hurried into the house.

Hector watched her departure with some resentment. What a proud, stubborn creature she was, not to recognise an olive branch when it was thrust under her nose! They'd rubbed along well enough when Jason was in danger. Now she was back on her high horse. So be it, then. There were plenty of girls as pretty

– and far more congenial – to be found nearer home. Miss Osmond might go to the devil, for all he cared.

Glancing up at the façade of the mansion, he saw that the Admiral and Jason were standing at the bedroom window. They both waved, and Hector raised a hand in salute.

A groom stepped forward to open the carriage door. Hector climbed in, the steps were put up, and the equipage rolled forward.

It was only as they passed through the gates that he remembered the parcel in his pocket. Opening it, he found it contained ten gold guineas – a full month's wage – and a testimonial lauding the tutorial skills, devotion to duty, and admirable personal qualities of Mr Hector Finch.

Serena returned to the house miserably confused. One part of her mind treacherously conjured up pictures of Mr Finch patiently teaching Jason to drive, or chatting comfortably with Lady Carey, or turning a sardonic eye on the idiocies of Crosby Nettlebed.

When he'd held out his hand to her, and smiled so warmly, she'd felt a lump rise in her throat. She'd longed to pour out her heart, apologise for the past, and beg that they might remain friends.

Yet at the same time a warning voice reminded her that Hector Finch was an Impostor. He had come to the Manor under false pretences and deceived them all merely to win a wager.

No doubt he thought his great rank and wealth entitled him to commit such deceptions. It was a case of history repeating itself. Once before she'd allowed herself to be taken in by a handsome face and easy manner. Lucius had possessed that same winning smile, that same air of assurance – and that same ability to lie to those who trusted him.

Never again, vowed Serena, would she be gulled into mistaking charm for solid worth, never again would she invite such pain and humiliation as Lucius Radley had caused her.

It was as well that she must soon remove to Brighton, for there could be small chance of meeting his lordship there.

The letter she'd received from her mama had been long and complaining. The tour of Europe's spas had been far from successful, the weather inclement, the hotels deficient in creature comforts, and Cousin Sybilla so homesick for London that she could talk of nothing else.

'To travel with such a wet blanket,' wrote Mrs Osmond, 'is past all bearing. We leave the Continent at once, and will go direct to Sybilla's house in Charles Street. I shall stay there until I can manage to find a house for rent in Brighton. There must be doctors there who will understand my constitution. I cannot remain in London, for the smoke and noise are more than my nerves can stand; nor will I go to Bath, as Sybilla urges, because it is dominated by a clique who believe they can play God to any newcomer who dares set foot on their holy ground.

'If I succeed in finding accommodation in Brighton – and that will of course depend upon Mr Guthrie, Heaven knows if he will find anything at this time of the year – then I shall go there immediately. I hope that you, Serena, will not be so blinded by the glitter of a Season that you will abandon me in my hour of need. Even if Sybilla accompanies me to Brighton, she is small comfort to one who suffers as I do. Though I do not insist upon your presence – I have never been one to harp upon what the world sees as a daughter's duty to an ailing parent – you may be sure that it is my sincere hope that you will find it in your heart to support me at this time.

'As I recall, your Uncle William planned to remove to Town at the end of the month. Sybilla assures me that it will be perfectly in order for you to stay with us in Charles Street, until such time as we can leave for Brighton. Pray write to me as soon as you receive this, to tell me when I may expect to see you.'

When Serena conveyed the message of her mama's letter to her aunt, Lady Carey said that of course Serena must do as she saw fit; but later, speaking to her husband, she said roundly that Hortense Osmond was a monster of selfishness, who was prepared to forgo her only child's chance of making a successful marriage, merely to suit herself.

'Serena has never had a Season,' she said. 'She's never had the opportunity of meeting gentlemen of the right sort. I know that if she were to stay with us, we should see her happily engaged in no time, for besides being well-bred, she's exceedingly pretty and has a comfortable income of her own.' A thoughtful look crossed her face. 'Of course, it won't do for her to marry a dullard. Serena has a mind of her own.'

'Mettlesome piece,' agreed the Admiral. 'I like a bit of spirit in a girl, myself, but she'll have to learn to curb her tongue a little.'

'She'll do so when her affections are engaged. She has great warmth of heart, and is never snappish with those she loves. I do so wish that Lord Hector . . .'

'No,' said Sir William firmly. 'Put that out of your head, Amelia. The Wycombes are top-of-the-trees, and you may be sure Lord Hector will choose a bride from among the blue bloods. It's probably cut and dried already. Besides, Serena didn't like him above half. Cross as a cat with the poor fellow.'

Lady Carey had her own view of that, but she didn't argue, only saying, 'I shall tell Hortense, when I see her, that Serena should remain in London with us.'

'You won't budge Hortense,' said the Admiral gloomily. 'That's one that puts her own comfort first, at all times.'

After dinner that night, the Admiral raised the question of how much might be told of his lordship's sojourn at the Manor.

'First and foremost,' he said, 'we must make no mention whatsoever of Piggott's share in the affair. Nor will we deign to discuss family matters. Those are our concern, and ours alone. Lord Hector won't say aught. He's far too much the gentleman to gossip.

'As to his lordship's sojourn at our home, the ideal would be to say nothing, but I fear that won't fadge. Too many people are in the know. Whatever we do, in time some facts will leak out, and when that happens we must expect to be quizzed by all manner of vulgar nosy parkers.

'What I propose is this. We remain silent for as long as we can. If taxed, we say merely that Lord Hector came to Kettleby and stayed in my house for some days. We make it plain that it was on a matter of business and that we claim no close association with his lordship. If there are any bold enough to press for more details, we refer them to Lord Hector. I dare swear they won't find the courage to badger him!'

He glanced about him for support, and Lady Carey said gently, 'Your plan is excellent, my dear, but I wonder if it will succeed with our close neighbours? A woman like Phoebe Nettlebed, for instance, will be all too ready to puff off her own consequence by boasting that Lord Hector visited her home. It will be quite beyond her to lose the chance to drop his name into her conversation.'

'You're quite right. I shall have a word with Henry Nettlebed. Drop him a hint that to displease his lordship by a lot of careless tittle-tattle could be injurious to young Crosby's career. I fancy that will stop Madame Nettlebed's mouth.'

Though the Careys wished to make the journey to Town as soon as Jason was recovered from his adventure, it was not a simple thing to close one large house and open another. Certain of the staff must remain at Kettleby while others went ahead to prepare the rented house in Bruton Street. Supplies of food and other necessities must be laid on at both addresses. Clothes must be packed, horses taken south by easy stages, accommodation secured at a good hostelry for the night the party would spend on the road, and financial arrangements made with bailiffs, stewards, agents and bankers.

Crosby was the first of the locals to leave for London, where his regiment was quartered. He came to the Manor the day before his departure, and indulged in an emotional farewell that reduced Laurel to tears, and the Admiral to speechless fury.

Mr and Mrs Nettlebed followed their son three days later, but it was a full week before the Carey cavalcade took to the road. Serena was of the party, and was set down late on Wednesday afternoon at the home of Mrs Sybilla Fortescue in Charles Street. While her trunks and bandboxes were being unloaded from the baggage-chaise and carried indoors, she turned to thank her aunt and uncle for all their kindness to her over the past months.

Lady Carey cut her short, saying briskly, 'No, now, don't speak as if we were never going to meet again! Our house is just round the corner, and we expect to see a great deal of you during the Season.'

'I'm afraid . . .' began Serena, but Lady Carey held up a hand.

'Don't give up hope, my love. I intend to keep you with us, if I can. Your mama will I'm sure see the advantages, once they're explained to her.'

Serena went into the house comforted but not convinced. Brighton, she felt, was to be her fate, but at least she was determined to enjoy whatever time was allowed to her in this great and exciting city.

XXIV

Hortense Osmond and Sybilla Fortescue had little in common beyond their interest in matters of health.

In appearance they were direct opposites, Mrs Osmond being small, pale and very thin, while her cousin was tall, stout and red of face.

Mrs Osmond had been driven to invalidism by a husband who was, not to put too fine a point on it, a miser. In his eagerness to save money, he demanded that his wife run a vast house and extensive gardens with few servants and a nipcheese budget. Hortense learned that the only refuge from drudgery was her bed. She became adept at producing the symptoms of influenza, bilious stomach and migraine. She was also a polished arthritic, and could at a pinch fall into palpitations that seemed to the ordinary viewer to be life-threatening.

Mrs Fortescue's preoccupation with health was of a different sort. Having watched her husband eat and drink his way into an early grave, she became resolved to fortify her own constitution by all possible means. She was not, like her cousin Hortense, a complaining invalid. Rather she pursued good health with devotion and vigour. She bathed in hot springs, and basked in the warm air of France or Italy. She tried every new cure that came her way, and was constantly on the lookout for food and drink produced in out of the way places, for she held that it was better to startle the stomach than to satisfy it. She believed a full social life to be beneficial, and attended a good many of the ton parties, as well as entertaining lavishly at home.

She always referred to Mrs Osmond as 'Poor Hortense'.

'Poor Hortense,' she would say to whoever cared to listen, 'is a horrid warning to us all. Eats nothing but pap, takes no exercise, sleeps with all the windows closed, I vow it would kill me in a week! Still, I'm fond of her, you know, and glad of her company. We widows must stick together I say! Have I told you about my new physician? Dr Strauss of Carlsbad? He advises a diet of nothing but vegetables. One par-cooks them and eats them like salad. Rather rabbity; to be honest, I don't think I shall stay the course.'

When Serena entered the house on Wednesday, she found both ladies awaiting her in the drawing room. Mrs Fortescue sprang from her chair, surged to embrace Serena and told her she looked decidedly peaky.

Mrs Osmond, who had no intention of allowing another peaky person in the family, offered her cheek to be kissed and said it was good to see her darling in such fine fettle.

'Myself, I am quite worn out with all the junketing and the foul air of this town. I shall leave for Brighton the moment I find a suitable house. Mr Guthrie is searching, but without success. I've never before experienced any difficulty in renting. Perhaps I shall have to employ another agent. It's all too tiresome and enervating.' She smiled bravely. 'Now you are here, dear child, I shall leave all those details in your capable hands.'

'We'll talk of it tomorrow,' said Mrs Fortescue. 'Serena my love, we'll dine early, at half past six, and afterwards you must tell us all about your stay with the Careys. How is my dear Amelia? Always so kind and sweet-natured, I declare I long to see her again.'

Chatting happily, she swept Serena away to the upper region of the house, showed her the bedroom allotted to her and the handsomely appointed dressing room next to it, adjured her not to dress fine as there'd be only themselves for dinner, and bade her call for Maggie Simmons should she require help of any kind. With a final beaming smile she bustled away, leaving Serena to acquaint herself with her surroundings.

The bedroom was spacious and charmingly furnished, the walls being hung with paper patterned with small circlets of spring flowers, while the sofa, chairs and bed were covered with a matching chintz. Curtains of blue corded silk were looped back from the two large windows, through which it was possible to see the verdant plane trees and elegant residences of Berkeley Square. Serena could not help wondering if Lord Hector's house was visible from here. She devoutly hoped not. She wished him to stay out of sight and out of mind.

She tugged on the bellrope, and when a neat young maid appeared, asked her to draw the curtains and unpack the trunk that held her evening gowns. She washed her face and hands, changed into a dress of lilac crêpe, allowed Maggie to dress her hair for her, and went downstairs.

The dinner presently served in the formal dining room was lavish, for Mrs Fortescue was far too good a hostess to impose her own dietary fads on her guests. While she consumed her meal of half-cooked beans and carrots, Mrs Osmond and Serena enjoyed poached salmon with salsify and mushrooms, followed by ducklings with roasted herbs and oranges, as well as a great many side dishes. The second course consisted of sweet omelettes, a floating island pudding with whipped cream, an apple pie, and a dish of hothouse fruits. Mrs Osmond picked at her food, but Serena ate heartily. It was pleasant to be in this house, so well-appointed and so well-run. She began to hope that her mother might not find a house in Brighton too quickly, and that she might enjoy at least part of the London Season before leaving for the coast.

During dinner the conversation was mostly of shopping, since all three ladies felt the need to replenish their wardrobes. Mrs Osmond, despite her delicate constitution, was an inveterate shopper, and as her taste in clothes was impeccable, Serena was glad to have her advice. Mrs Osmond decreed that Serena must go to Solange for her gowns, to Eugenie et Cie for bonnets, and to Monsieur Romilly for shoes and slippers. Since the end of the war, she declared, French artists and craftsmen had quite changed the face of British fashion; and while gentlemen might prefer to cling to their English tailors, most ladies now patronised the French houses. She warned Serena to buy generously, 'For I doubt we shall be in London next year, or for some years to come. My health won't stand it. We will have to survive on the camel's hump of what we buy now.'

When the shopping forays had been planned, and the covers of the last course cleared from the table, the ladies returned to the drawing room to exchange reports of their experiences over the past months. Both Mrs Osmond and Mrs Fortescue were anxious to have news of the Careys, and asked a great many questions, which Serena did her best to answer.

Great interest was shown in Laurel's infatuation with Crosby Nettlebed, and Sybilla said that she trusted nothing would come of it, for she'd met the young man and thought him quite addle-pated, as well as unbearably pompous.

As Mrs Fortescue enquired particularly about Jason's well-being, Serena felt obliged to refer briefly to the headlong flight of Ebenezer Bumper, and the consequent employing of Mr Finch. This led Mrs Osmond to say that she could not approve of Sir William's actions. 'To pluck an unknown from the hedgerow is the height of folly,' she said. 'You might all have been murdered in your beds!'

Perhaps it was a certain reticence in Serena that prompted Mrs Fortescue to probe more deeply into the saga of Mr Finch. She was much struck by his heroism in rescuing Jason from the caves, and said she hoped Sir William had shown his gratitude in a proper way. When Serena murmured that her uncle had written the tutor an excellent testimonial, Sybilla snorted. 'Tush, my dear, words are cheap! A tutor's wages are far from princely. William must make the man a suitable reward. I daresay he should go as high as a hundred guineas. I shall tell him so when next we meet.'

The image of Lord Hector being paid a hundred guineas by Sir William struck Serena as so humorous that she giggled.

'Why do you laugh?' demanded Sybilla. 'Mr Finch won't do so. He'll be grateful to accept. Very likely he supports an aged mother or an indigent brother. He may be laying money aside for his own old age. Money, my love, is always acceptable, provided it is given with tact and genuine goodwill.'

Serena hastily agreed, for Cousin Sybilla was watching her with the acuteness of a terrier at a rathole. She was quite capable of persisting with her questions until she uncovered the whole truth about Mr Finch – and then the fat would be in the fire.

The next morning dawned grey and drizzling and Mrs Osmond refused to leave her bed. Her chest, she said, would not allow it. Cousin Sybilla's chest being of a sterner order, she soon after breakfast carried Serena off to visit the Careys. They found that household in great disorder; the Admiral complaining that he couldn't find any of his possessions; Sudbury near to tears because the carriers had shaken the port wine; Cook about to give notice because the kitchens were full of blackbeetles; and Laurel on the fret because Ensign Nettlebed had not yet called.

Sybilla cut through these irrelevancies with the ease of long practice. She quietly directed Serena to deal with Laurel, asked a passing maidservant to bring tea to the morning room directly, and led Lady Carey away from the scene of strife.

'You and I,' she said, throwing a large arm about her friend's shoulders, 'have a great deal to talk about.'

Lady Carey, looking harassed, said that really she had no time to talk, but Mrs Fortescue shook her head. Reaching the morning room she untied the strings of her bonnet and cast it aside, saying firmly, 'Nothing, my dear, is of more importance than that Laurel and Serena should contract good marriages, and from what I've learned, they won't do so unless we take quick and resolute action.' She sat down on the sofa next to her hostess. 'Serena told us last night that Laurel is still daffy upon young Nettlebed. Surely William doesn't countenance the match?'

'No, of course he doesn't, but it's very difficult. The Nettlebeds are our close neighbours and friends, even if they do irritate William's nerves a trifle. What's more, Henry Nettlebed behaved with the utmost kindness when Jason was trapped in that dreadful cave. We can't offend him now.'

'No need to offend anyone. Just see that Laurel has a chance to compare that idiot Crosby with better men.'

'I know,' sighed Lady Carey, 'but I'm afraid I'm not well up in that regard. We come to London so seldom, I know very few of the younger set. I'm acquainted with Lady Sefton, as you know, and I hope she'll put in a word for our girls.'

'Takes more than that,' said Sybilla. 'There are hosts of ambitious mamas about, all set upon marrying off their daughters. Hope cuts no ice with anyone. What we have to do is pull every available string, twist every available arm. We must outmanoeuvre our opponents, we must drive them to the wall! The Season, my dear, is a war to the death!'

Lady Carey turned so pale that Mrs Fortescue broke into hearty laughter. 'There, don't look so worried! Remember that I have vast experience in the field. I've secured good matches for two sons and three daughters, and I know precisely what has to be done. In fact, I spent an hour last night drawing up a list of all those hostesses who owe me favours. We'll start with them. We'll make our calls tomorrow, and I assure you that by nightfall we'll be on several desirable invitation lists. We'll have to reciprocate, of course, but all that can be planned later.'

'Clothes,' said Lady Carey faintly. 'They must have the right clothes.'

'Indeed they must. Luckily both Laurel and Serena are blessed with good looks. My own dear Lizzie was not, you know, and I had to be particularly careful to choose garments that disguised her bad points. I'm happy to say that her sweet nature triumphed, and she found a husband with an amiable disposition and a very comfortable fortune. Laurel must join Serena and me on Friday when we visit the *couturières*; but before we come down to these little details, there's a matter of principle that must be settled.'

Lady Carey felt safer on moral ground, and nodded encouragingly. 'What is that?' she asked.

'Hortense,' said Mrs Fortescue. 'She means to carry Serena off to Brighton, and that would be disastrous. The only gentlemen to be found there are hardened old rakes suffering from gout, or shabby-genteels who can't afford to spend the Season in Town. Serena must have her chance, Amelia. She must!'

'If Hortense requests Serena to go with her, I don't see how we can prevent it.'

'We will find a way,' said Sybilla. She paused as a tray of tea and macaroons was carried into the room and set before them. When the maid had left the room, she settled herself more comfortably and said with an air of disinterest, 'I hear that Jason was in some scrape, and a tutor-person got him out of it?'

'Yes,' said Lady Carey, pouring tea into a cup and adding cream and sugar.

'A Mr Finch, I collect,' pursued Sybilla.

'Yes.' Lady Carey handed her friend the cup. 'Mr Hector Finch.'

'Hector Finch.' Mrs Fortescue frowned a little. 'Why does the name seem familiar?'

'I don't know.' Lady Carey was incapable of telling a deliberate falsehood, but she had learned to pretend ignorance in times of stress. Some day, she knew, she would have to tell Sybilla the truth. Someone would discover that Mr Finch and Lord Hector Wycombe were one and the same, but she did not feel equal to explaining that fact today. 'We were very lucky to find him,' she said. 'He did Jason a great deal of good.'

'But you haven't retained his services?'

'No. It was a short-term arrangement. He has . . . er . . . other commitments.'

Mrs Fortescue did not press for more information, nor did she let the matter rest. Her instinct told her that some mystery attached to Mr Finch, something that neither Serena nor Amelia wished to discuss. Topics of that nature were exactly what Mrs Fortescue found the most absorbing.

XXV

The following week was taken up with shopping on such a grand scale that Serena felt she had visited every emporium and boutique in Town. It was quickly borne in on her that what sufficed in the provinces was laughably inadequate for London. The bandboxes, packages and parcels poured into the house in Charles Street in such numbers that Serena began to feel ashamed; but her aunt and Cousin Sybilla saw the money they spent not as extravagances, but as necessary armament for the campaign ahead, which they were planning with the care and thoroughness of veteran generals.

Already the mantel in the drawing room was crowded with invitations to balls, assemblies, routs and musical evenings – and these were only the events Mrs Fortescue pronounced desirable. The undesirables had been firmly consigned to the wastepaper basket.

When she was not shopping, or being fitted for a gown or riding-habit or pelisse, Serena listened with folded hands to the advice of her seniors.

She was required to memorise the names of people of influence who must be treated with the utmost deference. She was warned against others, categorised as fortune-hunters, rakes, or debauchees, who must be shunned like the plague. She was rehearsed in the protocol of being presented at Court, and cautioned that on no account must she attempt to walk down St James's Street which was reserved for clubmen, or be seen in such areas as the quadrant of the Theatre in Haymarket, which was the haunt of women of ill repute.

There were so many do's and don't's to be observed that Serena found her head quite in a whirl. It was a relief to escape sometimes to the cheerful disorder of her uncle's house. Lady Carey, though she was busy with plans for Laurel's come-out, was not a militant, and said gently that if her dear girls remembered their manners, and behaved as they'd been raised to do, nothing could go amiss.

The Admiral's temper at this time was made brittle by the constant presence of Ensign Nettlebed. Crosby had learned from his mama the true identity of 'Mr Finch', and made it his business to raise the matter with Serena.

'I was never more surprised at anything,' he declared. 'I think I may call myself a sound judge of character. I hope I can tell a gentleman from a commoner, but I admit that Wycombe bamboozled me nicely. I shall explain all to him when next we meet – make my apologies, set the record straight. Embarrassing, of course, but I shan't fight shy.'

'I don't see why you should apologise,' said Serena. 'Lord Hector didn't wish to be recognised, so he can hardly take offence because his deception succeeded.'

'Lord, Serena, you speak like a greenling! Wycombe's opinion counts for everything here, and I don't intend to leave a black mark against my name. Why, his brother Robert is a colonel, who was on Wellington's staff! Think what damage could be done to my career if it got about that I'd been . . . well . . . a trifle heavy-handed with his lordship.'

'I doubt you've anything to fear. Though I hold no brief for his childish prank, I don't think he's the man to bear a grudge, particularly against the likes of us. He's far more likely to forget we exist.'

Here she was proved wrong, for a week later when she and Laurel returned from the library in Bond Street, they saw a curricle drawn by a splendid pair of match bays come to a halt outside the Careys' residence. The driver was Lord Hector Wycombe.

Serena's first impulse was to bolt for the mews behind the house, but it was too late. His lordship had already seen her, and handing the reins to a liveried groom, he sprang down to the flagway and advanced with hand outstretched.

'Miss Osmond, your servant, ma'am. Miss Carey, your most obedient. How pleasant to see you both.'

Serena responded with no more than a formal curtsey, but Laurel smiled delightedly.

'Good morning, sir! Have you come to visit us?'

'Yes, if your papa and mama are receiving?'

'They'll be happy to receive you, and Jason will be over the moon. He was becoming quite blue-devilled in case you'd forgot him.'

'I assure you, Jason is indelibly stamped on my mind! How is he? Recovered from his exploits?'

'Oh, he's right as a trivet,' said Laurel, dancing up the steps and sounding a peal on the doorbell. 'Only a little bored with London.'

When Sudbury opened the door, she led the way into the house, chatting happily. Serena followed in silence, struggling to compose her emotions. That first glimpse of Lord Hector had caused her heart to thump in the most mortifying way. She told herself not to be taken in by his lordship's friendly manner. It was tactless of him to arrive without warning, quite odious of him to look so very sure of his welcome. She would not allow herself to be impressed by the immaculate cut of his jacket, the exquisite set of his cravat, the perfection of his pale grey trousers and the glossiness of his boots. His finery could not disguise the fact that he was a gambler, untruthful, and very likely dissolute in his morals. She assumed an expression of stern disapproval, and was annoyed to see that it brought a gleam of pure enjoyment to his lordship's eye.

As Laurel had foreseen, the Admiral and his wife greeted their guest with open pleasure, and Jason, summoned from above stairs, came rushing down three steps at a time, and quite forgot to make his bow in the proper way.

The visit was not at all like the usual morning call. What with the Admiral wishing to be advised on the best place to buy wine, and Jason clamouring to know when he might expect his first driving lesson, and Laurel desiring to be given an account of Signor Morelli's attempt to fly in a balloon from London to Dover, the statutory half-hour raced past. It was only as he was about to leave that Lord Hector was able to enquire about their own plans, and to say that he hoped they would apply to him for any help they might need. 'I remember we discussed invitations to Almack's, once,' he said, with a glinting smile at Serena. 'Lady Jersey is a friend of long standing, and if you wish me to speak to her . . .'

'Thank you,' said Lady Carey warmly, 'but Lady Sefton has promised to send us vouchers for the next Assembly.'

'Then perhaps we shall meet there.' Lord Hector made his

farewells, cautioned Jason to be dressed and ready the following Tuesday morning at ten of the clock, and departed.

Sir William expressed himself much flattered by his lordship's visit. 'Very handsome in him to remember us,' he said, 'considering all the circumstances.' He turned to his niece. 'I must say, Serena, I was surprised to see you sit so glum and mum-chance!'

Serena coloured. 'I don't stand in Lord Hector's debt, Uncle, nor do I wish to. No doubt it amuses him to condescend to us mere provincials, but I certainly shan't kowtow to him!'

'Then you're more of a fool than I took you for,' said the Admiral roundly. 'A man of Wycombe's standing can make or break your fortunes, my dear. I hope that the next time he crosses your path, you'll treat him with rather more civility!'

'I doubt we'll clap eyes on him again,' Serena said. 'He's paid his duty call. Now he can forget us.'

This brought down a rain of protest on her head.

'We will see him,' cried Jason. 'He's promised to take me driving, and a gentleman never goes back on his word.'

'He said we should meet at Almack's,' reminded Laurel.

'He said "perhaps". It's easy to say "perhaps".'

Lady Carey brought an end to the squabble. 'We can hardly expect his lordship to pay us any special attention,' she said, 'but on the other hand it's likely we shall meet from time to time; and if we do, my love, remember what your uncle has told you, and be civil to him, if only because we're all indebted to him for saving Jason's life.'

XXVI

Mrs Fortescue's efforts had paid handsome dividends, and Serena found herself swept into the full flood of the Season's activities – and enjoying herself hugely. She was pretty, she had charm and vivacity, she was beautifully dressed, and she was not, like many of the younger debutantes, ill at ease with strangers.

Some few of the people she met were unpleasing to her – the men who were drunkards or fortune-hunters, the women who fought like harpies for social advantage – but for the most part her new associates were amusing, well-informed, and bent upon living life to the full. Serena found them delightful, and they in turn seemed delighted with her.

Though she had neither the beauty nor the material fortune to be counted a reigning toast, she attracted her own circle of admirers. Captain Lumley was always ready to take her driving or riding in the park, Mr Clinton Robins was eager to squire her to assemblies and the theatre, and within a month of arriving in Town, she was receiving flattering attentions from the eminently suitable Sir John Devenish.

All of this put Cousin Sybilla in alt. Serena, she said, would be betrothed before the summer was out, and would live happy ever after. Mrs Osmond did not share her satisfaction. The more popular Serena became, the more her mama conplained of her aching head, her unsettled stomach, her melancholy spirits. On being told of Sir John's marked interest, she suffered a migraine that lasted two days, and it was useless for Serena to point out that he had not yet offered for her hand.

Mrs Osmond employed more agents to house-hunt for her, and declared that if she could not move to Brighton soon, she would have to consider going to Bath, since London would be the death of her.

She became intensely resentful of any time Serena spent away from her, insisting that no one was able to care for her as well as her own daughter. On several occasions Serena was forced to cry off from parties in order to stay at home with her mother.

Mrs Fortescue, in a fit of irritation, told her cousin that she was being abominably selfish, which naturally set her back up. Mrs Osmond retaliated by refusing to act as Serena's chaperone, and consigned the task to Mrs Fortescue, who luckily found it exactly to her taste.

Lord Hector did not put in an appearance at Almack's, but he kept his promise to Jason, taking him out on several mornings for an hour's driving instruction. Jason looked forward intensely to these outings and bored his relations to distraction by his reports of what Lord Hector said, did, wore, and thought.

Serena was able to avoid meeting his lordship by visiting Bruton Street only in the afternoons or evenings, and her life was by now so full that she could, for the most part, refrain from thinking of him.

About three weeks after reaching London, she was bidden with Mrs Fortescue to an evening party at the home of Mr George Canning, the eminent politician. Mrs Fortescue warned Serena not to expect too much, as it would be a formal affair, packed with political pundits, and with few young people present. 'It is kind of Mr Canning to invite us,' she said, 'and it will be useful for you to be seen there, but don't, I beg, hope to enjoy yourself.'

Surveying the people gathered in the Cannings' reception rooms, Serena felt her cousin had been right. The gentlemen were all engaged in earnest conversation while the women, who had taken refuge in one of the side salons, looked a dowdy lot. She began to think she should not have put on the new gown of cream foulard that had been delivered to her that morning, since there was no one about to appreciate it.

She turned to speak to her cousin, and found that Mrs Fortescue had been ensnared by a wheezy old gentleman in a grey wig, and that her space had been filled by Lord Hector Wycombe. He was holding a glass of wine in each hand, and he offered one to Serena, saying with a bow,

'Pray take it, Miss Osmond. It may be your only chance of finding refreshment in this squeeze.' As Serena stared at him in confusion, he smiled. 'It's not poisoned, I promise. It was meant for Lady Ainsford, but I've no hope of reaching her, so you may drink it with a clear conscience.'

Serena accepted the glass, and remembering Lady Carey's

injunction, smiled politely at his lordship, and enquired how he did.

'As well as may be expected,' he answered, with a quizzical glance round the room. 'I'm very much out of place, here. It's the Tory stronghold, you know, and we Wycombes are Whigs.'

'My uncle says that if Mr Canning becomes Prime Minister, he'll bring Whig members into his Cabinet.'

'Yes, Melbourne perhaps, and Palmerston. It's not a fate I'd choose.'

'Oh? Why?'

'It will be a wasp's nest.' Hector nodded in the direction of a lanky man with restless eyes and a great beak of a nose who was holding a group of listeners spellbound. 'That's Brougham,' he said. 'He's brilliant, full of theories, and a schemer to his fingertips. They nickname him Beelzebub. Over there, the small man with the prim look? That's Lord John Russell. A man to be trusted, but not loved. And the fellow with the bushy eyebrows is Radical Jack Durham – though how one may see as a Defender of the Poor a man who has just refurbished his house at a cost of £90,000, I can't conceive. Those are Canning's closest cronies, and three more complete egotists you'd be hard-pressed to find. No ship with such a crew could hope for calm passage.' He set down his empty glass and said abruptly, 'Miss Osmond, I need your advice, if you please.'

She glanced up in surprise. 'Mine, sir?'

'Yes, about Jason. I'm afraid it may soon be necessary to discontinue his driving lessons.'

'Oh, no!' she said involuntarily, and then added quickly, 'Forgive me. Of course it's your decision, but he'll be so very disappointed.'

'I know, but with the Season reaching full spate, it's growing hard to find a safe place to take him. Even the lanes in Kensington and Shepherd's Bush are chock-a-block with traffic, and it's really not safe to let a beginner take the reins. However, it's in my mind to persuade Sir William to buy him a hunter. That would be some compensation. He could ride out sometimes with me and with my brother John's brood. They're in Town for a month and staying with me. Jason might enjoy their company. What do you think?'

'I think it would be an excellent thing,' said Serena at once.

'He's always longed to own a hunter, and I certainly agree that he should be mixing with children of his own age.' She paused, then said resolutely, 'Jason thinks the world of you, and we're all indebted to you for your kindness and consideration.'

Again she caught that gleam of amusement in his eyes, but he said gravely, 'Then I shall broach the matter with Sir William tomorrow and count on you to continue the good work. Now, if you'll forgive me, I must go and make my peace with Lady Ainsford.'

He bowed and moved away across the room – a slow progress, Serena noted, as everyone seemed anxious to exchange pleasantries with him. His target was evidently a lady standing in the doorway to the main reception room, who was watching his lordship with an air of frowning impatience. She was in her middle years, tall and full-bodied, dressed in a modish gown of dark-green satin cut very low across the bosom. Her features were aquiline, and there was a hardness and arrogance in her expression that Serena found distasteful.

She was recalled to herself by Mrs Fortescue, who arrived at her elbow in a positive flurry of excitement.

'Serena, my love,' she exclaimed in low but throbbing tones, 'what a triumph! To be in conversation with Hector Wycombe for nigh on ten minutes! I declare, you were the cynosure of all eyes! What a sly puss you are, not to tell me that you were on friendly terms with him. Strange, but I can't recall that Hortense ever spoke of knowing him.'

'She doesn't,' said Serena flatly. 'I'm not well acquainted with Lord Hector. He chanced to be at the Manor for a time, and I . . . I met him there.'

'Through the Careys?' demanded Mrs Fortescue, eyes shining.

'Well, yes. It was a . . . a business connection.'

'That makes it all the more remarkable that he should remember you, and take the trouble to converse with you tonight. My dear, it's the most gratifying circumstance! You've no idea how much good it must do you in the eyes of the ton. For a girl to be singled out by the Nonpareil is far more prestigious than for her to be presented at Court! Later I shall wish to hear every little detail, but for the moment we must strike while the iron's hot. I shall present you to those of my friends who've been backward in their attentions. They'll change their tune now, I'll warrant.'

Her florid face wreathed in smiles, Mrs Fortescue plunged into the sea of guests like a swimmer challenging the Hellespont. Serena followed in her wake, acknowledging introductions, curtseying, exchanging trite remarks with strangers. Her chief concern was to find a way to depress her cousin's euphoria, and when Mr Canning made a point of speaking to her and said kindly that he saw Serena knew his good friend Lord Hector Wycombe, Serena murmured that truly their acquaintance was slight.

Cousin Sybilla, far from being depressed, told Serena that she was very well pleased by her behaviour. 'It showed a proper modesty, my love, most becoming in a young girl in her first Season.'

They left the party an hour later. As they moved down the main stairway, Sybilla showed signs of wanting to discuss Lord Hector's sojourn at the Manor. Serena was forced to gain a temporary respite by saying that the heat of the rooms had given her a shocking headache.

There was a long line of carriages waiting to take up the departing guests. The one at the foot of the steps bore a crest on its panel and, as they watched, they saw the woman in green, accompanied by a pallid girl in white, climb into it.

'That is Lady Ainsford, I believe,' said Serena.

Mrs Fortescue sniffed. 'Yes, with her daughter Anna,' she said. 'The *on dit* is the girl's to marry Hector Wycombe, but I don't give it any credit. Lord Ainsford may have sixteen quarterings, but his daughter's an antidote. Looks as if she eats nothing but curds and whey and hasn't a word to say for herself. If you ask me, it's Lady Ainsford who set up the buzz of an engagement. A more odious, scheming, brass-faced liar I've not had the misfortune to meet.'

Serena made no answer. She was well aware that families like the Wycombes did not marry for love. They formed alliances that strengthened their social and financial position. Probably Lord Hector's bride had been chosen for him while he was still in his teens. Yet Serena thought he deserved better than the sour-faced Anna Ainsford, and found herself hoping that the rumour was false.

XXVII

Whatever arguments Lord Hector used on the Admiral, they must have been convincing, for when Serena called at Bruton Street a few days later, she found the Carey family in the stable yard, discussing a young roan horse. Mounted on the animal was Jason, his face wreathed in smiles. He slid to the ground and greeted Serena ecstatically.

'Serena, he's mine, my very own! Papa bought him for me at Tattersalls. Lord Hector came to help us choose him. Ain't he the most splendid horse you ever saw? Look at those quarters, those hocks! His name's Merlin. Lord Hector says I may ride in the Park with him and Matthew Wycombe.'

Master Wycombe, it seemed, was his lordship's nephew, the son of the Marquess of Fontwell. Jason described him as a prime gun.

'Matt is to go to Eton next year,' he confided. 'He has a boat of his own at Hove and says I may sail with him some day, and he means to ask his papa to take us to see the mill between the Jersey Battler and Mosey Malone at Bermondsey. I told him that perhaps we would take him to visit the docks, and he said he would like that above all things because he is set on joining the Navy, which he can do because he is the third son and not obliged to be a marquess or a duke.'

The Admiral cut short this flow, saying that Jason was not to become a nuisance to the Wycombes.

'Lord Hector's been uncommonly kind to you, but that's not to say he wants a pack of puppies at his heels all day long. By all means invite young Matthew to come with us to the docks, but he must have his papa's permission to do so – as you must have mine before you accept any more invitations. I won't have it said we Careys are trying to scrape an acquaintance with people who are quite above our touch.'

He later repeated this stricture to his wife. 'It's as plain as the nose on my face,' he said, 'that Wycombe feels obligated to us for having played that trick on us. All rubbish, of course. If he owed us anything, it was paid in full when he pulled Jason out of that hellish cave. He's no call to bother his head further with us, and we mustn't impose on his good nature. Make that plain to the girls, Amelia, as I have to Jason.'

Lady Carey duly conveyed the message to Laurel and Serena; yet though they treated Lord Hector with daunting circumspection, he showed no disposition to vanish from their lives. Despite the many claims on his time, he still managed to visit the Careys. When he came upon them riding in the Park, he did not tip his hat and canter past, but fell in with their party. When Laurel and her maid were caught in a shower of rain in Piccadilly, Lord Hector took them up in his carriage and brought them home. When he chanced upon Serena and her mama at the Royal Academy, he spent almost an hour strolling about the exhibition with them, listened attentively to Mrs Osmond's catalogue of her ills, and commiserated with her on the dearth of houses for rent in Brighton.

These attentions sent Mrs Fortescue into her seventh heaven. She refused to accept that they sprang from a sense of guilt. 'If he seeks your company,' she told Serena, 'it's because he likes you.'

'But he doesn't,' said Serena desperately. 'If you must know, I think he's trying to teach me a lesson.'

Mrs Fortescue started. 'Why?' she demanded.

'Because when first we met I . . . I took him in dislike. I wasn't very civil to him. I expect it's just pique that makes him want to . . . to bring me round his thumb.'

Mrs Fortescue became pensive. She knew Serena's temper. It was possible she had been high-handed. But surely Lord Hector wasn't the sort to bear a grudge, or seek a petty revenge for a slight? She continued to hope he would develop a serious interest in Serena.

Serena, for her part, found herself less and less able to see Lord Hector as a man of straw.

He was not at all like the typical man of fashion; he was not arrogant like so many of the high-flyers, he never snubbed his inferiors, he never seemed bored or cynical. She could not believe that all the people who flocked round him were mushrooms and tuft-hunters. When she heard his name mentioned, it was usually with affection or approval.

It would be extremely easy to fall in love with him. She had to remind herself sternly that it would be idiotic to do so. In a short while her mother would find a house in Brighton or Bath, and they would leave London, probably for good. In due course he would marry Anna Ainsford or some other high-bred female and forget all about the brief sojourn in Kettleby.

One thing she did earnestly hope ... that she might find a chance to apologise for having misjudged him. Then at least they might part friends. Somehow, though, the time was never right. Impossible to talk seriously when one was whirling about a ballroom floor, or pinned elbow to elbow in a crowded salon.

The days passed. In mid-June Serena and Laurel were presented at the court of His Majesty King George IV ... monstrously fat, Serena thought, and not at all like the Prince Florizel of legend.

The weather turned very hot and Mrs Osmond's health deteriorated. She became more and more demanding, until Serena thought that only the advent of a fairy godmother could save her from a life as a sickroom attendant.

In fact, though, help lay much closer to home.

One afternoon at the height of the heatwave, Serena walked to Bruton Street to borrow a book her mother wished to read. She found her uncle and aunt at home, though Laurel and Jason had gone out for a drive.

'It's far too hot to exert oneself,' Lady Carey said, motioning Serena to a chair. 'Try a glass of lemonade, my love. How is your mama today?'

'A little better, I think. She sleeps badly at night, and likes to doze during the day.' Serena untied the strings of her bonnet and dropped it on the sofa beside her. 'Uncle, I've been wondering if you know of anyone who might help us find a house in Brighton? It must be cooler by the sea, don't you think?'

Sir William looked frowningly at his niece. The poor girl was white as a ghost. A shame she was made to fetch and carry for that stupid, fractious female, when she should be out enjoying herself. He was on the point of saying as much, when the door burst open and Jason rushed into the room, brandishing a sheet of paper.

'Papa, Mama! The most famous thing! There's to be a display

tomorrow at Vauxhall! See, I have the broadsheet! It says there will be Tumbling by Mr Lantern and Mr West and their Troupe, and a Punch and Judy, and a Donkey Race, and Rope-Dancing. Papa, I have never seen rope-dancing. It says here that Signor Ferantino and Others will perform feats of unprecedented daring upon the high wire. May we go, please, Papa? I'm sure we shall all enjoy it excessively.'

The Admiral said tartly that to be jostled by *hoi polloi* was not his idea of enjoyment. 'These events are nothing but a field-day for vendors of cheap goods and sensation-mongers.'

Lady Carey, seeing the disappointment in Jason's face, said that perhaps there would be a place for carriages at the grounds. 'I recall that when we watched the balloon ascent in Hyde Park, we were allowed to remain in the landau, and felt quite safe and comfortable.'

'There will be space for carriages,' said Jason eagerly. 'Lord Hector said so. He's to take Matthew and Lady Fontwell. If the Wycombes don't condemn it, then it must be all level and above board. Please Papa, say we may go.'

The Admiral, while insisting that wild horses couldn't drag him to such a freak-show in this weather, agreed that Lady Carey might take the children, provided Wiske was in attendance to beat off rudesbys and pickpockets.

'I've a better scheme,' said his wife. 'Serena and Sybilla shall go in my place, and I will sit with Hortense.' As Serena began to protest, Lady Carey patted her shoulder. 'No, my dear, don't argue. It will spare me from sitting for hours in the sun, which I detest, and it will allow Sybilla and you to snatch a breath of fresh air. I see the events are set down to begin at three, so the carriage will call for you at Charles Street at quarter past two. That will give Tilley time to find a good place.'

XXVIII

Rather to Serena's surprise, Mrs Fortescue fell in happily with this plan, and the following afternoon saw them driving south across Westminster Bridge in the Careys' comfortable landau.

Jason took it upon himself to entertain Mrs Fortescue with a description of the many and varied delights awaiting her at Vauxhall. Laurel, in a fit of the sullens because Crosby Nettlebed had not been included in the excursion, maintained a tight-lipped silence, and Serena was free to think her own thoughts.

She was determined to make the most of her remaining time in London, and to enjoy this outing to the full. She had put on a gown of muslin embroidered with blue sprigs, and a bonnet of chip straw trimmed with ribbons of the same blue. A white parasol, white kid slippers and a blue silk reticule completed a toilette which she knew to be both modish and becoming.

The sun shone, the river glittered, and a soft breeze blew up-river to take the edge off the heat. She had never before visited Vauxhall, and found it far larger than she had expected, with capacious buildings, gardens with fine trees, gravelled walks and rustic arbours.

A section of the greensward had been roped off to form an arena for the entertainers, and as the landau joined the line of vehicles under a row of oaks, its occupants were able to see a number of displays already in progress: tumblers, a sword-swallower, and a man with a troop of performing dogs.

Over to the left was the high rope, strung between two specially erected poles. All about the arena people milled and jostled; prosperous Cits with their families, young fops on the strut, tradesmen and idlers, as well as a good number of fashionables. A barrel organ vied with a band thumping out one of Dr Arne's merriest airs, and over all could be heard the shouts of vendors selling hot pies and ale, sweetmeats and bread. Jason clamoured to be allowed to spend the guinea his father had given him, and Mrs Fortescue sent him off with Wiske, reminding him that he must return within half an hour if he wished to see the rope-dancing.

Serena alighted from the landau and strolled to the edge of the greensward to watch the troop of dogs. They were amazingly clever, leaped through hoops, climbed ladders, executed somersaults in mid-air, and even pirouetted on their hind legs. In general she disliked to see animals performing tricks, but these seemed so well-cared for, and so happy with their trainer, that she could not think the performance cruel.

Going back to the carriage she found Lord Hector standing beside it, conversing with a beaming Mrs Fortescue. With him was a tall young man, fair-haired and with a ruddy, good-humoured countenance. He was chatting to Laurel, who seemed quite to have forgotten her earlier megrims.

Lord Hector greeted Serena with a smile. 'Miss Osmond,' he said, 'may I have the honour to present my friend Frederic Lychgate? You've heard me speak of him, I think?'

'More than once,' agreed Serena, shaking Mr Lychgate's hand. 'As I remember, sir, you recommended Lord Hector to my uncle in glowing terms.'

'He forced my hand,' Mr Lychgate said. 'Wouldn't take no for an answer.'

'How very unhandsome of you, Frederic,' said his lordship. 'I'm glad to inform you that my business with Sir William went off very happily . . . and you may take credit for having put me in the way of meeting his delightful family. Miss Osmond, do you care to walk a little with me? It's pleasantly cool in the grove.'

Seeing a chance to speak with him in private, Serena nodded and slipped a hand through his arm. They set off along the shady avenue, which was almost deserted, most of the crowd having moved closer to the arena.

'This is an unlooked for pleasure,' said his lordship. 'Was it Jason who contrived to bring you to Vauxhall?'

'Yes. He told my uncle he shouldn't baulk at our coming, as the Wycombes were to attend.'

'Hm. Matthew told me that I should very likely find the Careys here. The young know how to cast a lure, don't they? Where have you been these last ten days, Serena? Almost I think you've been avoiding me.'

She looked up at him quickly. It was the first time he had called her by her given name, and though he spoke lightly, there was an intense expression in his eyes that made her pulse quicken.

She said confusedly, 'Oh, no, it's not that! I've not been about much this week. My mother feels the heat. I've been tending her.'

'I see. Does she still propose to move to Brighton?'

'Yes, or to Bath or some other spa. We leave London soon.'

'I'll miss you,' he said.

Serena stopped dead in her tracks. The conversation was not going at all as she intended. She said rapidly, 'Lord Hector, there is something I must say to you. It is that I regret the way I treated you at Kettleby. I took you for a cheat . . . and an impostor. I was mistaken . . .'

'But you weren't. You were perfectly right to suspect me. My motives were entirely selfish, entirely deplorable. It's I who must make amends, my dear, not you.'

'That debt was squared when you saved Jason,' Serena said, doggedly bent on speaking her whole mind. 'Since we came to London you've been most kind, most generous, and we're all very grateful for it but . . . but we wish you to understand that there's no need for you to do more.'

'We?' His eyes were amused. 'Are you using the royal plural, Serena?'

'No! I mean that all of us . . . all the family . . . agree that you're under no further obligation to us.'

Hector sighed heavily. 'Dear me, what an afternoon this has been! First Frederic gives me a set-down, and now you.' Seeing that Serena looked distressed, he laughed and set his hands on her shoulders.

'You goose, do you think I seek out you and your family merely from a sense of obligation? If so, kindly dismiss the notion. I like the Careys – and I like you, dear Miss Osmond, very, very much.'

Before Serena could speak, he leaned down and kissed her on the lips, first gently and then with such ardour that her senses whirled. A delicious languor filled her body, her arms lifted to encircle his neck and for a moment she leaned against him, eyes closed. Then with a gasp she tried to break from his embrace.

'Let me go at once, please.'

He released her and said contritely, 'I'm sorry. I didn't mean to distress you.'

'Did you not? What gives you leave to treat me like a . . . like a . . .'

He laughed. 'Serena, don't talk such fustian! You're a beautiful woman, with intelligence and spirit, who should be enjoying life to the full.'

'And I suppose you imagine you can teach me how to do so?'

'I might. I would certainly not encourage you to stay chained to your mother's sickbed!'

'How dare you! It's not for you to tell me how to conduct myself! If I need advice I shall seek it from a more reliable source than you!'

He coloured. 'I admit I behaved badly at Kettleby, but surely you don't mean to hold that against me forever! Serena – please – let us make a fresh start.'

He reached for her hands but she snatched them away. Tears burned her eyes. She was filled with unreasonable panic that the self-control it had taken her years to build might suddenly crumble away.

In a trembling voice she said, 'I wish to return to the carriage. You will please to take me there this instant.'

Lord Hector surveyed her in silence for a moment, then sighed. 'Of course, ma'am.'

He offered her his arm once more, but she shrugged away from him. Side by side and in silence they made their way back along the avenue.

The crowd at the greensward had increased considerably, and now pressed close to the carriages, so that Hector had to exert some muscle to clear a way through. Mrs Fortescue and Laurel were still seated in the landau, Mr Lychgate stood guard beside it, and Jason and Matt Wycombe had climbed to the vantage point of the coachman's box. As Hector and Serena approached, Mr Lychgate called out, 'Finch! The Careys' groom has been searching everywhere for you. Seems in a bit of a pucker. You'd best speak to him.'

Hector handed Serena up into the carriage and gazed about

for Wiske. He spied him presently at the edge of the crowd, and made his way towards him.

'What is it, Wiske?' he asked.

'M'lord, I saw that monkey-face – Piggott's man.'

'Laval? Where?'

'Over by the skittle alley. Young Master wanted to try 'is 'and, an' while 'e was a-bowlin, I saw the Frenchie watchin' us from the 'edge 's if 'e didn't wish to be noticed. I never let on I seed 'im, but came straight to find you.'

'Was Piggott with Laval?'

'No, but there was a woman – a mort wi' yaller hair.'

'Did you see her face?'

'No sir, she was too far off. She'd a blue mantle on. Blue velvet, it was. Strange, I thought, on such an 'ot day.' Wiske ran a nervous finger round his collar. 'I don't like it, my lord, that's God's truth.'

'No more do I. Come, let's make a search – though by now they're probably both off and running.'

They walked together to the now thinly populated area of the amusement stalls. In the arena the first of the rope-dancers had begun his climb up the ladder, his balancing-pole in his hand. All eyes were riveted upon him, save those of Mrs Fortescue. She gazed at Lord Hector's retreating back with an expression of brooding speculation, as if she were trying to recall something from the depths of her memory.

Hector and Wiske searched the grounds and buildings for over half an hour, but they found no trace of Laval, or his companion.

'Reckon I was mistook,' Wiske said at last. 'Mebbe it was one o' them pesky gipsies I saw.'

'I don't think so,' Hector answered. 'The blue cloak, Wiske; can you describe it more exactly?'

Wiske met his eyes. 'It were like the one in the picture,' he said, 'the picture o' Lady Georgina? But she's dead, sir. Admiral told young Jason, she's dead. He won't take that bait again, surely?'

'I don't know,' Hector said. 'He might. We must be on our guard. I want you to tell Sir William what happened, as soon as you reach Bruton Street. I'll call on him tomorrow morning, and see if we can devise some plan.'

'What about Jason? 'E should know.'

'I expect Sir William will tell him. In the meantime, keep your eyes peeled, and if you see anything of Piggott or his friends, let me know of it at once.'

XXIX

The Careys set down Mrs Fortescue and Serena in Charles Street a little after five o'clock. Serena went straight to her mother's room, but Mrs Fortescue lingered in the lower hallway, and when Lady Carey came downstairs she found her cousin lying in wait for her.

'I sent your carriage away,' said Sybilla without round-aboutation. 'Purdey will drive you home later. I want to talk to you.'

In the drawing room she sat down facing her captive and said, 'Now, my dear Amelia, why have you been trying to pull the wool over my eyes?'

Lady Carey, who had spent a trying afternoon listening to Mrs Osmond's grousing, tried to fend off this fresh assault on her nerves.

'Really, Sybilla, I don't know why you should say such a thing. I've never lied to you.'

'No, but you've side-stepped,' replied Mrs Fortescue. 'Admit it, Mr Finch and Lord Hector are one and the same person. I knew it the moment I heard Mr Whatsisname – Lychgate – call his lordship "Finch". All the Wycombes bear that name, you know. This one is Hector Amory Finch Wycombe, and I demand to know how he came to be playing tutor to your Jason!' As Lady Carey shook her head, Mrs Fortescue continued inexorably, 'It's no use pretending you don't know, Amelia, for of course you do, and if you won't tell me the whole, I shall find it out from someone else!'

Since this was undoubtedly the case, Lady Carey reluctantly entered into an account of Hector's arrival at Kettleby Manor, and the events that ensued. Mrs Fortescue listened with an air of growing excitement, and at the conclusion clasped her hands ecstatically.

'You can't imagine how happy this makes me. It's plain as a pikestaff that Wycombe's developing an interest in Serena. I suspected as much and now I'm sure of it. Such romantic circumstances, my dear, and such a splendid match for our girl. It will be an excellent thing for Laurel too, for if she's to be related by marriage to the Wycombes, her own chances will be . . .'

'Sybilla, that's enough.' Lady Carey spoke with such unusual vigour that her cousin checked in mid-sentence. 'You will please not leap to conclusions. Lord Hector has been kind to us because he felt indebted . . .'

'Poppycock,' said Mrs Fortescue roundly. 'Men do as they please, particularly men who have the world at their feet. If he pays attention to Serena, it's because he prefers her above the rest. Take my word for it.'

'Perhaps he does like her . . . but I fear she doesn't like him. At Kettleby, they were at daggers drawn.'

'You exaggerate. Serena treats him with ordinary courtesy.'

'Only because I bade her do so, for Jason's sake.'

'Heavens above,' said Sybilla in exasperation. 'It wasn't courtesy that made her go off for a private stroll with him this afternoon and brought her back as pink and shining as a sunset! I wouldn't be surprised if he made her a declaration.'

'Then he had no right to do so. A gentleman shouldn't attempt to approach a girl without first asking permission of her papa.'

'Serena's papa is six foot underground, as you very well know, and I hardly think he should apply to Hortense for permission. Besides, times have changed. These days young people have their own way of arranging things. I expect Serena will confide in you soon enough.'

'No, she won't,' said Lady Carey with conviction. 'I don't think she's ready to form an attachment with any man . . . and pray don't stare at me, Sybilla. All that concerns me is Serena's happiness.'

'It concerns me, too. It could hardly make her unhappy to marry Hector Wycombe. I promise you, London is full of mamas who would give their eye-teeth to see their daughters suffer such a fate! I don't know what's got into you, Amelia.'

'I'm trying to say,' said Lady Carey desperately, 'that Serena hasn't yet recovered from her break with Lucius Radley.'

'That was four years ago!'

'No matter. She was head over heels in love with him, and to discover that all the while he was courting her, he had a mistress in keeping, a slut of a woman who'd borne him four children and was pregnant with the fifth . . .'

'Yes, it was very bad. Her father should have learned Radley's circumstances before allowing the engagement.'

'Her father knew quite well what Radley was. He turned a blind eye to his shortcomings because of the title and the money.'

'If that's true . . .'

'It is true, and it explains why Serena speaks so harshly of her father.'

'How did she find out about this other woman?'

'The creature came to see her, told her that Radley was marrying only for a legitimate heir, and that if Serena didn't believe it, she should challenge him to choose between them. Serena was barely seventeen, not wise enough to send Radley and his strumpet packing. She believed he loved her, she trusted him. Two weeks before the wedding, he ran off with his mistress, to Ireland.'

Mrs Fortescue sighed. 'One sees how painful it must have been for the child, but, after all, it's over and done with. Surely now she can see that not all men are rakes and liars?'

'The trouble with Serena,' said Lady Carey, 'is that she no longer trusts her own judgement. She idolised Radley, and he proved to have feet of clay. Until she regains her confidence, I fear she won't give her affection to anyone.' Seeing a certain look come into her friend's face, she said warningly, 'Sybilla, you mustn't meddle! You mustn't try to dictate to Serena in any way. It could do more harm than good.'

'I shan't dictate to her,' said Mrs Fortescue cheerfully. 'I wasn't born yesterday. Besides, a man of Lord Hector's address needs no help from the likes of me. Mark my words, if he's in a way to fall in love with Serena, then we may leave all in his capable hands.'

XXX

When Hector visited Bruton Street next morning, he found the Admiral surprisingly reluctant to believe Wiske's report.

'The man has windmills in his head,' he declared. 'There's plenty of black-avised rogues that hang about the pleasure gardens and fairs looking for what they can steal. I'll be damned if I frighten Jason with bogeymen that exist only in Wiske's imagination.'

'I don't think Wiske imagined this,' Hector said. 'The man resembled Laval, he appeared to be spying on Jason and he took to his heels when he realised we'd rumbled him.'

'As any thief would do.'

'Sir William, Piggott's a dangerous man, and you've caused him serious injury by driving him from Kettleby. His employers in France won't take such a loss lying down. They'll strike back at you, and the easiest way to do that is through Jason.'

'They won't succeed. I can look after my own.'

'Can you, sir? Can you be sure they won't find some means to lure him away? What of the woman – a fair-haired woman in a blue cloak such as your late wife owned?'

'Coincidence. How many females in London have fair hair and a blue cloak? Thousands, I'll stake my oath.'

'At least set some sort of guard over Jason.'

The Admiral scowled, but in the end said testily, 'Very well, I'll tell the boy he's not to set foot outside the house unless it's in company with me or my wife; and I'll see that Wiske or Timmins goes with him on his rides or walks.'

'And if they see Laval, or the woman?'

'Then they must tell me at once; but it won't happen, my lord. It's all moonshine, this tale. Piggott won't trouble us again.'

As there was no sign of Piggott or his cronies over the ensuing weeks, Hector began to feel that Sir William had been right, and that Wiske had imagined seeing Laval.

Jason did not take kindly to the restraints placed on his freedom. 'I feel like a poodle on a leash,' he complained. 'I ain't scared of Piggott. If he tries to cut a wheedle with me, I shall plant him a facer!'

Matters weren't improved by Lord Fontwell's leaving London with his wife and children, for it deprived Jason of companions of his own age. Serena tried to console him by saying that Lord Hubert and his family would soon be coming to visit Lord Hector, and that Jason was bound to meet the young folk.

'Much good that will do me,' said Jason darkly. 'They're all girls, and Matt told me they do nothing but primp and snivel the livelong day.'

Although everyone tried to devise schemes for his entertainment, there were long hours in the afternoon and evening when he was left to himself. He became tetchy and rebellious, and Lady Carey would have taken him back to Kettleby, had she not felt obliged to remain with Laurel and Serena.

Neither girl lacked for suitors. Few days passed without the arrival of posies sent by John Devenish, Captain Lumley, Mr Robins, Ensign Nettlebed, et al. Mr Lychgate had several times invited Laurel to stand up with him in the dance, and Lord Hector continued to be quietly attentive to Serena.

Yet the melancholy truth was that neither of the girls was formally betrothed. Laurel no longer saw Crosby as her destiny, but basked like a butterfly in the sunshine of attention, flirting with this or that flower of manhood, but settling to none.

Serena had fallen into a listless mood. She seemed resigned to leaving London with her mama – a stoicism that at times brought Lady Carey close to screaming point.

Mrs Fortescue counselled patience. 'The Season,' she said, 'is purgatory for mothers; but believe me, dear Amelia, the prizes go in the end to those who keep their heads and seize their opportunities.'

'It's the gossip I detest,' said Lady Carey. 'Last night that obnoxious Lady Cunningham told me in the most insinuating way that it was all over town that Serena had ambitions to be Lady Hector Wycombe, and that I should warn her that the Duke will never allow a son of his to marry so far beneath him. Can you credit such rudeness?'

'Easily,' retorted Mrs Fortescue, 'when one remembers that Augusta Cunningham is sister to Lady Ainsford, who hopes to catch Wycombe for her bun-faced daughter. You must ignore such malicious talk, as will all people of sense.'

Lady Carey nodded. 'Happily I was able to advise Lady Cunningham that Serena is not drawn to Lord Hector romantically and there is no thought in the world of their forming a lasting attachment. I hope I put a flea in her ear, for she went away quite chap-fallen.'

Not surprisingly, this statement filled Mrs Fortescue with gloom; but her hopes revived considerably when Lord Hector called at Charles Street to invite the ladies and also the Carey family to dine that week at his home. He apologised for the short notice, explaining that his brother Hubert was to arrive a week earlier than expected, 'And once his brood moves in, the house becomes their stamping ground.'

He asked Mrs Fortescue whether he should invite Crosby Nettlebed as well as Mr Lychgate, and she said he should not. 'Crosby is as jealous as a cat,' she told him, 'and would very likely sulk and spoil everyone's enjoyment.'

'You don't favour the match?'

'No, not at all. Crosby is vain and opinionated, not at all the sort of husband Laurel needs.'

'What sort is that?'

'Oh – a man of mature understanding, who likes to live in the country in a well-run house with a great many children. Laurel is very capable when she wants to be.'

'I shall cross Mr Nettlebed off my list,' Hector said.

Ensuring Mrs Osmond's attendance at the party proved a difficult task. When Hector's invitation arrived, she said at once that her health would not allow her to go out at night. Mrs Fortescue was forced to remind her that to refuse the Nonpareil would be a gaucherie that would sink them beyond redemption, and urged her for once to sacrifice herself.

'If I go,' said Mrs Osmond, 'it will be to make plain to Wycombe that Serena is devoted to me, and won't think of being parted from me.' She complained all week that the mere thought of consuming so much rich food and wine was upsetting her digestion; and on Saturday evening she suffered such severe palpitations that even Mrs Fortescue despaired of getting her to Berkeley Square.

However, the goal was achieved, and the party went off

amazingly well. Lord Hector was an excellent host. Serena, who arrived at the house in considerable trepidation, found no trace of awkwardness between them. He greeted her with exactly the right degree of friendly detachment, and she was able to convince herself that he had put the unfortunate encounter at Vauxhall out of his mind. His other guests were not in the least top-lofty. Mr Lychgate kept the table in a roar with his anecdotes; Lord Hector's uncle, Lord Lyttelton, turned out to be an old flame of Mrs Fortescue; and an elderly valetudinarian named Arthur Cromer so entranced Mrs Osmond with his account of the cures achieved by the faith-healers of India, that she quite forgot her fade-away airs.

'This Cromer,' murmured Mr Lychgate to Hector as the gentlemen left their port and moved to rejoin the ladies. 'Odd bird, ain't he? Where did you find him?'

'I've known him for years,' Hector answered. 'He was one of the Carlton House set. Spends most of his time in Brighton, these days.'

'Ah!' said Frederic, enlightened. A thought occurred to him. 'When Hubert comes,' he said, 'shall you tell him how you won your bet?'

'Why not?' said Hector.

'Won't like it above half,' suggested Frederic. 'And Emily won't like it at all.'

'I look forward with keen anticipation,' returned Hector, 'to seeing Emily's reaction. It will be some compensation for sheltering her appalling offspring for a month.'

'And your father? Does he come to Town this year?'

'Yes, but not to me. He prefers to be independent.' The lightness had vanished from Hector's voice, and he glanced involuntarily to where Serena sat talking to the Admiral and Lord Lyttelton.

Wonderin' what the old martinet will make of her, reflected Mr Lychgate; but he kept his thoughts to himself. The coldness between the Duke and his youngest son was not a topic one raised in Hector's presence.

Next morning Lord Hector strolled into the office where his secretary Mr Purdon was busy with a pile of documents.

'Good morning, Horace,' he said cheerfully. 'You may consign all that paper to the waste-paper basket. I've a matter that must take precedence over all.'

'Yes, my lord,' said Mr Purdon, mentally calculating how he could shelve the pressing demands of his lordship's estate.

'I wish to secure a rented house in Brighton,' Hector said. 'It must be well-situated, with a view of the sea, and within easy reach of the Pavilion.'

'You're going to Brighton, sir?' enquired Purdon in a voice of some surprise.

'No,' said Hector easily. 'It's for a lady.'

Mr Purdon coughed discreetly. 'I understand, sir.'

'No, Horace, you do not. The lady is middle-aged and in frail health. She is Mrs Hortense Osmond, and she is anxious to leave London without delay.'

'At this time of the year, my lord, every suitable residence is taken. It will be very difficult to . . .'

'I'm sure it won't be beyond your capabilities, Horace.'

'Er . . . thank you, my lord. How much is your lordship prepared to pay for the accommodation?'

'Whatever is necessary. If you can't find a house for rent, buy one. I suggest you apply first to Mr Arthur Cromer. He owns several properties in Brighton. His direction is Twenty-seven Half Moon Street, but he will be in Town for a few days only. Visit him today. If he cannot help you, go to the general agents. Oh, and ask Mr Cromer who is the best doctor in Brighton.'

'And should I mention your lordship's name?'

'Yes, but discreetly, if you please.'

'Quite so, sir. Will that be all?' Mr Purdon could not keep the edge from his voice, and Lord Hector smiled encouragingly.

'For the moment, yes. Speed is of the essence. I look forward to hearing very soon that your efforts have been crowned with success.'

Despite his misgivings, Purdon found Mr Cromer most helpful, and two days later Lord Hector became the lessee of a small but elegant house, within sight of the Pavilion's bulbous roofs, and with a pleasant prospect over the sea.

'It cost a pretty penny to secure it, I can tell you,' Mr Purdon later informed his wife, 'but Lord H never turned a hair. I'll lay odds it's to do with Miss Osmond. He's daffy upon her.'

'He'll never think of setting her up as his mistress?' cried Mrs

Purdon, much shocked. 'Such a nice, respectable young lady as she is?'

'No, I understand it's her mama that's to occupy the house, though I can't for the life of me think why.' Mr Purdon took a thoughtful sip of claret. 'One thing's certain. There's method in his madness. His lordship's not the man to lay down his blunt for nothing.'

Having secured the high ground on the field of battle, Hector now looked for an ally. He penned a graceful note to Mrs Fortescue, inviting her to drive out with him that afternoon as he had something of importance to discuss with her.

Mrs Fortescue accepted with alacrity, and three o'clock saw them bowling along the Bayswater Road in his lordship's town carriage.

'You'll forgive the cloak-and-dagger approach,' Hector said with a smile. 'What I have to say is confidential. It concerns Miss Osmond.'

Mrs Fortescue returned a murmur that she hoped combined well-bred reserve with keen anticipation.

'You must have noticed,' continued Hector, 'that I have the highest regard – and respect – for Miss Osmond. In ordinary circumstances I would ask her mama's permission to pay Serena my addresses; but in view of Mrs Osmond's delicate state of health, I feel this is not the proper moment.'

'Quite right,' agreed Mrs Fortescue, lowering her eyes so that he should not see the excitement in them. 'Dear Hortense's nerves are sadly overwrought. She's in no condition to make decisions.'

Hector nodded. 'I'm aware,' he said, 'that Miss Osmond places great reliance on your judgement. It's for that reason that I come to you for advice. The fact is, Serena doesn't yet feel as I do . . . though I hope that in time I may persuade her to like me a little.'

'Indeed, she already does,' cried Mrs Fortescue. 'It's plain as a pikestaff she enjoys your company. It's years since I've seen her so much at ease with anyone.'

'"At ease" isn't enough,' said Hector bluntly. 'To be frank, ma'am, I've had my fill of ladies who are at ease with me . . .

and who value me for my title and my fortune. I've a strong desire to be valued for myself. If Serena can't warm to me . . .'

'Pray don't think that, my lord! You spoke of giving her time. I assure you, that is all she needs.' Mrs Fortescue hesitated a moment, then took the plunge. 'You must know that Serena suffered a bitter disappointment in love when she was very young.'

'Her former betrothal, you mean? I've wondered about that, but she's never spoken much of it.'

'She was betrothed at the age of seventeen to Lord Radley.' Mrs Fortescue looked up at Hector's frowning face. 'Perhaps you're acquainted with him, sir? I imagine he must be your senior by some years.'

'I've met him . . . and disliked him thoroughly. He's a rake, a drunkard and liar. What in God's name possessed her parents to consent to such a match?'

'He had a title and a fortune,' said Mrs Fortescue drily, 'and his lands marched with theirs. He could be very charming when he chose. He was strikingly handsome – a little like you – though in his case there was a weakness in the features that should have given us warning. Serena was deeply in love with him.'

'And you think,' said Hector deliberately, 'that she now sees Radley in me?'

'No. Not now that she's come to know you . . . but at Kettleby, when she suspected that you had . . . had . . .'

'. . . lied my way into her family's confidence?'

'Yes. It made her mistrust you, compare you perhaps with Lord Radley.'

Hector rubbed a hand over his eyes. 'What a fool I was,' he muttered. 'It's cost me dear, that idiotic impulse.'

'If you hadn't submitted to it, you'd never have met Serena,' said Mrs Fortescue.

'True. Tell me, what made Serena break with Radley?'

'He had a mistress, a vulgar creature he'd kept for years. They had four children and another on the way. The woman came to Serena and announced that Lucius loved her, would never desert her, and was marrying only to secure a legal heir. Serena refused to believe it, but a fortnight before the wedding, Radley absconded. He took the woman and their children to Ireland where he has a small property. He has never sent Serena a line of explanation or regret.'

'Poor child,' Hector said.

'Yes. It was a dreadful time for her. It wasn't just disappointed love, Lord Hector. For a woman to be jilted in such a way destroys her belief in herself, her faith in the whole institution of marriage.'

'I understand.' He sat silent for a moment, then said briskly, 'Well that exposes the first of my problems. I've a second . . . Mrs Osmond's wish to keep her daughter at her side, here and in Brighton.'

'Yes.' Mrs Fortescue sighed. 'I'm afraid Hortense is adamant on that score.'

'What if I were in a position,' said Hector carefully, 'to supply a house that would exactly meet Mrs Osmond's requirements?' He saw a flash of apprehension in his companion's face, and smiled. 'Naturally, I wouldn't offer it if it meant losing Serena.'

'She'll go to Brighton,' said Mrs Fortescue gloomily. 'She has a tiresome sense of duty. If Hortense plays on her loyalties, she'll go.'

Hector nodded, again appearing to reflect. Then he said, 'The owner of the house is Mr Arthur Cromer, whom you met at my home this week.'

'Indeed?' Mrs Fortescue watched him with sharp interest.

'He's something of a property owner,' Hector went on, 'but will only lease to his personal friends. He will be more than happy to accept Mrs Osmond as a tenant.'

'Indeed!' repeated Mrs Fortescue.

'I thought,' said his lordship diffidently, 'that Mr Cromer and Mrs Osmond dealt extremely together the other night. Got on like a house afire, in fact.'

'Indeed!' Mrs Fortescue cleared her throat delicately. 'Hortense was saying only yesterday what an excellent man Mr Cromer is. Such sensibility, such courtly manners. She couldn't praise him enough.'

'Salt of the earth,' agreed Hector. 'Well-read, well-travelled . . .'

'And a widower, I collect?'

'Yes, he lost his wife three years ago. He misses her sorely.'

'No doubt, no doubt.'

'His doctor,' said Hector casually, 'attends upon His Majesty the King when he's in Brighton. I'm sure he could be persuaded to take Mrs Osmond as a patient.'

Mrs Fortescue made no answer. Her eyes were shining, as if she beheld a glorious sunrise.

'There's one small fly in the ointment,' Hector said. She turned quickly towards him, and he smiled. 'Cromer,' he said, 'possesses every virtue save one. He dislikes young people. Says they're rackety and frivolous and upset his nerves. It might be better if Mrs Osmond were to be accompanied by someone older than Serena. Is there some trusted friend who can fill the bill?'

Mrs Fortescue needed no prompting. 'I'll go myself,' she declared.

'What if Mrs Osmond refuses to leave Serena in London?'

'Leave her to me!' Mrs Fortescue's mind was already busy with details. 'I think, you know, that the offer of the house should come from Mr Cromer himself. I shall ask him to dine with us. If you will but give him the hint to say nothing of your part in the transaction, I'm confident we shall triumph.' She gave Hector a beaming smile. 'How pleasant it is, my lord, to deal with someone as far-seeing and practical as yourself.'

'Serena mustn't know we've conspired like this, ma'am.'

'Of course she mustn't. It will be our little secret.' Mrs Fortescue sighed happily. 'I shall arrange a dinner that will send Mr Cromer into transports,' she promised. 'And if we don't see Hortense set off for the coast within the week, I shall be very much surprised.'

XXXI

Mrs Fortescue was as good as her word. Within a week, Mrs Osmond was looking forward with keen anticipation to quitting Town, and was quite reconciled to leaving Serena behind.

'You'll be as merry as a grig with the Careys,' she said, 'and I shan't repine, because I'll have my dear Sybilla to bear me company. Mr Cromer has been everything that is kind. He's promised to introduce us to his own circle of friends, and that, let me tell you, is a signal honour. His sister Lady Danbury is the doyenne of Brighton society, so I daresay I shan't miss London in the least.'

She kept Serena busy running to and fro to purchase items she required, cancel appointments and make up a hamper of nostrums in case Brighton should prove to be lacking in good apothecaries. She also ordered several new gowns, and three or four very dashing bonnets, so as to be ready for every social eventuality.

At last the boxes were packed, corded, and loaded on to Mrs Fortescue's baggage fourgon; the postillions stood to their horses' heads; the final farewells were said; and the two ladies set out for the coast.

Serena had already moved her own possessions to Bruton Street and had only to stroll round two sides of Berkeley Square to reach her uncle's home. As she started out, she heard her name called and glanced round to see Lord Hector approaching on horseback. He dismounted and came over to her, saying, 'So the great migration has begun! I saw the carriages as I came past Apsley House.'

Serena regarded him with a darkling eye. She suspected he knew a great deal more than he told about the sudden availability of a house by the sea.

'Your friend Mr Cromer,' she said pointedly, 'has been extraordinarily helpful.'

Lord Hector answered blandly that he was happy to hear it. 'Perhaps you'll permit me to drive you to visit your mama, some day?' he suggested. 'We might make up a party with Miss Carey and Frederic Lychgate.'

Serena thanked him, aware that once again she had been out-manoeuvred. Since that day at Vauxhall, Lord Hector had been most circumspect, never saying or doing anything to suggest amatory intentions. At parties he made no attempt to detach her from the general company, and he was careful to include Laurel or some other member of her family in any invitation. Yet despite this exemplary behaviour, she had the feeling she was being played like a fish.

In July he made a sudden decision to spend a few days at Fontwell. Serena missed him dreadfully. Dancing with John Devenish and her other admirers was very dull work, the people she met dead bores. She felt grouchy and out of sorts with the world.

When Lady Carey ventured to ask when his lordship was due to return, Serena said snappily that she neither knew nor cared.

'Why Serena,' reproved her aunt, 'what an unhandsome thing to say! I'm sure you don't mean it.'

'I do! I'm quite out of patience with him, if you must know. I'm out of patience with the whole Season. I'm tired of feeling that the only thing in life is to find myself a husband. It's degrading.'

'My love, if by some happy chance Lord Hector were to offer for you . . .'

'I should refuse him! Why does everyone think that Wycombe has only to cast his handkerchief to have every female in sight scrambling to pick it up!'

Since this was precisely what Lady Carey did think, she fell silent, saying later to her husband that she hoped Serena wouldn't dwindle into an old maid.

The Admiral chuckled. 'Lord, Amelia, she won't. She's head over ears in love, that's all. Leave her be.'

'It's all very well for you to laugh,' protested his wife, 'but if Serena keeps Wycombe dangling too long, someone else will snap him up.'

'If you ask me,' said Sir William, 'it's not Serena or Lord Hector we need fret about, it's that damned stiff-necked family of his. The talk is, they want him to marry Miss Ainsford. If the old Duke's set on the match, then we've indeed cause to worry.'

Lady Carey's anxiety increased when a few days later the Careys attended a performance of *The Marriage of Figaro* at Covent Garden. Shortly before the curtain rose, she saw Lady Ainsford and her daughter enter the opposite box, accompanied by Lord Hector and a tall, elderly grandee whom she had no difficulty in identifying as the Duke of Wycombe.

Lord Hector, catching sight of the Careys' party, smiled and bowed in their direction; but he did not come round to their box in the interval. Lady Carey took this as a very bad sign, but the Admiral pooh-poohed her concern.

'A gentleman,' he said, 'don't invite one lady to accompany him to the opera, and then dance attendance on another.'

'Serena was hurt,' said Lady Carey. 'She held her head up, but she was hurt.'

'Good,' said the Admiral with brutal frankness. 'Since honey don't fetch her, maybe salt will.'

'I find that a very vulgar metaphor.'

Sir William was unrepentant. 'Hector Wycombe knows what he's about,' he said. 'Just leave them be.'

XXXII

Two days after, Serena and Laurel attended a rout at the London residence of Lord and Lady Lychgate. Lady Ainsford and her daughter Anna were among the guests, and Serena saw that Lord Hector spent some time chatting to them. Privately she considered that Anna Ainsford behaved in a ludicrously coy manner, placing a hand on his lordship's sleeve and gazing up at him with great cow eyes.

Serena felt quite out of patience with him, and when at last he came over to greet her, she assumed an air of studied indifference. She dismissed his compliments on her new gown with a shrug, and answered his friendly questions with quite oppressive politeness. Finally, when he invited her to accompany him the following evening to a musical evening at the Fox-Lamberts' home, she replied that she was already engaged to attend a theatrical pageant.

His lordship looked puzzled. 'Oh, is there one? Where?'

Serena improvised wildly. 'At the Yorkshire Stingo, in Marylebone.'

Hector blinked. 'Truly? Won't you find the company a trifle rough, there?'

'I shall be perfectly safe,' returned Serena. 'John Devenish is to escort me, and my cousin and Mr Nettlebed will be of the party.'

Glancing at Laurel, his lordship surprised a blank look on her face. He smiled. 'Well, I hope you will enjoy a pleasant evening. Is there to be a melodrama, Miss Carey?'

'I . . . I don't know,' stammered Laurel, and Serena cut in quickly.

'Yes, there is, but it is the singer, Miss Nelly Bloom, that we are particularly anxious to hear. A quite remarkable soprano, I'm told, who's making a name for herself among the *cognoscenti*.'

Lord Hector knew that Nelly was making a name for herself among other than music-lovers, but he merely nodded blandly, and soon after moved away to converse with Lady Jersey.

Laurel looked accusingly at her cousin.

'Serena, what made you tell such a whisker? I never heard of this Yorkshire Thingummy before.'

'It was the first name I could recall,' said Serena, 'and I shall make sure it's not a lie. I shall ask John Devenish to take me there, and you must persuade Crosby to join us.'

'I won't! I don't wish to encourage Crosby. I'm tired of all his posturing and boasting. Mr Lychgate says he's a popinjay.'

'If you renege, John and I will go alone.'

'You can't, it wouldn't be proper to visit such a place without a gentleman who's a close relation. In fact, I doubt if it's a proper sort of place in any circumstances. Papa told me that the pleasure gardens have become shockingly debased. He'll never give us permission.'

'You're not to tell him of it,' said Serena feverishly. 'Laurel, I've never asked you for a favour, but I'm asking you now. I can't be caught out in a lie. Not by Lord Hector, of all men.'

Nothing could make her change her mind, and at last Laurel agreed to fall in with her plans, and issue an invitation to Mr Nettlebed.

Later that evening, Hector informed Frederic Lychgate of Serena's determination to visit the Yorkshire Stingo, and Frederic said at once that it was a hare-brained scheme. 'The place will be full of raggle-taggles come to ogle the Blackbird. But there's no need to worry. Devenish will never be fool enough to escort her.'

Hector shook his head. 'I fear Devenish is putty in Serena's hands,' he said. 'He'll do anything she asks.'

This proved to be the case, and the next evening the party of four set out for Marylebone.

The Yorkshire Stingo had in the past century been one of the best known of the rural tea gardens. It took its name from a remarkably strong ale brewed in Yorkshire, and that beverage had long since replaced tea as the patrons' favourite tipple.

Large gardens and a bowling green surrounded the inn, and an arena had been built behind the saloon, where entertainments of all kinds were staged. To keep out undesirables, the proprietors demanded an entry fee of sixpence which could be exchanged for refreshments within the gates. In short, once inside, a man was able to drink himself to the point of stupor.

There were boxes, though, for which one paid a shilling, and it was to one of these that Sir John led Miss Osmond, Miss Carey, and Ensign Nettlebed.

They were not what could be called a happy party. Sir John, when he saw the type of person streaming into the arena, said at once that he thought they should leave.

'It's worse than I imagined,' he said. 'To remain might be to subject you ladies to unpleasantness. Let us depart before the performance begins.'

'No,' said Serena obstinately. 'We'll be perfectly safe in the box, and I've quite set my heart on hearing Miss Bloom sing. Please let us stay.'

Sir John capitulated. He liked strong-minded women – his mother was one – and he saw that to find a way out through the press might be more unpleasant than remaining in their seats.

The gentlemen procured wine for the ladies, and ale for themselves, and the four settled themselves, Sir John and Serena in the front places with Laurel and Crosby behind.

The floor of the arena was now crowded with revellers who whistled and stamped their feet and shouted to one another in a very free way. Presently the band struck up a popular air, and the audience joined in enthusiastically, swinging their pint pots, and roaring out the choruses. There was a section quite close that was particularly noisy, and two or three of them, rough fellows in shabby frieze coats, looked leeringly at the women about them and yelled coarse endearments. Serena was glad to see that the management had set guards armed with stout cudgels at points around the pit.

The curtains of the stage were raised, and a group of tumblers burst from the wings, leaping and turning and climbing on one another's shoulders with incredible skill.

Sir John explained that they were Italians, but Serena could hear little of what he said, as the noise of the crowd was now deafening.

The tumblers gave way to a pageant depicting the Heroes of Waterloo, and then to a melodrama with a plot of such complexity that it was impossible to understand it. At last a gentleman in a swallowtail coat and pantaloons stepped forward to announce that the Blackbird of Marylebone, the inimitable Nelly Bloom, would now sing.

The announcement brought a crescendo of catcalls and whistles from the audience, the drummers rolled out a rattattoo and out from the shadows sailed Miss Bloom, mounted on the model of a swan.

She was dressed in a black gown whose décolletage was so low as to display large portions of her ample bosom. A cleft in her skirt exposed her legs; black boots laced with silver ties to the knee, and a great deal of plump white thigh above. Her face was thickly powdered and heavily rouged, and on her golden tresses was perched a shovel hat trimmed with ostrich plumes. Striking a provocative pose, she burst into such a series of trills, arpeggios and top notes that the rafters rang. It was the signal for chaos.

As one man the patrons in the pit surged to their feet, chanting 'Nelly, Nelly,' blowing kisses, and inviting the diva to step down and join them. In reply, she removed her hat and tossed it to the most vocal section. At once a fight broke out, several draymen battling for possession of the trophy. Fists flew and oaths rang out.

Turning to glance at Laurel, Serena saw that she was sitting rigid, her face white and scared. The sight filled Serena with contrition, and she said quickly, 'Don't fret, dearest. We'll leave at once.'

Laurel shook her head. 'I don't think Crosby can,' she said. She was right. Fallen back in his chair, Crosby snored steadily, the victim of the powers of Stingo. John Devenish tried to shake him awake, without success.

'I must find a waiter,' said Sir John, 'to help me carry him.' But before he could move, the isolated fight in the pit turned to universal mayhem. All over the arena, men swayed and trampled in a punching, gasping mass. The armed guards struck out right and left, breaking the crowns of guilty and innocent alike, and numbers of women set up a screeching that they'd been robbed.

One doxy in orange satin lunged towards Serena, clambering up the front of the box and snatching at Serena's necklace. Without pausing to think, Serena punched her in the face, and the woman dropped back. Her place was at once taken by three burly ruffians, who scaled the rail of the box. Laurel screamed in terror, and John Devenish, laying about him with a will, quickly dislodged one assailant, who fell to the arena floor and stayed there. A second man wrapped his arms about John's chest and the two of them swayed to and fro, grunting and cursing. The third man fixed his gaze on Serena and, grinning, began to climb towards her.

It was then that Serena was overcome by a lovely, primitive bloodlust. Seizing Sir John's half-empty tankard, she hit the thug squarely on the nose. He let out a bellow of pain and swayed back but he did not relinquish his grip on the rail, and his eyes held a very ugly expression. Serena hit him again on the side of the head and he disappeared from view. Turning to look for Sir John, she saw that he had fallen unconscious across his chair, and that the man who had felled him was coming towards her.

She retreated, thrusting Laurel behind her and brandishing her tankard. The rowdy guffawed, showing black teeth, and reaching out, caught her by the wrist and dragged her towards him. She tried wildly to strike his hands away, but she knew he was too strong for her. Shouting to Laurel to run, run, she clawed at her attacker's face. She felt the breath was being squeezed out of her, and a dreadful dizziness assailed her. Just when she felt she could struggle no more, a fist swung past her head and smashed into the ruffian's jaw. Serena felt herself snatched up and borne out of the box. She saw that Laurel too had been seized, and she was opening her mouth to scream when a well-known voice said firmly,

'Be quiet, Serena. You're safe.'

Looking up, she saw Lord Hector's face above her. He smiled at her. 'Lychgate has Laurel,' he said. 'Hold fast and we'll get you out of this Bedlam.'

Somehow he forced a path through the crowds behind the box, and brought her out to the blessed fresh air. His carriage was standing close by, the groom holding the bays' heads, the coachman on the box. Mr Lychgate appeared, bearing a weeping Laurel.

Lord Hector set Serena down. 'You're all right, are you? Not hurt?'

'Only my pride,' she said. She glanced down at the torn lace of her gown, the beer-stains on her skirt. 'I was such a fool. I put them all at risk, coming to this place.'

'Write it off to experience,' said his lordship cheerfully. He handed her a handkerchief, and she wiped her face, tried to smooth the tangled mass of her hair.

'I feel a drab,' she said.

'You were magnificent. I've never seen a nicer style with a pint pot. Gentleman Jackson could take pointers from you.'

Against her will, Serena giggled. 'I enjoyed it,' she admitted. 'I never thought I could be so bloodthirsty.' She handed back the kerchief. 'I must go to Laurel,' she said.

'No need,' said his lordship easily. 'Frederic's shoulders are broader than yours.' Indeed, she saw that Laurel was leaning on Mr Lychgate's chest very contentedly.

Hector took her hand. 'Come, we'll take you home.'

Serena took a step, then remembered her obligations. 'I can't leave Sir John, and Crosby.'

'Why not? They deserve what they got, for bringing you here.'

'They didn't wish to come. I persuaded them, and I can't abandon them.'

The laughter died from Hector's eyes. 'I suppose not. Very well, Frederic shall escort you and Miss Carey to Bruton Street, and I'll undertake to salvage Devenish and Crosby.'

'Thank you,' she said warmly, 'and thank you for rescuing us. I've never been more glad to see anyone in my life.'

For a moment he hesitated, then he smiled and bowed and strode away towards the arena, where the sounds of battle were fast growing faint. Serena walked slowly across to Frederic and Laurel. She felt very much alone in the world.

By good fortune the Admiral and Lady Carey were from home that night, enjoying a game of whist with the Sherbornes. Serena and Laurel were able to creep up to their bedrooms unnoticed.

Serena found it impossible to sleep. She knew that it was not chance that had brought Lord Hector and his friend to the Yorkshire Stingo. They must have agreed the night before to protect herself and Laurel from the effects of her folly.

She tried to feel remorseful, and could not. Lying in her bed, she recalled her feeling of liberation as she swung that tankard, she remembered Hector's smiling eyes, and her own laughing response to his teasing.

Tomorrow, no doubt, this exalted mood would fade, but tonight, for a few short hours, she soared on the wings of a new-found happiness.

*

Next morning, Sir John Devenish and Ensign Nettlebed both called at Bruton Street.

Sir John, sporting a bruised eye and a cut lip, apologised repeatedly to Serena for involving her in such a fracas. He also asked for her hand in marriage. Serena refused him gracefully, using all the correct phrases. Sir John, though crestfallen, said he would not give up hope too easily, and begged that Miss Osmond would not deny him the continued pleasure of her company. They parted with mutual expressions of regard.

Laurel's interview with Crosby was far less amicable. He had, he announced, the very devil of a headache. Laurel said he deserved it. 'You were dead drunk,' she said hotly. 'You did nothing but lie and snore, while poor Sir John and Serena fought for our lives.'

'A lady does not indulge in fisticuffs,' said Crosby, unwisely. 'Serena should know better.'

'I suppose you would have preferred us to be outraged, or murdered? If it hadn't been for Lord Hector, and dear Mr Lychgate, we might not be here today – and nor might you, Crosby, for it was Lord Hector who went back to that dreadful inn and dragged you and Sir John out.'

'Of course Lord Hector is the hero of the piece. You've forgot how he tricked your papa at Kettleby. The man's a liar, a fraud.'

'You may spew your malice, Crosby, it's of no importance to me. I'm tired of your jealous tongue. I never want to see you again, do you hear? Never as long as I live.' With which Laurel swept from the room.

When it was borne in upon Lady Carey that her charges had destroyed the hopes of two suitors in one morning, she retired to her room and burst into tears, telling her startled husband that the world had run mad, that Serena and Laurel were doomed to die old maids, and that they had all better pack their bags and return home without delay.

XXXIII

Hector was finding the invasion of his house by Hubert and his family more trying than he had expected.

His sister-in-law lost no time in condemning all the arrangements he had made for her and her children. The maid assigned to the nursery floor was as clumsy as a bear. The day nursery was too large and the night nursery too small. The menus devised by Hector's French chef were far too rich for juvenile stomachs.

'I shall talk to the man myself,' she announced, 'and tell him what meals to prepare for the duration of our stay.'

'No,' said Hector firmly. 'You may talk to me, Emily, tell me what you'd like, and I'll convey your wishes to Leon.'

'Are you saying that your cook doesn't know how to take instructions?' asked Emily tartly. 'If so, I recommend you to dismiss him.'

'Out of the question,' Hector said.

'Why, pray?'

'I like his way of doing turbot.'

'I,' said Emily, 'would not allow myself to be dictated to by a servant. I suppose things are always lax in a bachelor establishment. You should marry, Hector. I gather the Ainsfords are ready to consider the match.'

Though Emily returned several times to the attack, he refused either to dismiss Leon, or to be drawn on the subject of Anna Ainsford. Emily turned to harassing the other members of his staff, and very soon had them on the point of rebellion. The situation was saved only when Hector conceived the brilliant plan of commissioning Sir Thomas Lawrence to paint a portrait of her children. Emily carried them off each morning for sittings at the artist's home in Russell Square, and Hector's household was able to get on with its business in peace.

It was during one of these lulls that Hubert in funning mood reminded Hector of his wager, and enquired archly whether he had any gainful employment in mind? Hector replied by producing the testimonial Sir William had given him.

Hubert read the document through several times, his face darkening to a rich plum colour. At last he looked up. 'I don't understand a word of this,' he said. '"Tutorial skills"? "Mr Finch"? What's it all about?'

'It means I was employed for some three weeks as tutor to the son of Sir William Carey. I was paid for the full month, however. Ten guineas.'

'You worked as a tutor? A tutor?! I am ... I am dumbfounded!'

'Thought you might be. I was surprised myself. Never thought I should recall so much of my Greek.'

'Don't be frivolous, pray. How could you, a Wycombe, so demean yourself as to hire yourself out as a jobbing pedagogue, merely to win a wager? And who are these Careys? Can they be trusted to keep their mouths shut about this sordid affair?'

'They have so far.' Though Hector spoke lightly, there was a glint in his eyes that should have warned Hubert to desist, but he was too indignant to heed it.

'You have always been irresponsible,' he cried. 'You have never had a proper regard for the dignity of the family name, or the feelings of its members. You have gone your own sweet way all your days, but this is the outside of enough! To expose us to vulgar gossip, to make us hostages of ... of a bunch of country bumpkins ...'

'Hubert, that's enough!' Hector bent to retrieve the paper that Hubert had tossed to the floor. 'Admiral Carey is a gentleman. His stock is as old as ours, and his wife is kin to Lady Sefton. Rid yourself of the notion that the Careys are some lower form of life.'

'Clearly they've bewitched you,' thundered Hubert. 'One can only hope that the incident is closed and that you will never have to set eyes on them again.'

'On the contrary, I see them frequently.' Hector rose to his feet. 'They're in London for the Season and reside just round the corner from here, in Bruton Street. You're bound to meet them sooner or later and when you do, oblige me by treating them with proper courtesy. Be particularly affable to Sir William's niece, Miss Serena Osmond.'

'Why?' demanded Hubert, rising too, and throwing out his chest like an outraged pigeon. 'Why should I pay the smallest attention to the girl?'

Hector regarded his brother with a faint smile. 'Because,' he said gently, 'I hope very much to marry her.'

XXXIV

'He's run mad,' declared Hubert. 'He actually hopes to marry this . . . this nobody.'

The other occupant of the room, who was seated in a wing chair near the window, did not at once reply. Julian, fourth Duke of Wycombe, was not given to hasty speech. Reticence was one of his most intimidating qualities, and many a mushroom had been sent scurrying for cover by the implacable stare of his deep-set eyes.

His countenance, though handsome, was austere, the nose high-bridged and the mouth set in an uncompromising line. His hair, thick and silver-white, was worn rather longer than was fashionable, and though his suits were made by Weston, he managed to invest them with the panache of a bygone, more flamboyant age. His waistcoat today was of deep red brocade, and a fine ruby pin glowed in the folds of his cravat.

He turned from his contemplation of Grosvenor Square to watch his third son pace about the drawing room. Hubert, thought his sire, had the knack of setting up one's hackles, even when he was in the right.

'Hector must not be allowed to commit this folly,' announced Hubert. 'You must prevent it, Father.'

'How?' enquired the Duke gently.

'You must forbid the banns. The marriage is impossible. No one has ever heard of these Careys.'

The Duke examined his fingernails. 'I have,' he said. 'I fancy William Carey was one of Nelson's most daring captains. As to forbidding the banns, I must remind you that Hector is of age, and free to do as he chooses.'

'Sir,' pleaded Hubert, 'do but consider what must be Lady Ainsford's sentiments if this story comes to her ears.'

'I trust,' said the Duke in a bored voice, 'that whatever they are, she will keep them to herself. I don't brook criticism of my sons from outsiders.'

'Lady Ainsford is an old friend, sir!'

'She's also an arrogant and encroaching female with a very poor ear for music. At the opera last week she persisted in humming the melodies, a trifle off-key. And her daughter is as stupid as she is whey-faced.'

'I thought you approved the match?'

'To my knowledge, the match doesn't exist, except in her ladyship's overheated imagination.'

Hubert stopped pacing and came to face his father.

'Papa, tell me honestly, do you consider Miss Osmond a suitable wife for Hector?'

'I don't know. I've never met the girl. I shall of course make it my business to do so – and to learn something of her background. But I shall be discreet, Hubert, and so must you be. Don't go huffing and puffing your objections all over Town. You're to speak of this to no one. Understand?'

'I must tell Emily,' said Hubert stiffly. 'We have no secrets from each other.'

'Then kindly warn her that if she breathes a word of the tale, she'll have me to deal with.'

'Very well. And you'll speak to Hector, sir?'

The Duke glanced down at his signet ring, which bore the engraving of a finch.

'I could wish,' he said, half to himself, 'that Hector would confide in me . . . but perhaps that's expecting too much.'

'I fear so, sir. When has Hector pleased anyone but himself?'

The Duke contemplated Hubert without sympathy. 'Hector has tried to please us all,' he said, 'and none of us has had the sense to recognise the fact, or the grace to appreciate his qualities. I for one intend to do what I can to make amends.'

As Hubert stared at him in amazement, the Duke sighed. 'Pour me a glass of wine, Hubert, and take one yourself. The weather's too hot for us to indulge in these lurid emotional scenes.'

The following night the Careys were bidden to attend a lecture at the home of Lord and Lady Grimsby, the lecturer being the Right Honourable Mr Thomas Grenville, and his topic the illustrated manuscripts of the Middle Ages.

The Admiral, who regarded all the antiquities with loathing, soon took refuge in an antechamber to the drawing room, and was about to fortify himself with a draught from his pocket-flask when he realised that he was not alone.

Standing a few paces from him, and regarding him fixedly through a quizzing-glass, was a tall, elderly gentleman of rather forbidding aspect.

The Admiral put away his flask, stuck out his jaw, and prepared to repel boarders. The stranger approached him in a leisurely manner, bowed slightly, and said, 'I believe, sir, that I have the honour to address Admiral Sir William Carey of Kettleby?'

'You do,' agreed the Admiral, staring hard. 'I fear, sir, that you have the advantage of me.'

'My name is Julian Wycombe.'

'The Duke of Wycombe?'

The Duke inclined his head. 'If you're willing to forgo the pleasures of the lecture room for a while, there's a matter I'd very much like to discuss with you.'

Sir William scowled. 'If it's about Lord Hector, I take leave to tell you, Duke, that I don't tattle about a man behind his back.'

'Very laudable,' approved the Duke. He indicated a pair of chairs set against the wall. 'Shall we sit down, Sir William? I won't keep you long.'

The Admiral complied, though still with an air of belligerence.

'I've been told,' said the Duke tranquilly, 'that Hector spent some time in Kettleby as ... er ... tutor to your son. Is that true?'

'Why don't you ask him?'

'I shall, of course.' The Duke gazed steadily at Sir William. 'However, it's a delicate matter. Before I raise it with Hector, I should like to have the facts straight in my mind.'

The Admiral grunted. A Roman Father, he thought, who's too proud to go cap in hand to his son. Aloud, he said:

'I'll tell you this much. I owe your son a debt I can never repay. He saved my Jason's life.'

'Indeed?' The Duke waited with an air of courteous expectancy, and against his will the Admiral found himself giving an account of the excursion to Merlin's Pot and Hector's heroic part in the rescue. When he had made an end, the Duke shook his head.

'Dear me, how little one knows of one's own offspring,' he murmured.

'Lord Hector's not like to tell you of it,' said the Admiral bluntly, 'not being one to blow his own trumpet.' He got to his feet. 'And now, if Your Grace will pardon me, I must rejoin my wife.'

The Duke rose and extended a thin white hand.

'I'm sincerely grateful to you, Sir William. Perhaps one day I shall have the privilege of meeting the other members of your family.'

He did not wait for an answer, but with a slight bow, strolled off towards the exit doors. The Admiral stared after him, his expression half-puzzled, half-resentful; then with a shrug of his shoulders, he made his way back to the lecture room.

Although Hector had naturally paid his duty visit to Number Twenty-two Grosvenor Square, he didn't thereafter expect to enjoy much of his father's hospitality. It came as a surprise when on Tuesday he received a note from the Duke, requesting him to call round for 'an informal chat' at five the same afternoon.

As the invitation was in the nature of a royal command, Hector cancelled his other appointments, dressed with particular care, and at precisely five o'clock trod up the front steps of his father's mansion. He was admitted by Manion, His Grace's steward, who had the reputation for being twice as starchy as his ducal master.

The Duke was in his book room, a copy of Virgil's *Bucolics* on his knee and a glass of wine at his elbow. He did not rise, but dismissed Manion and summoned his son with one graceful movement of the hand.

'Good afternoon, Hector,' he said. 'Before you sit down, pour yourself a glass of the amontillado. If you like it I shall bid Hodge send you a case, but I beg you won't waste it on Hubert. He has no palate, alas.'

Informed by this greeting that the interview was to be conducted on a friendly note, Hector poured himself a glass of sherry, carried it to a chair, and waited to be enlightened.

The Duke wasted no time. 'I hear,' he said, 'that you've won a hundred guineas in a wager?'

Hector nodded. 'I thought that must be why you sent for me. I suppose Hubert blew the gaff?'

'He told me part of the story. Admiral Carey filled in certain omissions – at my request.'

Hector coloured. 'I see. May I ask, sir, where you met Sir William?'

'At Lady Grimsby's, last evening.' The Duke closed his book and set it aside.

'Why did you do it?' he asked.

'Pique,' Hector answered. 'I was out of patience with Hubert and wanted to give him a set-down. The chance offered, and I took it.'

'The terms of the bet required you to work for a week. You were at Kettleby Manor rather longer. Why was that?'

Hector glanced up, expecting to see in his father's eyes the usual cold disapproval. He met instead an expression of polite interest. He said uncertainly, 'I became . . . involved . . . with the Carey family. I felt sorry for young Jason Carey. He's a good lad, despite his unfortunate upbringing.'

The Duke nodded. 'Some men create their own disasters. I fear Carey's one of them.'

As Hector remained silent, the Duke continued. 'One recalls the tragedy of his wife.'

'She died.' Hector spoke a little too quickly, and the Duke regarded him quizzically.

'She did indeed, but not before she'd cuckolded her husband. She eloped with the dashing Comte de Rennes. Carey gave out that she'd died of a fever in Marseilles. It was an effective face-saver. Deceived most people.'

'But not you?'

'No. I had the true story from the Comte's father, you see. The Duc de Rennes was my friend. I stayed with him many times in Paris, before the Revolution. When the Terror began, his family broke apart. His wife and four younger children went with him to take refuge in Switzerland. His oldest son and daughter declared for Napoleon. Etien became a colonel in the Imperial Guard, and the girl married some upstart princeling. They prospered until Bonaparte was crushed and exiled; then they were stripped of their ill-gotten gains. Etien scraped a living as a gambler. He met Georgina Carey in Marseilles, seduced her, and persuaded her to run off with him. She helped him run his gaming house in Paris, and died a year or so later. The Comte did not long survive her.'

'What?' said Hector, so sharply that the Duke raised his eyebrows.

'Do you mean to tell me,' said Hector, 'that Etien de Rennes is dead?'

'Oh, very. I imagine the brandy did for him.'

'Sir William never spoke of his death.'

'Probably never knew of it. It was hardly a loss to the world. Why does it disturb you?'

Hector shrugged. 'I'd formed a theory, and you've just exploded it.' He thought for a moment, then said, 'You mentioned a sister, sir.'

'Yes. Elise de Rennes.'

'What was she like?'

'Like no other child I ever met,' said the Duke. 'A witch in the making. Blonde hair that hung thick and wild to her waist, a skin as white as milk, delicate hands and feet. She kept her gaze downcast, but if she chanced to look up, one saw that her eyes were as bold and green as a hunting cat's.'

'Where is she now?'

'I've no idea. Is it important?'

'It could be.' Again, Hector saw in his father's face that expression of concern, and on impulse he said, 'I told you that at Kettleby I became involved in the Careys' problems. The chief of them was that William Carey was involved with a gang of smugglers. I imagined Etien de Rennes was at its head, but if, as you say, he's dead . . .' He thought a minute, then continued. 'This sister of his . . . would she be capable of directing such an operation?'

'Elise de Rennes is capable of anything. She's as avaricious as she's ruthless.'

As Hector looked anxious, the Duke said, 'What precisely is it that you fear?'

'I'm afraid that Piggott and the woman may strike at Carey through his son . . . hold him to ransom, or harm him in some way.'

'I would strongly advise the man to call in the Law.'

'He's unwilling to do so.' As the Duke looked incredulous,

Hector said quickly, 'There are reasons. I've persuaded him to set two of his servants to keep an eye on the boy, but it's wellnigh impossible to guard a lively eleven-year-old for twenty-four hours of the day. I wish I knew what's best to be done.'

Looking at Hector's troubled face, the Duke said carefully, 'You appear to have a more than academic interest in the family.'

'I do. I regard them as my friends – and I've a particular regard for Miss Serena Osmond, the Admiral's niece.'

'Ah. And does Miss Osmond return the sentiment?'

'Not yet. I hope to win her over.'

'I see. May I meet her?'

'Of course – but not, if you don't mind, till the moment is right.'

The Duke bent his head. 'Let us hope that that will be soon. In the mean time, Hector, if I can be of service to you, I rely on you to say so.'

'I will, sir, and thank you.'

Hector smiled and took his leave; but the Duke sat for a long time at the window, pondering on what he had learned.

XXXV

It was on the following afternoon that Wiske saw Laval for the second time. Knowing that the Admiral had taken Jason on the long-promised visit to Greenwich, he carried his news straight to Berkeley Square.

Ushered into the study where Hector was glancing through a pile of unanswered letters, he said thankfully, 'My lord, I'm right glad to find you home. I seed Laval, sir.'

'Where?' demanded Hector, motioning to Wiske to sit down.

The groom perched on the edge of a straight-backed chair. 'In Piccadilly,' he said. 'I was set to ride to the saddler's at Charing Cross to pick up some harness, when I see 'im comin' down Bond Street.'

'Was the woman with him?'

'Aye, she was.'

'Did you see her face?'

'I did, sir. She turned her head to look at some geegaws in a window, an' I seed her quite plain. Yaller hair, an' her eyes big an' bold as a cat's.'

This echo of the Duke's phrase sent a coldness down Hector's spine.

'Did they see you?' he said.

'No, for I hid be'ind a vintner's dray. I watched 'em walk a short ways down the road, and then they hailed a hackney carriage, an' she and Laval climbed in an' druv off towards the circus.' Wiske hesitated. 'I had to make up me mind, quick. I followed 'em. I hope I did right.'

'Quite right. Where did they go?'

'A good ways. Along the Strand, past Aldwych, up Fleet Street. I thought mebbe they'd lodgin's in the City. I'd a job of it wi' all the carts an' carriages, but I kep' 'em in sight. Came past St Paul's, an' Eastcheap, an' the Tower. By then, it was plain as a pikestaff where they was bound.'

As Hector looked puzzled, Wiske smiled kindly. 'Well, my lord, if Piggott's on the smugglin' lay, stands to reason he must bring 'is goods in somewheres. Reckon London Docks is as good a port as any.'

'Of course.'

'Like I said,' continued Wiske, 'they passed by the Tower, an' along Smithfield, an' then they turned off of the high road and made for the river. I took note o' the name o' the street. Nightingale Lane. Couldn't follow too close, down there, for there weren't so many folks about. The hackney stopped at the foot o' the lane. That's wharves an' then the water. I seed the pair on 'em climb down, an' pay off the hackney, an' go inter a buildin' on the wharfside. I waited till the hackney came back and passed by me. Then I moved close to take a good look at the place.'

'And?'

'An old 'ouse, none too grand, my lord. Not the kind o' place for such a fine lady. Paint peelin', and all the shutters up. Still, they went inside, the pair on 'em. I waited more'n an hour, to see would they come out again, but they stayed within. I thought of askin' at the inn, a bit further up. The Swan Inn. Then I thought no, it'd mebbe tip someone the wink, so I turned about an' came straight 'ere . . . seein' as the Admiral's from 'ome, my lord.'

Hector nodded. 'Very wise of you. When will he be back from Greenwich?'

'Five o'clock the latest, 'e said, my lord.'

'Then I shall call at quarter past. Be sure you're on hand, Wiske. Somehow we have to convince him that he must take action against these people.'

'Poppycock!' said Sir William angrily. 'Humdudgeon! Wiske has only to see a gipsy and a blonde woman for him to fall into a panic!'

'Wiske recognised Laval,' said Hector. 'He saw him come from Bond Street, which is a stone's throw from this house. Laval could well have been spying out the lie of the land. He was with a woman. Wiske tracked the pair of them to a run-down building on dockside . . . hardly the sort of place for a respectable female, let alone a lady of quality.'

'Unless she aimed to enjoy a tumble with her paramour,'

retorted Sir William. 'There's many a high-born lady likes the smell of the stable.'

'Sir,' said Hector impatiently, 'I'm convinced that the woman is Elise de Rennes, Etien's sister. If she was with Laval, that places her squarely in Piggott's camp. It proves beyond doubt that Piggott has sold you out. You can't ignore the danger to Jason. You must report the whole to the authorities.'

'And what am I to report, pray? That my head groom saw a pedlar at a fair, in company with a blonde female? That he saw them a second time, in Bond Street? Damme, I'd be laughed out of Town if I told such a rigmarole.'

'Not if you warn the Runners and the Excisemen that the pedlar and the woman are in league with Piggott to bring contraband into England.'

Sir William glared at Hector. 'And what proof should I offer of that?'

'The brandy and wine in your cellars, Sir William. I'll lay odds you've allowed Piggott to store his wares there these many years.'

The Admiral's face was clammy with sweat. 'If that were true,' he said, 'd'ye think I'd tell the Excisemen of it?' He struck his clenched fist on the arm of his chair. 'I'll not go crawling to a bunch of pettifogging clerks who lay safe abed while I and my shipmates were out fighting the French. I never made a penny from Piggott's trade, save on what I bought for my own consumption. If I help to bring wine and brandy to gentlefolk without feeding the Custom's carrion crows, so much the better! I'll not run to the authorities, my lord, I'll not run my neck into a noose and spoil my reputation, merely to satisfy you.'

'It's not your reputation that's at stake,' said Hector angrily. 'It's Jason's safety. God knows what these people want with him, but he must be protected. We can't do it ourselves, we must have help. Go to the officials, tell them whatever story you please, say that Piggott duped you, say you wish to make a clean breast of things. Tell them about the house on the docks, offer to co-operate with them any way you can, so long as in exchange they defend Jason.'

The Admiral met Hector's gaze. 'You don't understand,' he said dully. 'If I call in the Law, I'll make an open enemy of Piggott.'

'He's your enemy now. You know it, sir.'

The Admiral remained stubbornly silent.

'You've no choice,' Hector said, and the old man sighed.

'Very well. I'll go to Bow Street and the Custom House, and see what can be arranged.'

'And you'll warn Jason?'

'Yes,' the Admiral said. 'I'll warn him.'

Hector took his leave, but the day's trials were by no means over. He had taken no more than a few steps along Bruton Street when he saw Ensign Nettlebed hurrying towards him.

'My lord Wycombe,' cried Crosby, blocking Hector's path and glaring at him in a highly belligerent way, 'a word with you, if you please.'

'Make it brief, Mr Nettlebed. I'm engaged to dine out this evening.'

'Oh, I'll be brief, sir.' Crosby's face was mottled red and white, his whole frame quivered with resentment. 'I've but one thing to say to you, and it's this. You have come between me and the lady I love, sir, and I won't stand for it, d'ye hear? I won't stand for it!'

'What the deuce are you talking about?' said Hector coldly. 'What lady?'

'No, no, sir, that sacred name shall not pass my lips. I'm a gentleman, I hope!'

'You're foxed, Mr Nettlebed! Go home and sleep it off.'

'I am not drunk, sir, I'm sober as a judge, and I'm here to give you solemn warning to cease your interference in my concerns.'

Light dawned on Hector. 'If you're talking of Miss Laurel Carey,' he said, 'I assure you you're wide of the mark. I've no interest in her except as a friend.'

'Do not,' said Crosby awfully, throwing out his chest till the buttons seemed ready to burst. 'Do not presume to speak that angel's name! You are not worthy, sir! I know what sly tricks you've employed, these past weeks – encouraging every Tom, Dick and Harry to flatter and beguile that innocent child, dazzling her with your wealth and consequence, turning her against those who hold her in true affection! Well, my lord

Wycombe, it's gone far enough. Know that if you persist in these pernicious attempts, I shall demand satisfaction!'

'Not of me, you won't,' said Hector firmly. 'Miss Carey is free to choose her friends where she finds them. If you disapprove, take up the matter with her. Better still, keep your feelings to yourself. Nothing is gained by this sort of whingeing complaint. Now, if you'll excuse me, I've an appointment to keep.'

He made as if to walk on, but Crosby, losing the last vestige of his self-control, snatched at Hector's shoulder and aimed a wild punch at him. Hector parried the blow on his upraised arm and seized Crosby's wrist in a painful grip.

'That's enough,' he snapped. 'Much as I'd like to teach you a lesson, I don't approve of brawling in the street – and nor should you, if you hope to succeed in a military career. I'll bid you a very good day.'

With a final shake, he released Crosby, and strode away towards the square. Crosby hesitated a moment, glaring with open hatred at his lordship's retreating back; then he set off muttering to the nearest public house, there to drown his sorrows in a bottle of brandy.

XXXVI

The Admiral's detestation of what he termed pettifogging clerks was heightened by his dealings with the officials of Bow Street and the Custom House.

The Runners, as he had foreseen, refused point blank to take action on such slight evidence as he could provide. They insisted that no crime had been committed against him or any member of his family, nothing discreditable was known about the house on dockside, and the smuggling of contraband was in any case a matter not for them but for the Excisemen.

The Excisemen, on their part, showed intense interest in the Admiral's revelations, but insisted that the centre of Piggott's operations must lie not in London, but in Kettleby. They sent their agents *ventre à terre* to Leicestershire, and brushed aside all requests that they pursue the trail of Laval and Elise de Rennes.

Sir William was subjected to relentless questioning by sharp-faced men of the law; and when he asked what protection would be given to his son, he received such evasive answers that he was driven to the point of apoplexy.

Lady Carey, in hourly dread of seeing her husband hauled off to gaol, was quite unable to concentrate on anything else. She wandered aimlessly about the house, smelling-salts in hand, and left Serena to see that meals were ordered, tradesmen paid and the household kept from sliding into chaos.

However, by Friday evening, seeing that Sir William was still a free man and that the last of his inquisitors had departed, she agreed to take up the threads of her life again, and to accompany Serena and Laurel to the Seftons' dress ball.

'Not that I feel the least bit festive,' she told Serena, 'but dear Lady Sefton has been kind enough to lend us her support, and it would be the height of ingratitude to fail her now.'

Serena was glad of this decision, not only because she felt it would do them all good to be in cheerful company, but also because she wanted a chance to speak to Lord Hector.

So often during the past two days she had longed for his

support, his good-humoured and sage advice, his ability to make the most daunting obstacles seem of no account.

She dressed for the party with particular care, choosing a gown of cream brocade with an overskirt of fine lace that set off the warm tones of her hair and skin. She allowed Lady Carey's dresser to arrange her hair in a new style, knotted high on top of her head with curls falling over the ears. At her throat she fastened the delicate diamond necklace bequeathed her by her grandmother. A gauze scarf, long cream gloves, satin reticule and satin slippers completed her toilette, and in her hand she carried the posy of small pale roses his lordship had sent her that morning.

Sir William did not accompany his womenfolk, saying that he wouldn't leave Jason alone till Piggott's hash was settled once and for all.

It was just on ten o'clock when they entered the Seftons' house, and as the main press of guests had not yet arrived they were able to enjoy some conversation with their hosts. Lady Sefton, despite her restless and gossipy manner, was a kind-hearted woman, and tonight she was generous in her praise of Serena and Laurel. Watching them move away with Lady Carey, she remarked to her husband that of all the girls she'd sponsored over the years, none pleased her more than Miss Osmond and Miss Carey. 'They'll marry to advantage,' she prophesied. 'Hector Wycombe has been most particular in his attentions to Miss Osmond, and Sally Jersey tells me young Lychgate is showing a marked interest in Miss Carey.'

'Too early to tell,' opined her husband. 'The Wycombes and Lychgates may have something to say in the matter. Besides, I thought the Carey gal was soft on young Thingummy – that soldier-fellow.'

'A passing infatuation,' said Lady Sefton airily. 'What chit of sixteen isn't bowled over by a hussar uniform? But an ensign, my dear, can't compete with the son of an earl, and if Lychgate chooses to throw his cap in the ring, Mr Nettlebed's hopes are at an end.'

In point of fact the cap had already been thrown. Mr Lychgate was not only enchanted with Laurel Carey's beauty, he perceived in her all the qualities he desired in a wife: good humour, modesty of manner, and a love of the country life. Her lineage was respectable and her dowry would be handsome, factors which counted with his parents if not with him. He set himself to win Laurel's affections, showing far greater adroitness than the unfortunate Mr Nettlebed. While Crosby indulged in flourishing speeches, languishing looks, and reams of bad poetry, Frederic saw to it that Laurel felt cosseted and protected by his attentions. He gave her gifts she truly appreciated – a basket of fresh strawberries, a blue china bowl filled with pot-pourri – and took her to places she enjoyed, such as the beautiful gardens made by Queen Charlotte at Kew.

Tonight he came early to the ball, and was the first to welcome the Careys when they turned from greeting their hosts. Crosby, arriving later with the main flood of fashionables, found the high ground already lost. Mr Lychgate had not only settled his party in seats close to the ballroom, but had drawn in several of his friends, so that the girls' dance-cards were quickly filled. Crosby had to be content with one paltry country dance with Miss Carey.

His was not a nature that could accept disappointment. Since his brangle with Lord Hector two days earlier, he had spent his time brooding over his imagined ills and consuming an inordinate amount of brandy. This latest setback put him in such a rage that he could think of nothing but how to level the score, not only with Frederic Lychgate but with Lord Hector, whom he saw as the source of all evil.

His first thought was to find his lordship and call him out, but a search of the reception rooms established that Lord Hector was not yet present.

Thwarted in this, Crosby looked for another weapon and found it in Lady Ainsford, who was sitting alone in an alcove, watching the quadrille with a very sour expression. The gentleman she had coerced into standing up with her daughter was looking the picture of boredom, and Anna wasn't making the least push to entertain him. Lady Ainsford could not help noticing that Miss Osmond's partner was laughing and chatting in a most provoking way. Lady Ainsford was wondering how she could contrive to put the odious girl in her place, when she heard a discreet cough, and looked up to see Ensign Crosby Nettlebed at her side.

Crosby was by no means one of the young men Lady Ainsford

thought worthy of cultivation, and she fixed him with an arctic stare.

'Well, Mr Nettlebed? What is it?'

Crosby bowed obsequiously. 'If your la'yship permits . . . a few words with your la'yship?'

'About what, pray?'

Crosby lowered his eyelids. 'A subject of the utmost delicacy, ma'am. One that will interest you as a lifelong friend of His Grace of Wycombe.'

'Stop beating about the bush, Mr Nettlebed. Say what you have to say without roundaboutation.'

'It touches, Lady Ainsford, on the . . . shall we say friendship . . . between Lord Hector Wycombe and Miss Osmond.'

Lady Ainsford stared, torn between a desire to snub Mr Nettlebed and avid curiosity. At length she patted the chair next to hers. Mr Nettlebed sat down cautiously, since the dress trousers of the hussars did not permit of easy bending, and said portentously:

'It must have come to your notice, your la'yship, that Miss Osmond has been much in his lordship's company since she came to London?'

'What of it?'

'Miss Osmond is trying to fix the interest of Lord Hector.'

'No crime in that, I suppose.' Lady Ainsford's tone was snappish. She wouldn't allow this tuft-hunter to waste her time with stories she already knew by heart.

Crosby touched a finger to his moustachios. 'But are you aware, ma'am, how this very extraordinary friendship came about?'

'I believe they met at Admiral Carey's home.'

'They did indeed.' Crosby permitted himself a sly smile. 'And in very singular circumstances, which I'm persuaded have allowed Miss Osmond to exert a quite unnatural influence over Lord Hector. If I may acquaint you with the full facts . . .?'

Again her ladyship hesitated, and again the bait proved irresistible. She gave a curt nod, and Crosby recounted the tale of Hector's deception at Kettleby Manor.

Lady Ainsford listened in shocked silence; and when her daughter came over to her at the end of the quadrille, sent her away with a sharp command to go and find someone else to talk to as she had urgent matters to discuss with Mr Nettlebed.

When Crosby had made an end, Lady Ainsford said, 'Are you telling me that this disgraceful situation endured for over three weeks? That for that whole period Lord Hector was at close quarters with this . . . this adventuress?'

'Precisely, ma'am.' Crosby coughed delicately. 'Modesty forbids me to point out what . . . opportunities . . . must have been afforded her in such compromising circumstances.'

'Indeed.' Lady Ainsford stared at Serena, who could be seen some way off, talking to Lord Melbourne. 'Why, what an unprincipled Jezebel it is! No doubt she cast out her lures for him, and now he can't be rid of her for fear she might reveal the truth. How the tongues would wag if it became known that a member of the House of Wycombe had so demeaned himself! Tell me, Mr Nettlebed, who else knows of this?'

'Several people in Kettleby, I imagine, but few in London. Miss Osmond won't care to make it public, for that would destroy her hold over Lord Hector, would it not?'

'As you say.' A gleam of malice shone in her ladyship's eyes. Rising to her feet, she gathered up her reticule and fan.

'Leave all to me,' she directed. 'I fancy I can put an end to Miss Osmond's ambitions to be Lady Hector.'

Crosby bowed, and watched Lady Ainsford march away like a gladiator preparing to deliver the *coup de grâce* to his dearest foe.

XXXVII

Serena was about to take the floor in the waltz with Mr Lychgate when she found her path blocked by the formidable figure of Lady Ainsford. She dropped a polite curtsey, but her ladyship waved this greeting aside, and addressed herself to Mr Lychgate.

'I wish, sir, to speak with Miss Osmond in private.'

As Frederic started to protest, Serena laid her fingers on his arm and said quickly, 'Mr Lychgate will forgive me, I'm sure. I'm at your disposal, ma'am.'

Turning on her heel, Lady Ainsford led the way from the ballroom and through two antechambers to a room that had been set aside for the guests' cloaks. Here she closed the door and wheeled to face Serena.

'I have summoned you here, Miss Osmond,' she said, 'to warn you to cease your sordid liaison with Lord Hector Wycombe.'

Serena stared at the older woman in disbelief. Was it possible, she wondered, that her ladyship was subject to fits of insanity?

'I'm afraid I don't understand,' she said.

'Oh don't try to play the innocent with me, miss! I know how you contrived to trap his lordship. It's plain as a pikestaff what went on at Kettleby. Doubtless you thought that by luring him to your bed, you could secure an offer of marriage. Disabuse yourself of that notion, I beg. You will not be allowed to continue your shameless blackmail. I have the confidence of His Grace the Duke, and I promise you I intend to inform him of this whole sorry episode. He will very soon give you your *congé*!'

As she listened to this diatribe, Serena's amazement turned to icy rage. Drawing herself up, she said in as level a voice as she could manage, 'You're mistaken, ma'am. No liaison exists between Lord Hector and me. As to your carrying this story to His Grace, I fear he will find it stale news. Lord Hector has already told him what passed at my uncle's house, and it was nothing discreditable or shameful, as you seem to think. Lord Hector made an excellent tutor.'

'Don't bandy words with me, you insolent bawd,' cried Lady

Ainsford. 'I'll see you drummed out of polite society! I'll let your mushroom admirers know what sort of creature you are. I'll . . .'

'You will hold your poisonous tongue, Lady Ainsford! If you utter one lie about me, or any member of my family, I shall take pleasure in hauling you to court! I have nothing further to say to you. Pray stand out of my way.'

Lady Ainsford had expected fear in her victim, tears, even a plea for mercy. Instead she found herself face to face with an angry disdain that drove her to a frenzy

'You won't succeed in your schemes, Miss Osmond,' she said in a shaking voice. 'You will never marry Hector Wycombe. Tell me, has he made you an offer yet?' As Serena was silent, triumph lit her ladyship's eyes. 'I see he has not. Nor will he. A Wycombe may amuse himself with the likes of you, but will never marry beneath him, and so you will find.'

'Stand aside!' Serena was white-faced, her eyes blazed, she looked so fierce that her ladyship was suddenly afraid, and took a pace backwards; but before Serena could move, there was the sound of footsteps in the corridor outside, and the door was flung open by a flunkey bearing an armful of cloaks. Lady Ainsford moved aside, and Serena stalked past her without a word.

She did not return to the ballroom. She was trembling with rage, her cheeks burned, her hands were ice-cold. She walked blindly along the corridor, reached the stairway, and started down it.

Her mind was in turmoil. Lady Ainsford's coarse insults, her venomous threats, were not the cause of her distress. It was the creature's last thrust that had gone home.

Lord Hector had not proposed marriage, and never would. He had been amusing himself, no more. His gifts, his gallantries, even the pains he had taken to send her mama to Brighton, were all part of it. If at Vauxhall she had shown herself a little more compliant, he might by now have made her a very different sort of offer, one that included a house, a carriage and horses, expensive jewels, but not the Wycombe name.

The irony of it was that now at last she knew how much she longed to marry him. All these weeks when she had tried to pretend indifference to him, it had been nothing but self-deception.

Nothing remained but for her to retire to virtuous spinsterhood, or emigrate to China or High Brazil, where she need never be obliged to set eyes on him again!

Tears began to pour down her cheeks so that she could scarcely see the steps ahead of her. She stumbled and almost fell. A hand reached out to steady her, and a voice said, 'My dear Miss Osmond! I've been searching everywhere for you.'

Lifting her head, she saw Lord Hector gazing at her with anxious concern. She uttered the first words that came to her.

'Go away! Please go away!'

For answer he put an arm round her shoulders and gently turned her about.

'Let us find somewhere quieter,' he suggested. He led her up the stairs, past a group of guests, and through a door on his left. They entered what was apparently Lord Sefton's study. Candle-light shone on well-filled bookshelves, a large desk. An open window allowed cool air to flow in from the garden below. A row of crystal decanters stood on a side table.

Serena sank down on the nearest chair.

'Would you care for a little brandy?' asked Hector.

'No!' said Serena, fumbling in her reticule for her kerchief, and dabbing at her eyes.

He poured a glass of water and handed it to her. 'Please tell me,' he said, 'what's occurred to upset you so.'

She swallowed a sob. 'Nothing. It's nothing.'

Hector came to stand beside her chair. 'You know this is very disturbing! If "nothing" makes you cry your eyes out, how will it be when something serious befalls you! I can't have my wife behaving like a watering-pot, you know.'

Serena stared at him blankly. She could have sworn he'd said 'my wife'. She supposed her ears were playing her tricks. She drew a deep breath, intending to make a dignified response, but achieved only a loud hiccup.

'Drink some water,' advised his lordship, 'and then try holding your breath.'

Serena did as she was bid, glowering at him above the rim of the glass. To her alarm he went down on one knee beside her.

'Dearest Serena,' he said, 'I love you to distraction, and beg you will do me the honour to marry me.'

'I can't,' said Serena. 'Hup. You d-don't mean it. It's another of your hup-horrible jokes.'

'I promise you I was never more serious in my life.' Hector removed the glass from Serena's hand and took both her hands in his. 'I'm not a fly-by-night, you know. I don't resemble Lucius Radley. In general I'm truthful, well-behaved and commonsensical. Don't hold my single act of lunacy against me for the rest of my days.'

'Lady Ainsford said, hup, she called me a bawd. She said I must end my sordid hup liaison with you.'

'Avenge the insult. Say you'll marry me.'

As Serena tried to draw her hands away, he took her in his arms and kissed her. Against her better judgement, Serena returned the embrace, which seemed to inspire him to fresh efforts. At length he released her and regarded her with marked complacency.

'That did the trick,' he said.

'What do you mean?'

'Cured your hiccups,' he pointed out. 'Come Serena, no more quibbling. I love you and wish to marry you. I dare to think you love me. Say yes, I beg. We've wasted enough time.'

Serena sighed. 'Yes,' she said.

His face lit in a beatific smile. He rose and drew her to her feet.

'Shall we go and find Lady Carey, or do you prefer to go home and let your uncle be the first to hear our good news?'

'I don't want to meet Lady Ainsford,' said Serena, confused. 'But the Seftons . . . I should say goodnight . . .'

'You may write them a note tomorrow,' said his lordship, guiding her towards the door, 'and the butler shall convey a message to Lady Carey that I've taken you home.'

Serena made no further demur. She was content to float in felicity down the stairway, her fingers linked with Hector's; and as she rode beside him in the carriage through the lamplit streets, she thought that nothing in the world could dim the happiness of this night.

But when they reached Bruton Street, they found a scene of pandemonium. Lights blazed in every window, and as the carriage halted at the foot of the steps, the front door was thrown open and they saw Sir William beckoning to them urgently.

They ran to join him. In the hallway behind him a group of servants clustered round the prone figure of the butler Sudbury.

On one side of him knelt Wiske, nursing a basin full of bloodied water, and on the other a black-suited man was engaged in binding up a gaping wound in Sudbury's upper arm.

The Admiral cast an arm about Serena, clinging to her. His face was ashen.

'Those devils have taken Jason,' he said thickly. 'They left a message. They say if I don't call off the Law, they'll kill him.'

XXXVIII

Hector helped Serena bring the Admiral from the hall to the library, guided him to a chair and poured him a shot of rum. The liquor brought colour back to the old man's face, and Hector asked him if Lady Carey had been sent for.

Sir William nodded. 'Timmins went in the phaeton, first to fetch Dr Hastings to Sudbury, and then to bring my wife and the girls home. When I saw you and Serena, I thought you must have had the message.'

'No, but I'm sure her ladyship has it by now and will be with us shortly. Can you tell us exactly what happened?'

'It was a few minutes past midnight,' the Admiral said. 'I heard a commotion in the stable yard. Wiske was shouting for help. I ran through the house to the kitchen door and saw him near the mews gate, fighting off two Mohocks. They were masked and armed with cudgels. I snatched up the kitchen poker and ran to aid Wiske. Jason must have heard the shouting and come downstairs from his bedroom.

'While I was still in the yard, there was a ring at the front door and Sudbury went to answer it. He found himself facing two thugs with pistols. He tried to slam the door, but was shot. Jason turned to run back up the stair, but the men seized him and bundled him out of the house and into a waiting carriage. Sudbury saw that much before he collapsed.

'The Mohocks bolted when they heard the shot. We came into the house and found Sudbury. The note was on the floor beside him.' Sir William drew a crumpled piece of paper from his pocket and handed it to Hector.

' "We took the boy," ' Hector read. ' "Call off your dogs, or we kill him." '

Hector frowned. 'It's strange they make no demand for ransom. Perhaps that will come later.'

The Admiral looked up wearily. 'Oh yes, they'll demand their pound of flesh.'

'You must call in the runners,' said Serena urgently, but he shook his head.

'No. The note forbids that. These rogues know they must quit England. They've taken Jason, he's their safe-conduct ticket. They know I'll not do anything to endanger him.'

Serena put a hand on the Admiral's shoulder. 'They won't harm him, Uncle. How could they, he's only a child.'

Hector said quietly, 'A child who can identify them and testify against them in a court of law. We can't count on their releasing him.'

'There's nothing to be done,' muttered the Admiral in despair. 'If I make any move, Jason will be killed.'

'I agree it would be pointless to apply to Bow Street,' Hector said. 'They've already disclaimed responsibility, and we've no time to argue. Nor can you trust the Excisemen. Piggott evidently knows all about your visit to them. My guess is, someone at the Custom House tipped him the wink.'

As he spoke, rapid footsteps sounded in the hall, and Lady Carey and Laurel burst into the room.

'William,' cried Lady Carey, 'what's happened to Jason? Timmins gave me such a garbled story I couldn't make head nor tail of it.'

Sir William put his arms about his wife and daughter. 'Jason has been kidnapped by Piggott,' he said. 'The villain left a note. If we attempt to call in the Law, Jason will be killed. There's naught we can do, save watch and pray for his safe return.'

The two ladies broke into cries of protest. Hector said quickly, 'Sir William, we've a few shots in our locker yet.' As the Careys turned to face him, he continued. 'You're right in saying Piggott and his gang will try to leave the country. They will probably take ship for France as soon as possible.'

'Probably, yes.'

'We know that the woman de Rennes, and Laval, went to a house in Nightingale Lane. By Wiske's description, that lies close to the London Stillwater Dock at Wapping.'

'Aye.'

'It's likely that the house on dockside is Piggott's London warehouse – and that the ship that runs in goods for him is moored close to the Wapping wharfs.'

'Perhaps, but I don't see how that helps us.'

'If we go there . . . you and I and Wiske . . . we may be able to prevent Piggott from taking Jason abroad. They won't sail before daybreak, I imagine.'

'Have to wait for the high spring tide,' said Sir William, brightening a little. 'That'll be, let's see, half past eight tomorrow morning, at the earliest.' He sprang to his feet. 'Yes, by God, it's a chance. We'll leave at once. We must have pistols, shot. Where's Wiske?' He reached for the bellrope, but Hector caught his arm.

'A moment, sir. There's one other thing we must do.'

'What's that?'

'We must make sure that if we fail to stop Piggott, someone else will.'

Sir William's jaw jutted. 'I won't set on the Law, Wycombe.'

'There may be another way. I visited the Wapping docks last year. Lord Ranulph, who's a director of the London Dock Company, was kind enough to invite me to sample some of the wines in the bonded vaults. In the course of the visit he told me a great deal about the organisation of the dockyards. Each one has its own militia, I understand, and takes measures to prevent the plundering of its goods. If we alert them . . .'

'Out of the question. Piggott will learn of it.'

'Ranulph must be warned to act only in the last resort.'

'Oh? And who will warn him, my lord? You, or I?'

'My father,' said Hector coolly. 'Give me pen and paper and I'll write him a letter. Timmins can deliver it.'

'No,' said Serena unexpectedly. 'I will. There's a need for secrecy.'

Hector smiled at her. 'True, my love.' He slid his signet ring from his finger and placed it in her palm.

'Give him this,' he said, 'and my respects. Tell him that if all goes to plan I shall call on him in the morning.'

He sat down to pen his message, while Serena hurried away to put off her ballroom finery, and Sir William and Wiske collected weapons and clothes for their coming venture.

It was past one o'clock when Serena alighted from the Careys' carriage outside Number Twenty-two Grosvenor Square. She saw with relief that lights still blazed in the lower parts of the house, for to raise the Duke's household at this hour would have been daunting indeed. As it was, she felt the impropriety of calling on a gentleman so late at night, and unattended; but the need for secrecy had persuaded her against bringing a maid with her.

Summoning up her courage, she climbed the steps and rang the doorbell. It was answered with alarming speed by a black-clad butler of such impressive aspect that Serena was tempted to flee back to the coach; but she steeled herself and said with as much firmness as she could command that she had brought a letter from Lord Hector Wycombe, which she must give to His Grace at once.

The butler regarded her with icy disfavour.

'His Grace, Miss,' he said repressively, 'has retired to his bed. If you will give me the letter, I will see that he has it in the morning.'

He held out his hand, but Serena tightened her grip on the letter, and put up her chin.

'Tomorrow won't do,' she said. 'Pray inform the Duke that Miss Serena Osmond wishes to speak with him on a matter of the greatest urgency. You will also please give him this ring.'

The butler considered the ring and seemed to recognise it, for his expression became a shade less supercilious; but he still barred Serena's path.

'If Miss will wait,' he said, 'I shall enquire if His Grace is able to see Miss.'

He was about to turn away, when a voice spoke behind him.

'Who is it, Hodge?'

'Miss Serena Osmond, Your Grace.'

'Then admit her at once, man! Don't keep her waiting on the doorstep!'

Hodge seemed taken aback by the order, but he complied with a murmured apology, and Serena moved into the hall.

It was magnificently appointed, the tessellated marble floor, the grand sweep of the staircase and the immense chandelier all suggesting the opulent taste of a past era. Two gentlemen stood facing her. One was portly, rubicund, dressed in the sombre garb of a man of God. The other had exchanged his evening coat for a jacket of dark brocade, and his shoes for embroidered slippers. He came towards Serena, and as she took his outstretched hand, and made her curtsey, she saw that in features he very much resembled Hector. She said quickly,

'My lord Duke, please forgive this intrusion. You don't know me, but . . .'

'I know of you, Miss Osmond. Hector has spoken of you, and this week I had the pleasure of conversing with your uncle, William Carey. I think you've not met my third son, Hubert?'

Serena curtsied again, and received a stiff bow from Lord Hubert. She turned back to the Duke.

'Hector . . . Lord Hector . . . desired me to give you these, sir.' She held out the letter and the ring. The Duke took them, watching her sharply.

'Is he in trouble, ma'am?'

'No. That is, not yet. If . . . if we might talk in private, sir.'

The Duke glanced at Lord Hubert, who was looking scandalised.

'I'm sure you will excuse us.'

'Papa,' said Hubert, 'I really don't think you should . . .'

'Is it not time you returned to Berkeley Square, Hubert?' said his father gently. 'I wish to speak to Miss Osmond.'

Hubert moved away, disapproval in every inch of his bearing. The Duke ushered Serena into a small parlour, set a chair for her, and broke the seal on Hector's letter. He read it through twice, his brow furrowed. At length he looked up.

'Jason Carey has been kidnapped by smugglers?'

'I know you must find it hard to believe, Duke, but . . .'

'I believe you, but I confess I don't grasp the motive. Did they demand ransom?'

'Not yet. That'll come, not a doubt of it. In the meantime, Jason's to serve as hostage till they're safe in France. My uncle and Lord Hector and our groom, Wiske, have gone to Piggott's house on the docks. They will try if they can to free Jason . . . prevent his being forced aboard a ship. But if they fail, someone must intervene to see Piggott doesn't get away.'

'I would have thought an appeal to the regular Law . . .'

'That won't serve. There's too little time, too many complications. So if you will be so good as to use your influence with Lord Ranulph . . . ask him to alert the company's militia, and instruct them that Piggott's ship mustn't be allowed to sail. Lord

Hector said that perhaps a revenue cutter could be called into play. Lord Ranulph would know how to arrange it.'

'I see. I'll send word to him at once.'

'That won't suffice,' said Serena impatiently. 'We must act with all speed, sir. My uncle's gone by boat with the others . . . he said it would be quicker and attract less attention. They should be almost at the Hermitage wharfs by now. That's at Wapping. I do beg you to go yourself to Lord Ranulph and impress on him the need for haste!'

The Duke's eyebrows rose a fraction, but he said blandly, 'You're quite right, Miss Osmond. I'll have the carriage brought round at once.'

'A plain carriage,' warned Serena. 'No crest on the panel. We don't want to advertise our presence to the whole of Wapping.'

'Our presence?'

'Yes,' said Serena impatiently. 'Oh, do hurry, sir, there's not a moment to lose.'

'Miss Osmond,' said the Duke, 'understand one thing. While I see it's my duty to engage Ranulph's support, and thereafter to post off with all speed to Wapping, nothing will persuade me to take you with me.'

'But I must go!'

'Not with me,' said the Duke firmly. 'This could be a highly dangerous undertaking, my dear. For any female to . . .'

'I am not "any female",' cried Serena furiously. 'I am betrothed to marry Lord Hector, and I mean to do everything in my power to help him and my cousin Jason Carey, so let us waste no more time arguing. If you won't take me, I shall make Timmins drive me, though I daresay that will be a lot more risky, for he's country-bred and will very likely lose his way in those back streets.'

'Did you say "betrothed", Miss Osmond?'

'Yes!' Encountering the Duke's stare, Serena had the grace to blush. 'I'm sorry, I shouldn't have blurted it out in that hoydenish way. Hector said he would call on you tomorrow morning . . . and . . . and he will very likely tell you himself and seek your blessing. I know you must feel angry with me, but if you will only . . .'

'I'm not angry,' interrupted the Duke, reaching out to tug the bellrope. 'Amazed, rather, that you should consent to marry my ramshackle son. No, no,' he added hastily, as Serena showed signs of leaping to Hector's defence, 'I've no wish to criticise him. I'm delighted that he's chosen a woman of spirit as well as beauty, and think you've already done him a power of good.'

The butler Hodge appeared in the doorway, and the Duke said briskly,

'Have the plain carriage brought round at once, Hodge. Bid Kyle harness the bays, and see the horse-pistols are loaded. He must also provide himself with a gun. And bring me my old Hessians, and a drab-coat, and the pistols from my duelling case.'

Hodge looked as if he could hardly believe his ears, but he rallied and said, 'Yes, Your Grace. And if . . . if anyone should enquire where Your Grace has gone, what should I answer?'

The Duke gave him a glinting smile. 'You may say,' he replied, 'that I've gone out with Miss Osmond, that we're going first to call upon Lord Ranulph in Curzon Street, and then to visit the London Stillwater Dock at Wapping.'

XXXIX

Like most men of fashion, Hector had never devoted much thought to the City or the river east of Westminster. That was the domain of Trade, and quite beneath the notice of Quality Folk. A wealthy Cit might be permitted to contribute handsomely to charity, to patronise the arts, or bail out indigent members of the Royal Family, but he was certainly not encouraged to mingle with the ton.

Tonight though, as he travelled downstream in the boat hired at Lambeth by Sir William, Hector understood for the first time that here beat the very heart of London.

The landmarks he knew – Lambeth Palace, the Palladian façade of Somerset House – soon fell away, to be replaced by an endless succession of wharfs backed by warehouses, churches, inns and jostling houses. Most were in darkness, but at Billingsgate small craft crowded the quay, and a swarm of porters in aprons and billycock hats laboured to bring ashore baskets of fish under the oily light of flares.

The face of the river itself was thick with ships at anchor . . . barques and brigantines, schooners and ketches, their furled sails and rigging skeletal against the full moon, the lamps at their prows throwing long ribbons of light across the black water. Over all hung the pungent river smell, composed of mud and sewage and the salt tang of the sea.

The Admiral, who had been silently watching the flow of the water, spoke suddenly:

'What's the depth here, Wiske? Thirty feet?'

Wiske nodded. 'Aye, Cap'n, at the high.' He pointed to a stretch of exposed mud on the south bank. 'Tide's turned. Comin' in fast.'

The Admiral turned to Hector. 'If Piggott's craft is small, he could sail in an hour or so. If she's over fifty tons, though, he'll have to wait for the flood, and we'll have a bit more time.'

They passed the bulk of the Tower, and the Admiral said to the oarsmen, 'Pull in to the Hermitage jetty.'

The boat edged towards the north bank and a few moments later nosed against the landing stage at the foot of a flight of stone steps. The boatmen were paid off and the three passengers made their way up the stairs to the head of the quay.

The moon, now soaring high, gave a good light, and Hector was able to discern to his right the high wall that marked the boundary of the London Dock, with beyond it the lock that led to the stillwater basin. There were lights in the lock-keeper's blockhouse, and in the windows of a distant mansion which he knew to be the home of the Dock Superintendent.

Over to the left the wharf stretched bare and deserted, save for the unwieldy bulk of a crane. No light showed in the blank faces of the warehouses.

Directly ahead was the mouth of Nightingale Lane, bordered on the west by a row of mean dwellings and on the east by a dilapidated building two storeys high under a roof of broken slates. Across its river frontage stretched a faded sign, bearing the legend, JAS THOROGOOD SHIPS' CHANDLER. The windows of the building were shuttered and showed not a gleam of light.

Wiske said in a hoarse whisper, 'There's a yard round the back, Cap'n. Mebbe a guard, too.'

The Admiral nodded, and the three moved quietly along the quay, keeping in the shadow of the building, and reached a wide gate, closed and padlocked. Beyond it was a square yard with sheds on three sides, all of them shut. Close by the gate and facing it was a watchman's box; but the occupant was plainly lacking in a sense of duty, for he sprawled on his chair with legs out-thrust and mouth snoring widely. A lamp stood at his elbow, and under his limp hand rolled a black bottle.

The Admiral touched Wiske's shoulder.

'Take him,' he said softly, 'but don't kill him.'

Wiske's face split in a wolfish grin. He slid a wicked-looking knife from beneath his jacket, clamped it between his teeth, and noiselessly climbed the gate. Next instant he had reached the watchman's box and clamped a hand over the snoring mouth, the point of his knife caressing the man's throat.

The watchman made one convulsive movement, then lay stiff, his eyes bulging in terror. Wiske lifted him bodily to his feet and bundled him to the gate.

'Open up, cully, and no tricks.'

The man found the key and released the padlock. The Admiral and Hector stepped through the gate and contemplated their captive.

He was a small man, with spindly legs and a pot belly. His face, under layers of dirt, had the purplish sheen of the hardened drinker, and he smelled strongly of rum.

The Admiral smiled at him.

'What's your name, blubbergut?'

The man did not answer, and Wiske tightened his grip, letting the knifepoint bite into the grubby throat.

'Chubb,' gasped the man. 'Jeremiah Chubb. You don't 'ave no call ter . . .'

'Shut your teeth,' rasped the Admiral. 'Where's Piggott?'

'Not 'ere.' Chubb attempted bluster. ''E'll 'ave yer liver an' lights, 'e will, for breakin' of 'is property.'

The Admiral took a step forward and seized hold of Chubb's greasy hair, forcing back his head. The bluff country gentleman had quite vanished, and in his place stood the Will Carey who had harassed the pirates of the Caribbean and driven Boney into exile.

'Now hear me, you scum,' he said softly. 'Piggott kidnapped my son. He took my boy, d'ye understand? Tell me where Piggott is, before I cut out your lying tongue.'

'I dunno! I dunno nuffink about no boy, I swear it!'

'Liar! You're Piggott's jackal and you'll hang with him – unless I slit your throat for you, here and now. Yes, that would please me, I think.'

Facing that flinty glare, Chubb quailed, sagging back against Wiske.

'No!' he whimpered. 'Don't! Please!'

'Where's Piggott?'

'Not 'ere, yer honour, an' that's Gawd's truth. Left last evenin', 'e did. Said 'e'd be back at daybreak.'

'Who else is with you?'

'Nobody, nobody, I swear.'

The Admiral thrust him away in contempt.

'Lord Hector,' he said, 'lock the gate and bring the lantern. Wiske, haul the blubbergut inside. We'll see for ourselves how Piggott conducts his business.'

*

'Ali Baba's cave,' said Sir William, gazing about him, 'but only one thief to guard it.' He glanced at Chubb, sitting trussed to a chair. 'Piggott's running out on you, matey. Leaving you to face the music alone.'

They had searched the lower regions of the building and found them to contain nothing but sacks of coal and a few rats. Wiske had been left in the lane to keep watch. Hector and the Admiral, with the shivering Chubb, were in the long room that occupied the whole of the upper storey. Chubb's lantern dangled from a hook in the roof-beam. There was no danger that its light would penetrate to the street, for the windows were entirely covered by the crates, barrels and sacks piled against the walls from floor to rafter. The air was heavy with the smell of wine and molasses, tobacco, spices and coffee beans.

The Admiral nudged a dark sack with the toe of his boot.

'Black strap,' he said. 'Full of sugar, I'd say, stolen by Piggott's henchmen.'

Chubb said nothing, his eyes glued to the pistol in the Admiral's hand. The Admiral came and stood over him.

'So Piggott's a lighthorseman, eh, Mr Chubb?'

Chubb began to shake his head and the pistol jerked forward to brush his nose.

'Don't lie to me! Piggott's a lighthorseman, with his own little troop of thieves like you. He owns a mate or two aboard the merchant ships, am I right? He pays 'em good money, as much as thirty guineas a time, so they'll let his pretty boys open casks and packages in the holds, and carry off as much as they can, all in the dead o' night. Eh? Am I right? And then Piggott must pay watermen with boats to bring the goods ashore, and lumpers to carry the goods from the holds to the boats, and coopers to fill the bags of black strap which won't show up in the dark, to give the game away? Ah, and another thing, Piggott must have a brace of Revenue Men in his pay, the sort who'll be kind enough to go early to bed when Piggott's making his raid. Aye, it takes a smart man to set up such a team, and run it, too. Ain't it so, Mr Chubb?'

Chubb's mouth worked, but no sound emerged. The Admiral leaned closer to him. 'I see you're a lumper, Chubb. That badge on your arm says you work for the London Dock Company, but I doubt if your name's on their roll. You're a fraud, Chubb. A thief. An arrant rogue, and you'll hang for it.' The Admiral's tone hardened suddenly. 'Where's the woman?'

Chubb swallowed desperately. 'I dunno what yer mean.'

'I think you do. A woman with yellow hair and green eyes, a Frenchwoman, who was seen to enter these premises on Wednesday evening last. Where is she now? Answer me, you dog!'

Chubb gasped. 'Reckon she went aboard Wednesday night.'

'Aboard which craft?'

Chubb began to whimper. 'Sir, I dursn't tell 'ee. Piggott'll kill me if I blab.'

'And I'll kill you if you don't.' The muzzle of the Admiral's pistol hovered near Chubb's right eye. 'Which craft?'

'The *M-Marguerite*, out of Calais.'

'Who owns her?'

'They say the woman.'

'Does she own Piggott, too?'

'In a manner o' business, mebbe. No more. That's a fancy piece, wouldn't be wi' no workin' man.'

'Where's the *Marguerite* moored?'

'Hermitage reach, midstream. I wouldn't lie t' yer, Cap'n.'

'What's her tonnage?'

'Forty, Cap'n.'

The Admiral surveyed Chubb coldly. 'What do you think, Lord Hector, has the scum told us all he knows?'

'I doubt it.'

'I 'ave, I 'ave!' The words tumbled out of Chubb's quivering mouth. 'I wouldn't lie to yer, noble sirs! I dunno nuffink about your boy, Cap'n. I dunno nuffink about no kidnappin'. I don't 'old wiv such, never did nor never will lay 'ands on a ninnercent child!'

'It makes no difference,' said Hector in a bored tone. 'You'll be hanged for a smuggler, if not for a kidnapper.' He paused, then said casually, 'Unless, of course, you choose to turn King's evidence.'

'Don't waste your time, my lord,' said the Admiral, cocking the pistol and squinting along its barrel at Chubb's forehead. 'Better we save His Majesty the cost of a hanging.'

'No,' screamed Chubb, 'I'll turn King's squealer, I will, I'll tell yer anyfink yer wants ter know, gennelmen, on'y don't shoot me. Don't shoot poor old Chubb, as never meant yer no 'arm.'

The Admiral made an impatient sound, but Hector held up his hand, watching Chubb.

'Tell me, does Piggott mean to embark tonight?'

Chubb nodded wordlessly. Tears ran down his face.

'What's his plan?' demanded Hector. 'The truth, Chubb. Tell us the truth and perhaps we may put in a word for you with the Crown.'

Chubb gulped. "E'll come at dawn, same as allus. Ship's light, nuffink in 'er old. Tide'll be 'igh enough for 'er ter sail at five.'

'Does Piggott keep a boat here?'

'They'll send from the ship. Piggott won't trust no watermen, not if 'e's got yer boy, like you say.'

'How will he summon the boat?'

'Signal the *Marguerite* wiv 'is lantern from the quay.'

'Will he enter this building?'

Chubb chewed his cheek. His rheumy eyes dilated suddenly. 'Not if I warns 'im off,' he said.

'And how will you do that?'

"Ang a light in the cellar winder. 'E'll know summat's wrong, an' go on by.'

'How will he arrive? In his wagon? In a carriage?'

Chubb shivered. 'Not 'im. 'E'll come afoot, an' quiet as a liddy snake. You'd best watch out, or yer'll be food for the fishes.'

There was a brief silence. Then the Admiral leaned down, pulled the soiled neckcloth from around Chubb's neck, stuffed it into the man's mouth and used his own scarf to secure the gag.

Staring Chubb in the eye, he said, 'Gallow's-meat though you are, we'll give you your chance. If you sit quiet and try no tricks, and if Piggott doesn't get to you to cut out your cowardly heart, you shall be allowed to turn King's evidence. Cross us, and you're a dead man. Do you understand?'

Chubb nodded vigorously.

'Come,' said the Admiral to Hector. 'We've not much time.' He unhooked the lantern from the roof-beam. 'We'll set this in the cellar window as we go out.'

XL

The lamp shone in the cellar window, casting a band of light across the mouth of Nightingale Lane. On the dark quayside, the Admiral, Hector and Wiske held council of war.

'We can do nothing about the *Marguerite*,' the Admiral said. 'The tide's rising, the wind's in the right quarter, she could sail within the hour. If Lord Ranulph's done as we asked, there'll be a revenue cutter with a boarding party waiting for her, but it won't be in the Hermitage reach. Too many craft about, too little room to manoeuvre. They'll take her on the Limehouse reach, or maybe Blackwall.

'Our task is to prevent Piggott from taking my son aboard. There must be no wild shooting, though – nothing that will give Piggott cause to harm Jason.

'We don't know how many men Piggott will bring with him. Perhaps only Laval, perhaps more. He may even come alone. We must deal with whatever comes. Wiske, take the musket and guard the entrance to the yard. Keep an eye on the Hermitage Basin and the lock. If the militia ignore our advice and start to mobilise there, you must get to them somehow and warn them to lie low. Let Piggott but glimpse a uniform, and he'll carry out his threat.

'Lord Hector, you and I will station ourselves to the west of the lane. You'll find cover over there by the crane. You'll command a view of the steps to the landing stage.

'I shall stay in the doorway of the warehouse, on the corner, there. If I can take Piggott quickly and safely, I'll do so, and you must give me what support you can. That's all. Look to yourselves, lads, and God be with you.'

They separated, the Admiral concealing himself in the deep embrasure of the doorway, Wiske crouched in the shadows by the gate, and Hector hiding behind the solid base of the crane. As the Admiral had said, he was able to see both the expanse of the quay and the steps down to the water.

It was dark now, for the moon had set and the sun was not

yet risen. On the face of the river, little stirred, except for a wherry and a line of barges making for the Isle of Dogs. The *Marguerite* was a black swan, asleep with wings furled.

It was hard to imagine any evil could be at large in such a tranquil world, yet Hector knew Piggott must be close. He thought of Jason, and the terror the boy must be feeling. It steeled him to do whatever might be necessary.

An hour passed. Once he fancied he saw movement along the banks of Hermitage Lock, but whether it was troops or labourers he couldn't tell.

The darkness lessened slowly, the eastern sky gathered that opalescence that precedes the dawn, and suddenly a footfall sounded in Nightingale Lane, and a man stepped quietly on to the wharf.

It was Laval. He carried a lantern in one hand, which cast grotesque shadows on his monkey features. For a moment he stood utterly still, staring out at the *Marguerite*. Then he glanced over his shoulder, as if seeking instruction.

Piggott's there, Hector thought. But is Jason with him?

Laval must have received some command, for he now moved forward to the edge of the quay, raised the lantern high, and began to swing it back and forth in a wide arc. Watching the deck of the *Marguerite*, Hector saw the blink of an answering light. Soon a small boat detached itself from the black shape of the ship and moved slowly across the river. Hector saw there were two oarsmen, dressed in rough breeches and jackets, with knitted caps pulled low.

As they approached, the sky reddened, the water burned with oily fire, rooftops and spars were edged with flame. The boat reached the jetty at the foot of the steps, and one of the sailors caught hold of a mooring ring to hold her steady and beckoned to Laval, who turned towards the alley and raised an arm.

Piggott and Jason stepped from the mouth of the lane.

In the inferno of dawn, Piggott seemed to be the Devil himself, his skin pallid and eyes shining red. In his right hand he held a pistol, its nose pressed against Jason's head. The boy's hands were tied by a rope, one end of which was in Piggott's left hand.

'Move,' Piggott said, at the same time giving Jason a sharp thrust so that he almost stumbled. They began to walk towards the edge of the dock. Hector levelled his pistol, but he knew he could not fire. None of them could without the risk of hitting Jason, so close did Piggott hold him.

A few more paces and they would reach the steps. One of the boatmen was already standing up, ready to help them aboard. In despair, Hector prayed for help and the prayer was answered.

The rim of the sun rose above the horizon, its light poured across the face of the water and glinted on metal along the dock to the south. Laval's eye caught the flash and he turned, stared, then yelled:

'Piggott! Blue-jackets!'

Startled, Piggott broke stride for just a moment, but it was enough. Feeling his grip slacken, Jason twisted free and ran like a rabbit back towards the lane. Piggott swore and raised his pistol, aiming at the boy, and Hector fired. The bullet caught Piggott in the shoulder and spun him round. He fired towards Hector, the ball smacking into the oakwood of the crane.

Laval caught Piggott under the armpits and began to haul him towards the head of the steps, but Wiske and the Admiral were closing in, firing simultaneously. The two smugglers fell, locked together, toppled over the edge of the dock and rolled down the steps. Laval was already dead, his head shattered by the blast of Wiske's musket, but Piggott made an attempt to claw his way towards the boat. Hector fired his second pistol at the standing boatman. The shot went wide, but the man leaped backward and seized his oar, shouting to his companion to pull away. The boat dipped wildly, swung, began to move off.

Piggott collapsed, rolling over on to his back. His white eyes stared at the sky, his jaw sagged.

Hector saw that the Admiral had snatched Jason up and was holding him in a tight embrace. Wiske ran forward to the head of the steps, advanced down them and felt for the pulse in Piggott's throat. He looked up at Hector, grinning.

'Dead as a doornail,' he said with satisfaction. 'May he rot in hell.'

Men were running along the wharf from the Hermitage Lock; men in the blue uniform of the London Dock Company, with muskets at the ready.

Aboard the *Marguerite*, there was frantic activity. The anchor rattled up, sailors worked to set the sails. Hector saw the figure of a woman at the rail. The hood of her blue cloak had fallen back, and her yellow hair streamed in the wind. She stood motionless for a space, then turned and went below.

One of the militiamen ran up to Sir William and saluted.

'Beggin' yer pardon, sir, would you be Admiral Carey?'

'Yes.' The Admiral set Jason down. 'What of the *Marguerite*, man? She mustn't be allowed to quit port.'

'Don't worrit yerself over her.' The man was grinning broadly. 'The cutter will see she doesn't pass Blackwall.'

'Excellent.' The Admiral nodded towards the steps. 'You'll find two dead rogues down there, and a live one in the building. Handle him carefully. He's to turn King's witness, and can tell a fine tale of plunder on these docks.'

The militiaman despatched troopers to take Chubb in charge, and to load the bodies of Piggott and Laval on to a handcart. That done, he returned to Sir William and his companions.

'Compliments o' the Dock Superintendent, sirs, and will you do 'im the honour to jine 'im at 'is 'ome? It's nobbut a pace from 'ere, an' there's a gennelman and leddy mighty keen to see you safe an' well. The gennelman sent this, which I was to give to Lord 'Ector, most particular.'

He spread out his calloused hand to display Hector's signet ring.

Later, over a substantial breakfast served in the superintendent's dining room, Hector gave a report of the events leading to Piggott's death. He omitted that part of the story that involved Kettleby Manor, feeling that Sir William would prefer to tell it in his own good time.

The superintendent, a considerate man, had not felt it necessary to detain the Admiral and Jason, since the boy was exhausted by his ordeal, and Sir William naturally wished to take him home to his family with all speed. They had set off in the company's own carriage, with Wiske in attendance.

A clerk sat at the superintendent's elbow to record Hector's account, which would be handed to the proper authorities, so that the rest of Piggott's ring might be rounded up and brought to justice.

Towards the end of the meal, a message arrived from the superintendent's opposite number on the East India Docks at Blackwall. The *Marguerite* was in the hands of His Majesty's

Customs and Excise, and a certain Elise de Rennes had been taken into custody, to be charged with a number of crimes, including the kidnapping of Master Jason Carey.

'She'll hang for it,' the superintendent said. 'Stealing a child from his home by force, attempting to take him out of the country. She'll hang, and good riddance.'

His Grace the Duke of Wycombe, who had listened to his son's narrative with an air first of surprise and then of quiet appreciation, shook his head.

'Though I agree with you that hanging's too good for such a woman, I fear Madame de Rennes won't face an English court. She has important connections in France and Italy. The likelihood is, she'll be deported.'

The superintendent, though he found the proposition repugnant to his sense of justice, had to agree that His Grace was very likely right. He then diplomatically turned the conversation to pleasanter things, saying that he hoped his guests would return to the London Dock again, when he would make it his business to see they sampled the best wine in the company cellars.

They parted from their host with expressions of goodwill and esteem on both sides. It was only when they were driving back to Bruton Street that Hector remembered he had news to impart.

'Father,' he said, 'there's something I must tell you. Miss Osmond and I . . .'

'. . . are betrothed. Allow me to offer you my congratulations, Hector. Come and see me this evening, both of you, so that I may drink to your health. I suppose you'll be off to Brighton tomorrow to tell Mrs Osmond and Mrs Fortescue of your plans?' He leaned back in his corner with a sigh. 'I dislike Brighton, the air is so enervating – but not, I think, so exhausting as that of Wapping.'

It was broad daylight when the Duke set down Hector and Serena at the Careys' house. Hector wished to assure himself that Jason was well, and also to ask the Admiral, as the senior member of the family, for permission to become formally engaged to Serena.

Sir William replied with a laugh that he could see all was already signed and sealed between them, and that he wished them both very happy.

Laurel expressed herself delighted with the news, while Lady Carey burst into tears and said that to have Jason safe and Serena betrothed all in a few hours made her the happiest woman in the world. She then begged them to go and talk to Jason.

'Dr Hastings has given him a draught to make him sleep,' she said, 'but it seems to have had no effect. His nerves are too much at stretch, I think. Perhaps you can calm him a little.'

They found Jason lying on the couch in the library. He looked tired and feverish, and was unwilling to say anything of his ordeal, or even to speak Piggott's name. They did not press him, knowing that his reticence would wear off in time. He received the news of their engagement with obvious pleasure, but entered a *caveat*.

'No satin,' he said. 'I won't wear white satin breeches at the wedding, or a lace collar, or rosettes on my shoes.'

'You shall wear what you choose,' Serena promised, 'and you and Matthew shall ride to the church in the bridegroom's party.'

This Jason found acceptable, and Hector then suggested he accompany them on the drive to Brighton. He agreed to it at once.

'Perhaps,' he said sleepily, 'if the road is dead straight, and there's not too much traffic, you'll let me handle the ribbons for a space?'

'I expect I will.'

Jason began to ask what time they would leave, and whether Hector planned to drive his bays; but even as he spoke, his eyelids drooped, and in no time he was fast asleep.

Hector and Serena stood together at the foot of the couch, arms linked.

'You know,' said Hector softly, 'without that imp, I should never have come to Kettleby Manor, nor met you, nor enjoyed so many adventures.'

Serena gazed at him fondly. 'Mr Finch,' she said, 'it's a strange thing, but I feel an attack of the hiccups coming on. Can you find a way to prevent it?'

Mr Finch could, and obligingly did.